11/19

the Exact Opposite of Okay

of

Okay

Laura Steven

HARPER TEEN
An Imprint of HarperCollinsPublishers

HarperTeen is an imprint of HarperCollins Publishers.

Library of Congress Control Number: 2019932659

ISBN 978-0-06-287752-9
Typography by Jenna Stempel-Lobell
19 20 21 22 23 PC/LSCH 10 9 8 7 6 5 4 3 2 1
❖
First Edition

To Toria and Lucy—aka the Coven—
because in the immortal words of Kelly Clarkson,
my life would suck without you

HELLO

Look, you probably bought this book because you heard about how I'm an impoverished orphan at the heart of a national slut-shaming scandal, and you thought, *Oh, great, this is just the kind of heart-wrenching tale I need to feel better about my own life*, but seriously, you have to relax. I am not some pitiful Oliver-Twist-meets-Kim-Kardashian type figure. If you're seeking a nice cathartic cry, I'm not your girl. May I recommend binge-watching some sort of medical drama for the level of secondhand devastation you're looking for.

Either that or you saw the nudes, which, y'know. Most people have. My lopsided boobs have received more press attention than your average international epidemic, which I bet the supervirus population is furious about. All that hard work attempting to destroy the human race gone unnoticed.

But here it is, the unvarnished account of everything that went down my senior year, taken straight from the journal entries on my blog. Which is a big win for me because putting this together for you was practically no work on my part. When in doubt, always do the least amount of work possible, in order to preserve energy for important things like laughing and sex.

Don't look at me like that. This is a book about a sex scandal, did you really expect me to be a nun and/or the Virgin Mary?

TUESDAY, SEPTEMBER 13

6:51 a.m.

Going back to school after summer is, at the best of times, the absolute worst. So when you combine back-to-school melancholy with the literal hellscape that is being a high school senior—i.e., being asked "WHAT DO YOU PLAN TO DO WITH YOUR FUTURE???" six billion times per day—it's a recipe for unprecedented misery and suffering.

We're only a month in, and already I'm in the midst of an existential crisis. Hence starting this blog. I have little to no idea what I'm doing with my life, and I'm hoping typing up every single minor occurrence will help me figure it out. A flawless plan, I'm sure you'll agree.

9:47 a.m.

Just had a career counseling session with Mr. Rosenqvist, who is Swedish and very flamboyant. The dude tries really, really hard to make sure everyone FOLLOWS THEIR DREAMS [he is very shouty, hence the caps lock] and

TAKES THE PATH LEAST TRAVELED and STOPS INJECTING HEROIN ON WEEKENDS. [I hilariously added that last one myself. To clarify: nobody at Edgewood High is in the habit of injecting heroin on such a regular basis that it would be of concern to our guidance counselor. In fact if you are a lawyer who's reading this, please ignore every such allegation I make, because I really don't need to add a libel suit to my spectacular list of problems.]

We're sitting in Rosenqvist's minuscule, windowless office, which I'm pretty sure is just a repurposed broom closet, if the lingering scent of carpet cleaner is anything to go by. He sits behind a tiny desk that would be more suitable for a mole person. There are filing cabinets everywhere, containing folders on every single student in the entire school. I would imagine there's probably some sort of electronic database that could replace this archaic system, but thanks to endless budget cuts, my school has to do things the Old-Fashioned Way™.

So he's all: "Miss O'Neill, have you given mach thought to vat you vould like to study ven you go to college next fall?"

[I'm going to stop trying to type in dialect now as I don't want to appear racist. If you can even be racist to white Scandinavian men, which I am not sure you can be.]

Breathing steadily through my mouth in a bid to prevent the bleach smell from burning away my nostril hair, I'm all: "Um, no, sir, I was thinking I might do a bit of traveling, you know, see the world and such." This is not actually a thing

4

I'm considering, but it seems like something people say to career counselors when they have no idea what they're doing with their life.

"So do you have money saved up to fund your flights, at least?" he asks, completely unperturbed by the decades-old feather duster that's just taken a nosedive from the top shelf behind him. As an aspiring comedian and all-around idiot, it is very challenging for me to refrain from scoring the duster according to Olympic diving standards: 8.9 for difficulty, etc.

But back to the issue at hand: my negative bank balance. "No, sir, for I am eighteen and unemployed."

Patiently moving the feather duster to a more secure location in his desk drawer, he shoots me a sympathetic look. A waft of moldy apple stench floats out of the open drawer, and he hastily slams it shut again. This place must violate at least a dozen health codes. "I see. And have you tried to find a job?"

"Good god, that's brilliant!" I gasp, faux-astounded. "I had not previously considered this course of action! Have you ever considered becoming a career counselor?" [This may seem like a pretty ballsy thing to say to a teacher, but honestly, they're used to my snark at this point.]

In all seriousness, my unemployment is a sore point. For the third time this year, I just handed out my résumé to every retailer, restaurant, and hotel in town. But there are too few jobs and too many people, and I'm never top of the pile.

He sighs. "I know it's stating the obvious. But, well . . . have you?"

Grinding my teeth in mild irritation, I sigh back. "Yessir, but the problem is, even the most basic entry-level jobs now require at least three years' experience, a degree in astrophysics, and two Super Bowl trophies to even be considered for an interview. Unfortunately, due to my below-average IQ and complete lack of athletic prowess, I am fundamentally unemployable."

So ultimately, thanks to my lack of money and/or job, we both agree that jet-setting to South Africa to volunteer in an elephant sanctuary, while very noble and selfless, is not a viable option at present. Since, you know, air travel is not free, which I personally find absurd and unreasonable.

Rifling through my shockingly empty file, Mr. Rosenqvist then tries another tactic. "What subjects do you most enjoy in school?" He tries to disguise the flinch as he spots my grade point average.

I think about this for a while, tugging at a loose thread on the cushioned metal chair I'm perched on. "Not math, because I am not a sociopath."

He laughs his merry Swedish laugh.

"Or science. See above."

Another endearing chuckle.

As a feminist I feel immediately guilty, because everyone is trying to encourage girls into STEM subjects now, but to be honest I'm not dedicated enough to the Vagenda to force myself to become a computer programmer. Sometimes you have to pick your battles.

The thing is, I know exactly what career I'd like to pursue, but I'm kinda scared to vocalize it. Most guidance counselors are interested in one thing and one thing only: getting you into college. Schools are rated higher according to the percentage of alumni who go on to get a college education, and so career guidance is dished out with this in mind.

Plus the chances of success in my dream job are not high. Especially for a girl like me.

Rosenqvist continues his gentle coaxing. "What about English?"

Nodding noncommittally, I say, "I like English, especially the creative writing components. And drama." Before I can talk myself out of it, I add, "Sometimes I write and perform comedy sketches with my friends. You know, just for fun. It's not serious or anything." Judging by the tingling heat in my cheeks, I've flushed bright red.

But despite my pathetic trailing off, he loves this development.

"FANTASTIC! FOLLOW YOUR DREAMS, MISS O'NEILL!" [Told you.]

So now, despite the fact that it's not exactly a stable career path, I have a backpack stuffed full of information on improvisation groups and drama school and theaters that accept script submissions. I'm actually pretty grateful to Rosenqvist for not immediately dismissing my unconventional career ambitions, as so many teachers have before.

He even told me about his friend who does reasonably priced head shots for high school students. Granted, this sounds incredibly sketchy, but I am giving him the benefit of the doubt here, because I would be quite upset to discover Mr. Rosenqvist was earning a commission by referring his students to a pedophilic photographer as a side business.

11:24 a.m.
Geography is, as suspected, a snooze fest of epic proportions. I think if you offered me $500,000 right this second to tell you what it was about, I couldn't, and that is saying a lot because for half a million dollars I could both go to college and pay to have Donald Trump assassinated. [Apparently this is an illegal thing to say, so it's important to clarify: I AM JOKING. In fact it is fair to assume that any legally dubious sentences at any point are jokes. I am not sure if this gets me off the hook or not, but I'm hoping so because otherwise I'm almost certainly going to jail, where I will rot forever because I do not have the patience for a Shawshank-style escape. In fact without Netflix it is perfectly possible my general will to live would just evaporate within the week.]

At some point when Mr. Richardson is droning on, I make eye contact with Carson Manning, who's sitting in the next row. He's a professional class clown so I instantly know I am in trouble, because my ability to resist laughter is non-existent.

Carson smirks and holds up his pad of paper, revealing a ballpoint-pen doodle scribbled in the margin of his sparse notes. I would have guessed it'd be a drawing of a penis, because teenage boys love nothing more than sketching their own genitals, but I'm pleasantly surprised to see a charming caricature of Mr. Richardson. Doodle-Richardson has giant jowls and a tattoo of an alpaca on his arm. This is funny not because our geography teacher actually has such a tattoo, but because he reminds us at least once every thirty seconds about the time he went trekking in Peru and climbed Machu Picchu.

I snort with ugly laughter, but Mr. Richardson is too busy talking about tectonic plates or something to scold me.

Carson looks genuinely pleased by my reaction and smiles broadly, tiny dimples setting into his smooth brown skin. The black shirt he's wearing is tight around his arms and shoulders—he's the star player on the varsity basketball team and is in tremendous shape—and his blue beanie is slightly lopsided.

Even though we hang out in different social circles—him with the jocks, me with the hilarious people—I feel like I already know Carson. Like, as a person. Is that weird? We have a ton in common. We'll both do anything for a laugh, and if the rumors are anything to go by, his family isn't exactly rolling in cash either. In fact I think I might remember seeing him at the soup kitchen a few years back, when Betty had the shingles and couldn't work for a while.

So yeah, Carson Manning. He's good people. And not

exactly terrible to look at. And . . . maybe he feels the same about me? I mean, why else would he show me his doodle? Or am I just an incredible narcissist? Probably the latter.

Either way. Interesting development.

5:04 p.m.

On Mr. Rosenqvist's enthusiastic recommendation, I find myself staying behind after school to talk to Mrs. Crannon, our drama teacher, about possible career paths. Like, I am actually spending more time on campus than is absolutely necessary. Of my own free will. This is clear, unequivocal evidence that mind control is real, and that my lovely albeit shouty Scandinavian guidance counselor is in fact some sort of telepathic dark lord. It is the only explanation. Well, not the *only* explanation. For those who do not believe in the supernatural, it is of course possible that Rosenqvist performed some sort of lobotomy on me during our session.

For all my cynicism, I do actually genuinely care about writing. But, as much as I would love to be, I'm not smart in the traditional bookish way—more in the "watches a lot of movies" and "is very talented at mocking everything" way. Which means academia is not exactly my preferred environment. It's almost like teachers don't *want* to be told their subject of expertise is a cruel and unusual punishment.

Anyway, Mrs. Crannon's office is up a random back staircase behind the theater. I traipse up there once the final bell has rung and all other students have evacuated the premises. I'm armed with a notepad, a sample script, and a crap-ton of peanut butter cups, since talking to teachers in your spare time is a lot like getting a tattoo—you have to keep your blood sugar consistently high so you don't pass out from the pain.

Though as far as teachers go, Mrs. Crannon is pretty great. She dresses in purple glasses and Birkenstocks and crazy tunics, and veers toward the eccentric side of the personality scale. And she always gives me great parts in school plays because I'm loud enough that the tech department doesn't need to supply a microphone. I'm currently playing Daisy in *The Great Gatsby*, for example, despite not being elegant or glamorous in the slightest.

I've always liked Mrs. Crannon, but in a Stockholm syndrome sort of way. I mean, do any of us *really* like our teachers?

When I walk in, she's sitting behind a desk piled high with playbooks, coffee mugs, and a massive beige computer that looks like it's from the nineties [good old budget cuts]. The whole room smells like dusty stage costumes and stale hairspray. My favorite smell in the world.

"Izzy! It's lovely to see you outside of rehearsals for once."

She ushers me in and I take a seat on quite literally the most uncomfortable plastic chair I've ever had the misfortune to encounter. It is the iron maiden of the chair world. I'm not exaggerating.

"Thanks," I say, trying to give the pleasant expression of someone who is not in severe physical discomfort at the hands of a chair-cum-torture-device. "I brought peanut butter cups to compensate for the fact that I'm keeping you from getting home to Mr. Crannon."

"Actually, I have a Mrs. Crannon." She grins, waggling her left hand at me. Her engagement ring has a Dwayne Johnson of a diamond on it, and an elaborate wedding band sits next to it.

"Oh! Awesome. But let me get this straight." [Or should it be "let me get this gay"? Honestly, what a minefield.] "You're both called Mrs. Crannon? Doesn't that get confusing?"

She laughs, cracking heartily into the packet of peanut butter cups I've plonked in front of her. "Yes, in hindsight we probably should've kept our own names. But I had to do something to keep my traditional Catholic parents happy."

I grin. "Aren't you tempted to write some sort of farcical sketch about two wives with the exact same last name?"

Mrs. Crannon smiles warmly. "Which leads us nicely on to your writing. Mr. Rosenqvist told me you've been writing your own comedy scripts? That's great! Tell me more about that." She leans back in her chair.

Suddenly I feel a little embarrassed, mainly because I can tell I'm expected to hold a normal adulty conversation at this point, not one that's peppered with inappropriate gags and self-deprecating humor. And I've sort of forgotten how to do that.

Mumbling idiotically about Nora Ephron, my all-time hero, I reach into my satchel, which is decorated with an assortment of pins and badges to give the illusion that I am halfway cool, and pull out the sample screenplay I brought along. It's a feature-length film I wrote over the summer, when I decided I wanted to branch out from comedy sketches of a couple minutes to a ninety-page comedy screenplay. Basically I just wanted to make people laugh, while also having the breathing room to tell an actual story.

The logline [i.e., a one-sentence pitch] is this: a broke male sex worker falls for a career-obsessed client with commitment issues. Essentially it's an updated *Pretty Woman* that challenges gender stereotypes while also telling an impressive array of sex jokes. [Be honest. You would *so* see this movie.]

"You've already written an entire screenplay?" Mrs. Crannon gapes at me, clapping her hands together. "Izzy, that's fantastic! So many aspiring screenwriters struggle to even finish one script. When I was a working theater director, I used to despair of writers who seemed incapable of seeing an idea through to the end. You should be very proud of yourself. Writing 'fade out' is quite the accomplishment."

"Really?"

"Really!" She takes the script from me, examining the professional formatting and neatly typed title page. [My best friend Danny pirated the software for me on account of my severe brokeness. Don't tell the internet police. Or, you know, the *actual* police.] "I'd love to take it home with me to read. Can I?"

This show of unbelievable support catches me way off guard. "You'd do that? Spend your own free time reading my work?"

"Of course I would!" She crams another peanut butter cup in her mouth, tossing the paper in the overflowing trash can behind her. It's full of empty candy wrappers and soda cans. Obviously she is just as nutrition-conscious as me, which is precisely not at all. "I know how talented you are through working with you on school plays. You have me in stitches with your clever ad libs and witty improv."

I blush fiercely. Again. "Thank you. It irritates the living hell out of most people."

"Well, most people aren't budding comedy writers in the making. Have you given much thought to what you'd like to do after leaving school? College? Internships? If you wanted to do both, USC is incredible for screenwriting—Spielberg is an alum—and you could intern during spring break and summer vacation while you're in LA. Best of both worlds."

I fidget with the zipper on the fake leather jacket I picked up at a thrift store last fall. This is the part I dread: coming clean about my financial situation. For the second time this afternoon. It shouldn't be a big deal, and in day-to-day life it doesn't bother me that much, but now that it's actually having an impact on my future, it's kind of uncomfortable to discuss.

But like I say, Mrs. Crannon is good people. So I tell her the truth. "Actually, I'm not sure I can afford college. I figured I'd just get a job here to support me and my grandma, and write in my spare time. Film a few comedy shorts if I can scrape together the cash."

She frowns. The sound of her computer putting itself to

sleep whirs through the quiet room. Even technology has zero interest in school after the final bell. "Have you looked into loans? For college, I mean." Figures that'd be her next question.

"Kind of. But the idea of being in that much debt scares the crap out of me. Especially with no parents to fall back on."

She rolls up the purple sleeves of her wild tunic, revealing a set of black rosary beads triple tied around her wrist. Another peanut butter cup bites the dust. She's plowing through them with impressive speed. If consuming chocolate were an Olympic sport, Crannon would be on the podium for sure.

"I get it," she says, in a way that entirely suggests she doesn't get it at all. "I do. But you have to think of it as an investment. In yourself, in your future. It's so clichéd, and I know you'll have already heard it all with Rosenqvist, but you're young, you're bright, you're ambitious. You have to go for it."

I nod, but I feel a little deflated. It always leaves me feeling kinda empty when people preach "follow your dreams" to those with "do what you gotta do" kinds of lives, even though I know their hearts are in the right place. Maybe being reckless and risk-taking is an option for them, but for me it just isn't.

Mrs. Crannon senses the shift in mood, even though I try my best to hide it from her. Showing vulnerability is about as appealing to me as sticking my face into a bucket of worms.

Wiping a smear of chocolate away from the corner of her mouth, she says, "I'll help you in whatever way I can, Izzy. Dig out old contacts, keep an eye out for paid internships, recommend some places to submit your work while you're still a high school student. USC would be great, but traditional college education isn't the only way into the industry." She smiles at me, and I can't help but smile back. "We'll figure it out. I promise."

When I leave twenty minutes later, stuffed full of Reese's and silently praying Mrs. Crannon actually enjoys my screenplay after all that hyperbolic encouragement, I realize that I don't just like her in a Stockholm syndrome way. I like her in a human way.

So I do have a heart. Who knew?

7:58 p.m.

I'm chilling at the diner with Ajita and Danny, my two best friends in the world. We have a mutual love of nachos and making fun of everything.

Martha's Diner is super old school, with neon signs and jukeboxes and booths and checkered tiles. You have to take out a small mortgage to afford a burger, but their fries have been cooked at least eighteen times and are thus the most delicious substance on earth. Honestly, you should've seen the hype all over town when Martha's opened. Largely from those people who post Marilyn Monroe quotes on social media and go on about how much they wish they were born

16

in the 1950s. Like, calm down. We still have milk shakes and racism.

Anyway, we go there because the milk shakes are actually pretty good. And whenever I'm here, I like to embrace old-fashioned language, not just from the 1950s but also the whole of human history. It doth be a very enjoyable activity. [I have little to no ability to use medieval lingo in the right context. You just have to roll with it.]

Incidentally, Martha's is also where my grandmother Betty begrudgingly moonlights as a pancake chef. I mean, it's not exactly moonlighting when it's her only job. But it sounds more glamorous if you say it that way. In reality she works twelve-hour shifts on bunion-addled feet and is in almost constant pain because of it, but there's just no way she can afford to retire. That's another reason I can't go to college. Not just because of the tuition fees, but because I need to stay in my hometown and work my damn ass off to give her the rest she deserves after so many years of hard graft. It's my turn to support her for once.

Anyway, I've just filled my pals in on my chat with Mrs. Crannon, and explained how I'm not as dead in the soul department as previously thought.

"And so, it transpires, I do in fact possess an organ of the cardiovascular variety," I finish, triumphant.

"Interesting hypothesis, but I'm not sold," Ajita replies, tucking a lock of black hair behind her ear and slurping her candy-apple milk shake. The henna on her hands is beginning to fade after her cousin's Hindu wedding last month. "I mean, it's pretty off-brand for you to care about people. In fact, short of an alien parasite feasting on your brain, I'm not convinced you have the capacity to like more than three individuals at any given time, and those slots are already filled by me, Danny, and Betty."

"Valid point," I concede. Smelling burned pancake batter, I peer past the server station into the massive chrome kitchen, trying to see if Betty's knocking around. There's no sign of her. She's probably swigging from her hip flask out back while telling dirty jokes to the unassuming dishwasher. [To clarify, the dishwasher is a person. Not an appliance. My grandma may be nuts, but even she doesn't engage kitchenware in conversation.]

"That's cool of Crannon to read your script, though," Danny says, stirring his salted caramel banana milk shake with three jumbo straws. He's wearing a grubby Pokémon T-shirt I got him for his twelfth birthday, which still fits due to his scarily low BMI. "She didn't have to do that."

I nod enthusiastically. "Right? And she was so complimentary. She even likes it when I spontaneously ad lib during rehearsals. I did attempt to show some self-awareness and reference the fact that it renders most people homicidal, but she was adamant. She genuinely likes my banter."

"Clearly the woman is unhinged," Ajita points out helpfully. I flick a blob of whipped cream at her face. It lands on her nose and she licks it off with her freakishly long tongue. She's about three feet tall, but her tongue is like that of a Saint Bernard. If I spilled my entire milk shake on the floor, for example, she could just vacuum it right up with her tongue without even bending down. It's truly remarkable.

"Well, I think Izzy's funny," Danny mumbles, blushing furiously before disappearing under his unruly platform of matted hair.

Confused, Ajita and I exchange looks. Danny has literally never complimented me at any point in his life. Even when I was five years old and my parents had just died, ours was a friendship built on good-natured antagonism.

"To look at?" Ajita suggests.

"Shut up," he says, not looking at either of us. "I'll go pay for these milk shakes."

And then he slides out of the booth and walks up to the cash register, where a large-of-breast freshman greets him with as much enthusiasm as she can muster for minimum wage.

"What on earth was that about?" I whisper to Ajita, too shocked to crack a joke. "He thinks I'm *funny*? What's next, he thinks I'm also a fundamentally decent human being?"

"Let's not get carried away," she says hastily. "But wait, he's paying for the milk shakes? Danny. Buying us things. Why? I think the last thing he bought me was a box of tampons, and that was just his pass-agg way of telling me I was overreacting during an argument."

Having forked over the moola, Danny walks back across to the booth, tucking his wallet into his jeans pocket and looking rather pleased with himself. The Pikachu on his shirt smirks obnoxiously as he almost collides with a waitress carrying three club sandwiches. She shoots him a dirty look, but his gaze is fixed so intently on me that he barely notices. Then he smiles this weird bashful smile I've never seen before. *Smiles.* Danny. I mean, really.

I'm so stunned that all I can do is whisper unconvincing medieval lingo to Ajita.

"What, pray tell, the fuck?"

WEDNESDAY, SEPTEMBER 14

7:01 a.m.

Honestly, I swear I'm the only person in the universe who realizes how pointless life is. People act like mere existence is some beautiful gift, completely overlooking the fact that said existence is nothing but the result of a freak accident that occurred a cool 13.7 billion years ago.

I mean, yes, said freak accident did bring about some awesome things, such as dogs and nachos and starry skies and daffodils in spring and peanut butter cups and laughing with your best friends and turning your alarm off on weekends and pizza and snow days and milk shakes and movies and waffles. [Should I be concerned that so many of these things are food related? Is my endless appetite really my raison d'être? Probably.]

But still. We're all doomed to a limited number of sun orbits before we finally kick the bucket and end up in the same infinite hell as Donald Trump and Adolf Hitler. Perhaps I'm overthinking it, but what we do between now and then barely seems worth getting out of bed for.

Maybe I'm being melodramatic. I just really hate getting out of bed.

7:16 a.m.

That last post is exactly why I created this blog. Can you imagine if I subjected my loved ones to such histrionics on a daily basis? I would almost immediately be banished to a cabin in the woods with nothing but birdsong for company. [For the record, birdsong is not on my list of awesome things brought about by the big bang. I find it obnoxious.]

So yes, the obvious solution to my ludicrous inner monologue was to start a blog in a random corner of the internet nobody is ever likely to find.

Also, I have little to no ability to voice my innermost feelings in real life. Why is it so much easier to type out your emotions and upload them into a bottomless void than it is to share them with your friends and family? It is truly one of the greatest philosophical questions of our time.

Seriously, the universe is weird. My parents were perfectly healthy and happy when their car was hit by a drunk truck driver [and obviously the truck too, not just the driver himself, that probably would've ended differently]. Boom, dead in an instant. But my grandmother, Betty, the woman who raised me from that day forth, is told repeatedly by doctors that she's going to die soon, on account of her significant BMI. And she's still kicking ass and taking names.

Anyway, even though the doctor repeatedly tells her she has to cut down on fat/sugar/carbs/basically everything fun,

Betty makes French toast for breakfast this morning. She's absolutely incredible at it, due to making delicious batter-based goods 807 times a day at the diner. Our tiny kitchen, full of ancient appliances so retro they're now back in vogue, smells of sweet cinnamon and maple bacon. The old radio is playing a tacky jingle-based advertisement in the corner.

"What's going on at school today, kid?" Betty practically whistles, ignoring the fact I'm feeding Dumbledore under the table. [Dumbledore is our dachshund, by the way. I'm not hiding the ghost of the world's most powerful wizard in my kitchen.]

"Oh, the usual. Feigning interest in the periodic table. Pretending to know what a tectonic plate is. Trying and failing to be excused from gym class for the thousandth time this semester." I stir sugar into the two cups of coffee perched on the batter-splattered counter. [Try saying that five times without giving yourself a tongue injury.]

This is our morning routine: she makes breakfast, I make coffee, and we chat inanely about our upcoming days. It's been this way as long as I can remember.

"Would you like me to write a note?" she asks. "I'll explain how your parents just died and you're having a hard time."

I snort. "Considering that was thirteen years ago, I'm not so sure they'll buy it. Besides, a couple of teachers have actually been pretty cool about my career potential lately. That's kinda motivating me to show up to class a little more often."

We sit down at our miniature wooden table, tucking into stacks of French toast that slightly resemble the Leaning Tower of Pisa. She listens intently as I tell her all about my meeting with Mr. Rosenqvist yesterday, and about how delightfully Swedish he is, and also about his excitement over my sketches, which I have repeatedly told Betty not to watch even though I know she will anyway. Then I brief her about the subsequent awesome session with Mrs. Crannon, and about how the enthusiasm from them both has made me feel slightly more optimistic about my strange brand of social commentary combined with dozens of dirty jokes per page.

"They're right to be excited, kiddo," she agrees. "You're hilarious. But how come you've never mentioned this screenplay of yours?"

"I guess I was just embarrassed," I admit. "Like, what does some random teenager from the middle of nowhere know about writing movies?"

I almost confide in her about my fears of sticking out like a sore thumb in New York or Hollywood, if I ever make it that far, but I don't want her to feel bad or anything. She knows I don't care about being able to buy fancy things, and it's not like I blame her for our financial predicament. But if she knew it was a big obstacle in my career path, she'd only end up feeling guilty. And that's the last thing in the world I want.

"If your mom were here, she'd say . . ." Betty trails off, blinking fiercely. She almost never manages to finish a sentence about my mom. As predicted, she fixes a neutral expression back onto her face, and I let it slide. "You shouldn't feel like a fraud. Everyone starts somewhere, right?"

Right. But for most successful people, somewhere isn't here.

"Maybe we could look at buying you another camera," Betty suggests, slurping her milky coffee through a straw. "I've been working so many doubles at the diner lately that I'm not actually behind on rent, for once. You may notice that the bacon we're currently consuming is actually within its use-by date. We are practically living in the lap of luxury here. So I'm sure I could scrape together the pennies for a secondhand DSLR and a lens or two. You know, if you want."

The suggestion sends a pang through my chest. Earlier this year, when I'd begun to realize how much I wanted to make it as a comedian, Betty bought me a nice camera and a light box so I could start up a YouTube channel. I filmed a couple videos, and I loved it. People responded pretty well too. One went vaguely viral. But it was a long, cold winter that stretched all the way into early April. Tourism was non-existent because of the snow, and unemployment is high in our town. Plus the holidays always leave everyone broke for months. And when you're broke, you generally don't indulge in seven-dollar milk shakes. As a result, Martha's was so quiet there wasn't enough work for Betty, and I ended up having to pawn the camera to cover our gas bill. It sucked, but you do what you have to do.

"Nah, it's all right," I say to Betty. "I'm just gonna focus on writing scripts and skits for a while. All you need for that is a working computer, and if worse comes to worst I can always use the library." I smile gratefully. "But thank you. I promise I'll pay you back when I'm a comedy mogul."

We chat about my weird brand of comedy for a while longer, which is fun because I get my wildly inappropriate sense of humor from her. She tells me about how back when she was young, it was considered unattractive for a woman to tell dirty jokes or do ridiculous impressions of political figures. And how that made her want to do it even more.

Every time I catch myself moping about my general lack of parents, or our dire financial situation, I just remind myself how lucky I am to be raised by such an incredible human who's always taught me how to laugh, no matter what's going wrong in my life.

I love my grandma. Especially when watching her feed crispy bacon to our chubby wiener dog and listening to her sing her own special renditions of popular nursery rhymes. Today it's: "Little Bo Peep has lost her sheep and doesn't know where to find them, largely because Little Bo Peep is fucking irresponsible and should not be in charge of live-stock." It's tough cramming all those extra syllables into the last two lines but she really makes it work.

7:41 a.m.
Danny meets me at my house so we can walk to school together, as we've done every weekday for a decade. I decide to forget all about the weirdness of last night in the diner and

26

write it off as a strange anomaly that will most likely never be repeated.

"Morning," he chirps, like a cockatoo or something similar, I don't know. Like most people with better things to do, I'm not that clued up on bird species. And then—THEN!—he hands me a paper coffee cup with steam billowing out the top. "Picked you up a mocha."

He doesn't have one for himself. Only for me.

And just like that, any attempt to overlook his sudden and deeply disturbing personality transplant goes out the window.

"Oh. Um, thanks."

"Don't mention it," he grins.

Sorry, but wtf. Danny and I have been friends since forever, and I've never seen him like this before. And we've been through a *lot* together. Especially right after my parents died. While the court was deciding who to grant custody to, his parents got temporary custody, since his mom is my godmother and all, so I lived with him for a few months. We played outside in his family's sprinklers, running around in just our underwear and spraying each other with water from the hose. I remember liking it because nobody could tell I was crying almost constantly.

For a while we all thought I'd end up living with them, since the government had concerns over Betty's ability to support me financially. Let the record show that I'm eternally grateful they chose her instead of the Wells. I mean, they're amazing people, don't get me wrong. But I can't imagine being with anyone but Betty.

Anyway, all I'm saying is that if anyone's gonna pick up on Danny being weird, it's me. And he's definitely being weird.

Regardless, the rest of the walk is fairly uneventful. We chat about the geography homework we both struggled to complete without slipping into a coma-like state. We discuss plans for tonight—torn between filming a skit or binge-watching *Monty Python* for the gazillionth time—and speculate about what movies will garner the most Academy Award nominations in a few months' time.

He's forgotten to pick up a cardboard sleeve for the coffee and it burns into my palm as we walk, making it impossible to forget. As usual we meet up with Ajita halfway to school, and she eyes the coffee like it's a grenade with the pin pulled out. Neither of us addresses it, but I know she's thinking exactly what I am:

What's going on with our best friend?

1:25 p.m.

It's Danny's turn for a careers session with Rosenqvist this lunchtime, so while he's off justifying his plan to become a hotshot surgeon despite his mediocre GPA, Ajita and I take the opportunity to brainstorm some new sketch ideas.

Ajita bites into her veggie hot dog. "I kinda want to do something controversial and political. Like, as much as your idea about a pet goldfish scheming to take over the world is entertaining, it's kind of silly."

"First of all, your face is kind of silly. I mean, come on, you really set yourself up for that one." The meat-filled hot dog I'm shoveling into my face is slathered with enough hot mustard to kill a small horse. My nostrils sting aggressively. "Second, I fail to see how a neo-Nazi shubunkin is not political."

"What in god's name is a shubunkin?"

"Honestly, it's almost like you're not an expert on goldfish breeds. Why do we even hang out?"

Before I can unleash the remainder of this sarcastic spiel on my long-suffering best friend, however, an extraordinarily tall girl I don't recognize plonks her tray down next to Ajita and smiles familiarly. She's got insanely curly auburn hair and freckled white cheeks.

"Hey, Ajita," she says cheerily. "Hey, Izzy."

Pardon me?

"Iz, this is Carlie," Ajita says, suddenly staring intently at the ravaged remains of her hot dog. I can only assume this ashamed expression translates as: *I am so sorry, dearest Izzy, for having people in my life you do not know about, for I understand how rude and inappropriate this is considering we're supposed to be best friends, and I can only endeavor to be a better pal in the future, one who keeps you abreast of any and all new friendship developments as and when they unfold, lest I be condemned to an eternity in geography class, aka hell.*

You know, something like that.

But really, wtf. Ajita and I inform each other of every single minor thing that ever happens to us, including but not limited to: bowel movements, disappointing meals, new and freakishly long hairs we find on our bodies. So it's utterly bizarre that she knows mysterious tall and pretty people and just forgets to mention it to me.

[On closer inspection, it is possible I have friend jealousy.]

"Hi, Carlie," I finally reply, once I've gotten over the unspeakable betrayal of the situation.

She smiles, all straight white teeth and naturally pink lips. "Nice to finally meet you."

FINALLY????

I repeat. Wtf.

"So, Ajita," she says, spearing some lettuce on her fork and crunching into it loudly. Seriously, she is eating a salad. I'm not kidding. An actual *salad*. I was not aware this was a thing people did in real life. "Are you excited for tennis tryouts later?"

I absolutely die laughing at this, to the point where I am so hysterical I fear a little bit of fart might slip out.

Both Ajita and Carlie stare at me as though I am having some kind of seizure. Without, you know, making sure I'm not in any immediate physical danger. All I'm saying is they're not the sort of people you want around in a potential medical emergency.

Once I finally wipe my tears away, I splutter, "Ajita? Sports? *Tennis??* You must be new here."

"Actually, I am new here," Carlie replies, popping a cherry tomato in her mouth.

Ajita clears her throat. "Um, Iz, I actually . . . I thought I might go and try out. I think I might actually enjoy tennis. Serena Williams makes it look like an excellent thing to do." A sheepish smile. "Carlie's the new captain."

And then they just look straight at each other. It's like I'm not even there, and neither is the rest of the cafeteria. [This might not sound weird, but think about it. How often do you actually do nothing but LOOK at the person next to you without saying anything? It's intense.]

I swallow the last mouthful of hot dog and resign myself to the fact that my best friend has been replaced by someone who likes *sports*, of all things, and that I am but a mere distant memory thanks to the sudden arrival of a Victoria's Secret model in our lives, and that Ajita undoubtedly has absolutely no interest in me or my existence now that she has a new best friend to scheme with.

Obviously I know it's irrational to be jealous, but I can't help it. I think it's human nature to feel vaguely territorial over your best friend. Not in a canine, pissing-all-over-them-to-mark-your-scent type way, but more in a childish not-wanting-to-share-your-favorite-toy type way. Yes, it's selfish. Yes, I'm immature.

Both of my best friends are behaving way out of

character. Which sucks because I very much prefer when things stay the same. What's that biological term? Homeostasis? Does that apply here? Can we please find a way to make it apply to friendship circles?

It really has been a wtf kind of day.

4:32 p.m.

Mrs. Crannon calls me into her office at the end of school. Her computer is wearing several of the 1920s wigs she sourced for our *Gatsby* production, and she's combing them as I walk through the door. Before I've even taken a seat in the iron maiden chair of doom, she offers me a cup of coffee and a triple chocolate chip cookie, which is how I know my instincts were correct and she is in fact a fantastic human being on all fronts.

"So! I finished your script," she says, all warm and friendly.

Through sheer nerves and stress, my stomach almost plummets through my asshole. [I realize this is a hideous thing to say, but you all know exactly what I mean, and I shall not apologize for vocalizing the sensation.]

"Oh, did you?" I sip the coffee, immediately giving myself third-degree burns, and try to resist the urge to flee the room banshee-screaming with my arms flailing in the air and a trail of cookie-based destruction behind me.

She abandons the wigs and leans forward onto her elbows in a very teachery way. "Izzy, I promise you I'm not

32

just saying this because you're my student and I'm trying to be encouraging. You have an unbelievable talent."

"Really?" I grin insanely, like an insane person.

"Really! I fully planned to only read the first ten pages last night and make some notes for you, but before I knew it, it was after midnight and I'd finished the entire thing. *And* I'd completely forgotten to make any notes. That's how good it is. It's smart and super funny, and your social awareness really shines through. I didn't feel like I was reading the work of a high school senior."

The cynical side of me feels like she's laying it on a little thick at this point, but I'm so happy I just don't care. I beam even more. "Thank you, Mrs. Crannon. That means the world."

"I'm glad," she says, smiling back just as proudly. "Now, I've been thinking about next steps for you. You're unsure about college, which is totally fine, and you're not in a position to take on unpaid internships just yet. Again, that's okay. But I did have a few ideas. Firstly, I really think you need to get this script into industry hands, whether agents or producers."

I sigh. "Right. But no agents or producers accept unsolicited submissions. I already looked into it."

"Maybe not," Mrs. Crannon agrees. "However, there are a lot of screenplay competitions out there that have judging panels made up of exactly those kinds of people— agents and producers and story developers who're looking out for fresh new talent. I did a bit of research over lunch, and there's a fairly established competition running in LA, aimed specifically at younger writers. You only have to submit your first ten pages, and if you make it to the shortlist, you get a ton of feedback from people who really know their stuff. And guess what the grand prize is?"

I shake my head, hardly believing what I'm hearing. How could I not have heard about this? It sounds like a dream.

"A college scholarship!"

I blink, wondering if I heard her right. "What?"

She hands me a printout of a web page [literally something only old people ever do] that has all the competition info on it. Across the top is bold branding: The Script Factor.

But my eyes land on one thing.

Entry fee: $50.

"This is great, Mrs. Crannon, but . . . I can't afford it." My voice is all flat and echoey. "The entry fee, I mean. I could never ask my grandma to give me fifty bucks. That's, like, seventeen hours of work at the diner." [I did mention math not being my strong suit.]

Without a trace of condescension, she replies, "I thought you might say that." And then the unthinkable happens. She reaches into her purse, pulls out a leather wallet, and hands me a fifty-dollar bill.

I stare at it in her hand, stunned. "Mrs. Crannon, I . . . I can't take that. No. Thank you so much, but no. No, I can't."

"You can, Izzy. I want you to. My father recently passed

away, and he left me some money. He was a teacher too. English literature. He'd love to know he was helping a talented young creative find their way."

Her crazy tunic is all orange and pink and yellow flowers, but all the colors blur together as my eyes fill with hot tears. To have a near-stranger take such a massive leap of faith in me? It's overwhelming.

"I don't know what to say. Thank you. Thank you so much."

"I'm glad to be able to help. Just remember me when you're famous, won't you?" She grins and boots up her ancient computer, which still has an actual floppy disk drive. "Now, let's fill in this entry form together, shall we? The deadline is tomorrow, so we have to move fast."

11:12 p.m.
I hang out with Danny and Ajita tonight—you know, once she finishes tennis tryouts with She Who Must Not Be Named, i.e., Carlie.

Danny and I actually beat her home, so we spend the first twenty minutes of the visit chatting with Mrs. Dutta in the kitchen as she pads around whipping up fresh cardamom curry. She's making a double batch to deliver to her elderly neighbor, who fell and broke her hip last week.

While we wait for Ajita to arrive, the three of us talk about her love of cooking and how her mom used to set aside every Sunday to teach her family recipes—and also about how Ajita would rather remove her own eyeballs with a skewer than spend a weekend with a pestle and mortar. Then Danny makes Mrs. Dutta hoot with laughter with his llama impression, and she accidentally adds too many green chili seeds to the curry. As punishment, Danny has to perform a taste test. His face goes so red and sweaty we briefly consider taking him to the emergency room.

Once the tennis-playing eyeball-skewerer returns, we head down to Ajita's basement, which is bigger than my entire house, to play pool and watch this obscure Canadian sketch show we all love. The conversation drifts toward school gossip, as it so often does, and I make an offhand comment about how Carson Manning is hot in a sexy-yet-unintimidating way.

Danny is incredulous. "Carson Manning?" He gapes at me, pushing his thick-framed glasses up his nose so he can actually see the red ball he's trying to pocket. His mousy brown hair is doing that weird frizzy thing he hates.

"But he's . . ."

"What?" Ajita asks, chalking up her cue. Blue dust hangs in the air around her, giving a vaguely demonic vibe.

Danny mutters. "He's just . . . well, he spends his whole school day pretending to be an idiot just for laughs. I didn't think feigned stupidity was your jam."

As it happens, feigned stupidity and general hilarity are precisely my jam, but I feel like this is beside the point.

I try explaining that finding someone hot does not necessarily imply a deep emotional connection, but this just seems to annoy him. An uncomfortable prickling rolls up and down my arms. If I didn't know any better, I'd say Danny was jealous. But why would he be jealous? I've talked about guys with him and Ajita for years.

Maybe he's just grouchy. His grades have been slipping lately, and his dad has been kind of a dick about it. I'm sure that's all it is.

In any case, instead of dwelling on yet another confusing development, Ajita and I continue to systematically destroy him at pool for what must be the seven millionth time this year. Ajita goes on an impressive pocketing spree and buries four stripes in a row. I whoop delightedly. We complete a complicated fist-bump routine we devised freshman year. Danny rolls his eyes and smiles. It seems like we've all moved past whatever emotional crisis he's dealing with, until . . .

Ajita: "So, Izzy, I heard a rumor today." She sinks a fifth. Danny is almost apoplectic. He's not great at losing.

"Yeah? Did Carlie tell you?" I try to act uninterested, but Ajita knows I am deeply nosy, and while I don't like to be directly involved in conflict itself, I must know absolutely every detail about other people's drama or else I will spontaneously combust.

Ajita ignores my petty jab and says, "Zachary Vaughan wants to ask you out."

I snort so hard that soda exits my nose in a violent manner. My brain is fizzing. Is that a thing? It feels like a thing.

Now, it's important for you to know how utterly despicable Vaughan is on practically every level. He's pretty but he knows it, he's rich and he flaunts it, and his über right-wing daddy is a Republican senator known for his shameless racism and general assholery.

"That's ridiculous. Has the dude ever even spoken to you?" Danny takes aim at the white pool ball and misses entirely. He sighs and thrusts the cue angrily at Ajita. Instead of catching it she just leaps out of the way, which if you ask me speaks volumes about her athletic abilities.

I say nothing, flabbergasted by Danny's outrage.

Ajita, deftly steering the conversation away from potential developments in my love life, turns back to the pool table and pockets the black ball, securing our victory. "Aaaaanyway. Whaddaya wanna do for your birthday this year, D?"

It's Danny's birthday next month, and while mine is usually a subdued affair due to my lack of funds, Danny always does something cool for his. He's an only child, so his parents don't mind forking out for me to tag along, too. Last year we went paintballing, the year before it was go-karting.

"I was thinking maybe zorb soccer?" Danny says, pushing his glasses up his nose for the thousandth time, looking relieved now that we're no longer discussing senators' sons who have crushes on me. "You know, where you run around in inflatable bubbles and attempt to kick a ball around a field while crashing into each other like bumper cars. It looks hilarious."

"Oh yeah, that looks incredible," I enthuse. "And is the only circumstance in which I would consider participating in sports. One of us will almost certainly die a gruesome death, but I'm game."

38

Ajita pipes up, "Speaking as the person who will most likely die that gruesome death, I'm willing to take one for the team."

Danny grins. "Perfect. And I think your brother would love it too, Jeets." Ajita's brother, Prajesh, is fourteen and already an amazing athlete.

"You wouldn't mind inviting him along?" Ajita asks, plonking herself down on the sofa. I nestle in next to her while Danny racks up the pool balls to practice not being awful. "That's so sweet of you. He would love that."

"Of course," he says. The balls spread and rattle around the table as he strikes the white ball in the perfect break. Two plop into pockets, and he smiles with satisfaction. "I think he's having a rough time at school at the minute."

Ajita frowns, half confused, half upset. "He is?" I share her concern. Prajesh is like a little brother to me too.

"I mean, it's nothing sinister. I don't think he's being bullied or anything. But the last few times I've seen him in the hallway, he's been by himself, looking a little lost. And I know what it's like to be a slightly awkward and nerdy fourteen-year-old."

"Doesn't he have friends on the track team?" I ask. Prajesh is a total track and field hotshot. He runs faster than most people can even imagine themselves running.

"I guess not," Ajita says, lowering her gaze. "He's so much quicker than everyone else, you know? They're probably jealous. Plus he's kind of awkward and introverted. And then there's his OCD." To say Prajesh likes things clean would be the understatement of the millennium. I remember the time he was taken to the hospital with bleach burns on his hands, back when he was six or seven. It was heartbreaking. "Not that it should matter, but fourteen-year-olds can be cruel. Maybe they think he's weird."

Danny squeezes her shoulder and says gently, "It's going to be okay. He's an awesome kid. I don't mind looking out for him for awhile, if you want. Hanging out and stuff."

"Thanks. I'd appreciate it." Ajita smiles, but it doesn't reach her eyes. I can tell she's going to worry and obsess over this. Her big, tight-knit family is her whole world.

A flash of envy catches me off guard. Fleetingly, I wonder what it must be like to have so many people to love and care about, but I shake the thought away like I always do. Self-pity isn't my style.

THURSDAY, SEPTEMBER 15

<u>1:23 p.m.</u>

Carson comes up to our bench in the cafeteria at lunch. Ajita kicks me under the table because of what I confessed last night, and in response I throw a french fry at her perfect face. Seriously, how are anyone's lips that full and skin that smooth and eyes that dark. It's possible I'm kind of in love with my best friend. She's ridiculously attractive. [It's funny that the horny teenager stereotype tends to refer only to boys. Things I have been aroused by lately: cherry-flavored lip balm, a fluffy blanket, a particularly phallic lamppost.]

Anyway, Carson. He loves the potato-throwing incident and begins to hypothesize what other vegetables would make suitable weaponry, until Danny rudely asks him what he wants, which is an act of douchebaggery not often associated with Danny Wells.

I try to flutter my eyes seductively/apologetically at Carson, but Ajita kicks me again, which I assume means *Izzy, stop doing that, you look like you're standing in front of that torture device at the eye doctor's that blows air into your eyeballs* so

I immediately cease and desist. When you've been pals with someone for basically your whole life, you learn to decode their secret messages based on the severity of their physical violence.

"Soooo," Carson says. "There's a party at Baxter's this weekend. You guys in?"

"Sure," Ajita replies on behalf of us all. I'm grateful because I suddenly feel like my tongue is glued to the roof of my mouth. I take a desperate gulp of orange soda and pretend to be uninterested in the entire conversation, watching as a gaggle of freshmen attempt to navigate the complex seating hierarchy in the cafeteria.

Carson, unperturbed by my lack of response, grins. "Awesome. See y'all there."

And then he disappears, and I'm free to resume normal respiratory function. I'm kind of disappointed by Carson's lack of eye contact with me, especially after our doodle hilarity in class the other day, but I figure I'll be able to dazzle him with my unbelievable wit and sarcasm once we've both had a few beers at the party. [Sorry, police officers. I meant Capri Sun. The best of all the conversational lubricants.]

Afterward I ask Danny why he suddenly looks as though he's chewing a dung beetle, but he just mumbles incoherently about history homework and disappears to the library for probably the first time in his life.

Ajita and I go to the bathroom so she can examine her eyebrows for fry shrapnel and I can text Betty about the party. Not for permission—I can't think of a time she's ever prevented me from having fun [perks of being a tragic orphan]—she just likes to be kept in the loop about my social engagements so she can plan when to get drunk herself. Betty says this in response:

Cool . Baxter, is he the arrogant mofo with the micro-penis complex ? I met his mom at parent-teacher night, think her doctor injected her lip fillers with a cattle syringe !

Honestly, the one thing I hate about my grandma is the space she always inserts between the ends of her sentences and subsequent question/exclamation marks. Though at this point I just have to be grateful she gave up on text speak and calling me "hun." Shudder.

I show Ajita the reply as she's wiping away rogue mascara smudges in the bathroom mirror, and she cackles her witchy cackle. "I'm so jealous," she says. "I want to be raised by your grandma."

I helpfully tell her that if she wants, I can arrange for her entire family to be killed in a terrifying road accident, but despite all her big talk she doesn't seem too keen on the idea.

Anyway, I'm half tempted to interrogate Ajita about whether she thinks Carson went out of his way to invite us because he's into me, but the mere thought makes me feel arrogant and self-involved. Also, that would mean admitting that I, Izzy O'Neill, am capable of having romantic feelings for another human being. Which, gross.

Instead, like the true high school cliché I am, I imme-diately begin to plan my outfit and strategize on how to convince the boy I like of my brilliance, pushing all thoughts of Danny to the back of my brain.

8:48 p.m.

Danny's hanging out with Prajesh tonight to make sure he's doing okay. I think he plans on showing him his collection of vintage Nintendo consoles and having a Mario Kart marathon, so he rain checks on me and Ajita. To be honest, I'm pretty glad for the girls' night. With everything that's going on with Danny's new weirdness, I'm finding myself monitoring my jokes and general behavior around him. It'll be nice to just relax and not have to worry about making things worse.

We're chilling and eating junk food in Ajita's basement, and I decide to fill her in on the latest developments in the screenplay competition and Mrs. Crannon's unbelievable generosity. I mean, fifty bucks. *Fifty bucks.* I've never been in possession of fifty bucks in my life. I'm practically Bill Gates.

"Ajita, consider this. What if—and hear me out, please, because I know this is going to sound absurd—but what if not all teachers are Dementors in human clothing?"

"You're right, that does sound absurd." She tosses a pretzel M&M into the air and catches it in her mouth. This sounds impressive but you forget her ridiculously long tongue. She's basically like a lizard catching flies.

"I'm kinda scared, though," I admit. "About entering this competition."

"Why?"

I pick at some stray lint on the sleeve of my sweater, despising the admission of vulnerability but needy for my best friend's reassurance. "I just keep thinking that I'm too working class. Too 'common.' They'll write me off as trash. These opportunities are not for People Like Me, you know?"

Ajita has a funny kind of smile as she pours the remaining M&M's down her throat straight from the package. "I'm Nepali American. Trust me, I know."

"Right," I agree. "Do you ever just feel like the deck is stacked against you?" I ask, digging my fist into a bowl of salted popcorn. [It may seem like we're always eating, but that's because we're always eating.]

"All. The. Freaking. Time." She crumples up the bag and shoves it down the side of the sofa for her parents to uncover in about a year's time. "And I think I'll feel that way as long as I live in this country. But what are you going to do—not even try? What's the worst that can happen if you enter a competition and it doesn't pan out?"

I think about it, and my fear really comes down to this. "I'll be laughed at. And not in the good way."

Turning to face me head on, Ajita replies, "So what?"

I smile. I know what's about to happen. When one of us is scared to do something for fear of rejection, this is how we talk each other around it. By asking "so what?" and forcing ourselves to justify the fear, we soon realize there's rarely anything to actually be afraid of.

"So I'll feel stupid."

"So what?"

"It'll be embarrassing."

"So what?"

I'm already struggling to come up with more answers. "So it might make me want to give up writing."

One more time: "So what?"

Watching as she tucks her legs smugly under her butt, I concede, "All right. You win."

"No, *you* win," she grins. "No matter what. Just by putting yourself out there. Look, it's human nature to shy away from situations where we might experience shame, especially in public. There's something primal about wanting to avoid embarrassment at all costs. It's about preserving your ego—and thus your sense of personal identity."

"Calm down, Freud," I say. "Spare a thought for the idiots in the room."

"Sorry, I forget about your below-average IQ. All I'm saying is that self-preservation and resistance to shame is natural. But it's also not logical. And because it's not a logical fear, it can't be countered with a logical response. You have to face emotion with emotion. So channel all your passion and bravery and wildness, and shove them in fear's face, okay?"

"Okay," I grin back even harder. "You're the best. Even though you're far too intelligent to be my best pal."

"I know. I tell myself this on a daily basis."

Trying my best to appear nonchalant but in reality just looking stoned, I ask, "What's up with Danny, by the way? He's been acting so weird lately." I hope by keeping it deliberately vague, I'll be able to judge whether Ajita really has noticed or whether it's just me being a paranoid narcissist as per usual.

"Oh good, you're not as oblivious as you look," she replies simply.

"What's that supposed to mean, d-bag?"

"Well, it's just that your head is usually so far up your own ass that your nose essentially is giving you a colonoscopy. So for you to notice the behavior of others is something of a revelation." Ajita gives me a half-disdainful, half-sympathetic look. "I have to say it, dude. And I know it'll make you cringe, and I know you'll disagree vehemently on account of your fundamental distrust in my judgment, but I think it's fairly obvious what's happening here."

"It is?"

"The guy's blatantly harboring a newfound crush on you. It's thrown him way off guard since he's known you for, like, a million years, but now he's developing The Feels and is unclear how to proceed."

My stomach sinks as I mull this over. "So he just keeps buying me beverages and complimenting personality traits he's previously expressed extreme disgust at, all in the hope that I will somehow fall in love with him in return?"

"Look, I never said he was particularly subtle with his tactics. I just think he's in trouble in the romance department. And honestly? This is not going to end well."

FRIDAY, SEPTEMBER 16

2:45 p.m.
I'm writing this post from computer science instead of doing the assignment because I am a fearless rebel who cannot be tamed. Usually I would wait until I got home and was safely in my cardboard-box-sized bedroom with a small mountain of peanut butter cups, but this is a legitimate emergency.

Having obsessed over the potential crush situation all morning, I decide to speak to Danny at lunch. As an extremely nonconfrontational person, this causes me actual physical pain, but I can't just stand by and let my relationship grow weirder and weirder without doing anything about it. So I'm going to put the feelers out there and try to gauge how true Ajita's theory may not be. Nothing drastic, but enough for me to get a sense of how bad this thing may or may not be.

Anyway, it's true. He's in love with me. Which is catastrophic on a number of levels. The conversation goes like this:

Me: Dude, what's going on? You've been so weird lately.

Danny: What? No.

Me: Danny.

Danny: It just bugs me when you and Ajita gossip about guys all the time.

Me: Ajita and I have gossiped about guys since the age of seven. It's never bothered you before.

Danny: *long silence while blushing*

Me: *reciprocates long silence because of aversion to conflict*

Danny: Well, it bothers me now.

Me: Why?

Danny: I don't know.

Now, I know you may think this does not sound like your average declaration of love, and yes, while I was typing out the exchange I began to wonder whether I'd misunderstood the whole situation, and perhaps I am simply an incredible narcissist, but I'm sticking to my guns. He's in love with me. Let's examine the evidence.

Article A: When I confronted him about being weird, he replied defensively at the speed of light. Which means he preempted the question. Which means he knows he's being weird. And then when I applied the tiniest little bit more pressure, he folded like a poker player with a pair of twos. Trust me, I am fluent in Danny. This means he is hiding something.

Article B: He blushed. Danny has never blushed in his

life. In fact, due to his extreme paleness, I have kind of been operating under the assumption that his blood is colorless, like IV fluid.

Article C: He said "I don't know." Let me tell you, Danny is the most opinionated son of a preacher man on the planet. Possibly in our entire solar system. So for him to utter the words "I don't know" is utterly implausible. Of course he knows. He just doesn't want to say it.

I'm not sure how I feel about these developments. I think at the moment I'm mainly sad, because anything that jeopardizes our friendship is not okay, and everyone knows unrequited love is the cancer of friendship circles. And I do not even a little bit love him back. I don't think. I mean, I love him, like an annoying cousin or particularly needy hamster, but I am not *in* love with him. I don't think.

Or maybe I am in love with Danny? Maybe I'm just missing the signs. Maybe the fact that he often makes me feel queasy when he burps the national anthem is not a symptom of disgust, but deeply rooted infatuation. Maybe the fact that we're so comfortable around each other, to the extent that I often FaceTime him from the toilet, is actually a sign we're soulmates. It's not exactly how imagined my first great romance would unfold, but is it really realistic to expect an epic *Notebook*-style love story in this day and age?

How doth one know that one doth be in love? [I'm unconvinced by the accuracy of my "doth" usage in this sentence, but am leaving it in for authenticity.]

6:58 p.m.

Due to our incredible lack of originality, we're hanging out at the diner again tonight, with one key exception: She Who Must Not Be Named has joined the festivities. Although we each have friends outside of the tripod, this is the first time there has been an attempt to infiltrate the inner circle. And I'm not down. Not down at all.

I mean, Carlie is probably a very nice girl, but you might have noticed that I'm not super good at dealing with friend jealousy. So I like to imagine her with devil horns and a pointy tail to make myself feel better. [Don't give me that look. This approach is incredibly mature and I would recommend it to anyone.]

The four of us are crammed into a booth, Danny and me on one side, Carlie and Ajita on the other. For the first time ever, I'm painfully aware of the air between Danny and me. It seems to crackle like electricity, not with sexual tension, but because I'm constantly paranoid that I might accidentally close the gap and make direct contact with him, and if that happens he may misconstrue the touching as an indicator of my reciprocated romantic feelings. So, muscles tensed and back straight, I sit in the booth as stiff as a boner.

We get off to a bad start when Danny, Ajita, and I all order deliciously unhealthy milk shakes—two double chocolate brownie, one peaches and cream—and Carlie orders a sparkling water and a side salad. Seriously, what is this girl's cherry tomato fetish all about? She then proceeds to eye our milk shakes not with jealousy but with extreme disapproval. The temptation to pour my brownie shake over her salad like Thousand Island dressing is overwhelming.

Ajita and Carlie are talking amongst themselves about tennis and Grand Slams, whatever that means, and Danny and I are just kind of sitting there awkwardly, waiting for an opportune moment to join the conversation. I know zero about sports, and always make a royal fool of myself every time I attempt to discuss balls in a nonsexual manner.

"So, Carlie, which school did you go to before Edgewood?" I ask the second there's a tiny pause as Carlie tries to spear a green olive on her fork.

She flips her auburn hair over her shoulder and chews the olive daintily. "I lived in Southern California, so you won't know the school. But it was a *lot* bigger than Edgewood, that's for sure."

"So how come you moved here?" Danny asks.

"My mom grew up here. My grandma still lives downtown, and she's pretty sick. Cancer. So we moved back to be close to her."

"That sucks," Ajita says. She looks like she's considering squeezing Carlie's shoulder, or engaging in some other kind of physical affection, but decides against it. "I'm sorry."

Carlie shrugs, completely apathetic. "Don't be. I never liked my grandma."

When I think of how much I adore Betty, this statement seems cold and callous beyond belief. I'd be devastated if she died. "No?" I ask. "How come?"

"I'm gay. She's deeply Christian. Need I say more?"

Against all my better judgment, I find myself feeling kinda bad for the girl. Even though having no parents sucks, I can't imagine being so misunderstood by my own family.

Danny sighs. "That must be rough."

"Yeah." Carlie unscrews the cap on her sparkling-water bottle and takes a tiny sip. "I mean, I thought when we moved back to a dumb little southern town that it'd be way less accepting than SoCal. But so far, everyone's been cool except my own family."

Seriously. Is there any need to emphasize how big her last school was? Or to call our hometown dumb and little? All right, so it is both of those things. But surely it's not a great way to endear yourself to the town's residents.

Ajita, unconcerned by Carlie's dismissal of the place we grew up, fills the ensuing silence. "Did you play tennis back in SoCal?"

"Yeah! I actually met Maria Sharapova at a tournament last year."

"No way! Tell me more."

And just like that, Ajita and Carlie are back in their own little tennis bubble.

As they chatter away and ignore us, Danny's elbow jostles mine when he stirs his shake. As the snap of static bristles between us, I am 800 percent sure he did this on purpose. Sure enough, he does it again. And again. And then I realize he's not attempting to generate romantic energy—he's trying to get my attention.

I look up, and he's doing the llama impression that never fails to make me laugh. He has this weird ability to fold his lips back on themselves so his teeth look ginormous, then he makes his eyes go half-goggly, half-drowsy just like a llama. On this occasion, he attempts to slurp his shake through a straw while maintaining the absurd expression.

I laugh so hard I convulse and smack my knee of the underside of the table. The sudden jolt makes Carlie jump in shock. Then, with a chunk of cucumber halfway to her open mouth, she shoots Danny and me the dirtiest of expressions before turning back to Ajita. Like those two are the parents and we're the naughty toddlers, and she wishes we'd go and play quietly elsewhere.

Before I can get too angry at her clear disdain for non–tennis fans and/or llamas, a group of cheerleaders strolls into the diner. At the sight of them, Carlie leaps up as though suddenly realizing she's been strapped to an electric chair, and says, "Hey, mind if I go sit with my other friends for a bit?"

Not even waiting for a response, she drops a ten-dollar bill on the table to cover her fizzy water and salad, making it clear she has no plans to return, and sidles off toward her infinitely cooler pals. I wouldn't care, but Ajita looks utterly crestfallen.

"Well. She seems nice," I say, unable to keep the sarcasm out of my tone.

Ajita chews the inside of her lip and says nothing. Danny shoots me a please-stop-being-a-douche-for-just-one-second look, then takes the conversational wheel. "Seriously, though, Jeets, she's always welcome to hang out with us. Want to invite her to zorb soccer? I can't promise Iz won't charge directly at her like a bull at a red flag, but still."

I cross my arms, faux-haughty. "All I'm saying is you can't trust someone who consumes salad of their own free will."

And then Danny does his llama impression for Ajita, and pretty soon the weirdness has vanished, and we're all laughing, and I'm kind of confused. Because Danny is funny, and sweet, and even though I'm not attracted to him . . . maybe being his girlfriend wouldn't be so bad. I mean, sure, the thought of kissing him is roughly as appealing as flaying myself with a potato peeler, but still.

Oh god. I'm so damn confused.

10:16 p.m.

It's quarter after ten on a Friday night, and instead of head-banging at a gig and/or participating in recreational drug use, I'm chatting with Betty in the living room over a mug of hot cocoa. Rock and roll.

Our living room is the size of your average garden shed. The walls are covered in that weird textured wallpaper most commonly associated with old folks' homes. We found the velvet sofa on the street, had it examined for termites, and then promptly covered it with blankets and cushions from a thrift store. My grandma's diner wages don't quite stretch to IKEA, which Mr. Rosenqvist would probably be horrified to hear on account of his proud Swedish ancestry.

We also have one of those old TV sets, fatter than it is tall, without cable. Honestly, the battle I had to go through to get Betty to have Wi-Fi installed. Like Vietnam but with more waterboarding.

We're both piled on the velvet sofa in our sweatpants, and her wrinkly feet are in my lap as I give her a much-needed foot rub while she knits. This is her first night off in ten days, and I can tell she's feeling it. She groans as I bury my thumb in the pressure points caused by her bunions. For the thousandth time, I wish it was me working so hard instead of her. But when I got in from school, I called around to all the places I'd dumped my résumé, and none of them showed any interest in hiring me. Not even Martha's.

Once I've moved on to painting Betty's toenails a vivid shade of fuchsia, I tell her about the Danny situation, and she doesn't even have the common decency to act surprised. Even Dumbledore looks at me like "duh, it's been graffitied on the kid's face since the start of summer, now give me one of those peanut butter cups or I'll *Avada Kedavra* your ass."

She asks me how I feel about it, and I tell her the thing about unrequited love being the cancer of friendship circles, and how maybe I am actually in love with Danny but I've been mistaking it for a mild stomach flu. At this she appears deeply shocked.

"Izzy O'Neill, you are absolutely not in love with Danny Wells."

"No, I didn't think I was." I wipe a rogue smudge of nail

56

polish from her skin with a Q-tip. "How do you know?"

"Do you want to kiss his face with your face?"

"No."

"Do you want to marry him and grow old with him and help him tie his shoes when his arthritis gets the better of him?" Her knitting needles click together at the speed of light, which making it sound like there's a cicada chorus occurring in our living room.

"Not even a little bit. The thought is vaguely horrifying."

"Do you want to let him enter you?"

"Gross. No."

Apparently this is all the evidence she requires to deliver her final verdict: Danny's love is unrequited.

"You and Danny have always been close pals, especially in the beginning, when it was just the two of you." Sometimes I forget it was once just the two of us. Ever since we brought Ajita home in the third week of fourth grade, cramming on this sofa with giddy excitement over our first playdate, the tripod was secured. Ajita fit right in. "He's an only child, so he struggled a bit when he first had to share you, but he soon got over it. You all bounced off each other. Always cracking jokes, inventing games, and acting out elaborate stage shows with no solid plot arc whatsoever. Danny doted on you, even then, but you always kept him at arm's length. He's always been infatuated with you—I think he just finally figured that out for himself this summer. Poor kid."

"Well," I say. "Shit."

"Shit indeed." She *tsks* at a dropped stitch in the scarf

she's knitting, examining the damage between her thumb and forefinger. "Hey, has he talked to you much about his parents lately? Danny, I mean."

I frown, swiveling the lid back onto the nail polish and admiring my handiwork on her toes. They look vaguely less horrific. "No, I don't think so. How come? Everything okay with them?"

She shrugs. "Word at the community center is that their marriage is on the rocks. Could just be small-town gossip, but who knows." As she talks, Betty ditches the knitting needles and rubs her temples with her thumbs, round and round in circular motions. At first I think she's trying to summon the Holy Spirit, but judging by her pained expression, she's not feeling so great.

"Another tension headache?" I ask.

"It's those damn strip lights in the kitchen at work," she grumbles. "Staring at fluorescent bulbs sixty hours a week would give anyone a migraine."

People love to glorify sassy old women who work until they're a hundred years old. Look at them! Throwing shade at snarky regulars and serving day-old coffee grounds to their ruthless managers! So hilarious and inspiring! But *this* is the truth. More and more vulnerable old people can't afford to retire, and so they keep working at grueling service jobs because they simply have to. It's a matter of survival. They work through sore feet and headaches and bone-deep exhaustion, illness and injury and grief. It's sick.

Anyway, after the pep talk with Betty, my general confusion over the Danny situation has made way for crushing guilt. What am I supposed to do now? [I am asking this purely rhetorically. I almost never follow the advice of others due to my insane stubbornness.]

I would love to be brave enough to take matters into my own hands, like a soldier who proudly charges to the front line and faces enemy troops head-on. I should really just ask him, human to human, whether he has feelings for me, and if he says yes, I should be honest and say I'm not sure I reciprocate. But alas, I am instead going to hide out in my soggy trench until the problem passes, or I'm brutally murdered by a grenade. Either way I am fundamentally a coward and not the kind of person you want on your side in a battle zone. [There have been a lot of war metaphors in this post, which I think is a beautiful representation of my emotional turmoil and deep inner conflict. Imagery and whatnot. What a poet I am. Like T. S. Eliot but with better boobs.]

Seriously, though, I have no idea how to handle the situation, so I decide to stick with the tried and true method of ignoring the problem and hoping it disappears on its own.

Unreasonable though it may be, I feel a bit angry with Danny for potentially messing up a perfectly good friendship, even though I logically know it's not his fault.

Is it mine? Is my raw sexuality, infectious personality, and awe-inspiring modesty sending out the wrong message?

<u>11:59 p.m.</u>

Update: Just looked at myself in the mirror. My blond hair is more "terrifying scarecrow" than "glossy shampoo commercial," and I have raccoon eyes from three days' worth of mascara and eyeliner gradually building up and soaking into my skin. The bra I'm wearing doesn't fit properly, on account of me never having any money, so I have a slight case of quadruple-boob going on. My thrifted Hooters T-shirt [shut up, I bought it ironically] has cocoa stains all down the front, and also a patch of Dumbledore drool shaped like Australia.

It might not be the raw sexuality thing.

SATURDAY, SEPTEMBER 17

<u>**1:30 p.m.**</u>

Party day! Danny and I are spending the afternoon trailing Ajita around every clothing store imaginable in search of the perfect outfit for tonight, both providing helpful and educational commentary on her selections. So far we have vetoed the sequined overalls [like a cabaret show vomited onto a hillbilly], the high-waisted mom jeans [she's three feet tall and they come up to her nipples] and the distressed faux-vintage band tee [when challenged to name any song or album by Pink Floyd, she mumbled something about us being assholes, which is offensive yet accurate].

I'm super excited to wear my outfit for tonight—a gray silky shirt I've had for years and years, but I still feel like an absolute queen when I wear it. It's an original Armani with these silver studs all around the collar, and it's the only piece of designer clothing I own.

When I was fourteen and just starting to be painfully aware of how badly I dressed compared to everyone else, I found it on a weekend shopping trip with Ajita [I could never afford to actually buy anything, but I enjoyed hanging out with Ajita enough to tag along]. It was in Goodwill for $40, which is a lot of money for Goodwill, and I had nowhere near enough to afford it. I went home and begged Betty to loan me some cash, and she agreed to put aside a little money from her next paycheck to buy it for me. I spent every single night praying nobody else would buy it in the meantime. By the time we went back to get it, it had sold, and I was heartbroken.

But who'd bought it? Ajita, who had gotten it for my birthday. I honestly nearly cried when I tore open the carefully wrapped tissue paper and saw the silky gray material I'd fantasized over for so many weeks. I still only wear it on special occasions, because I never want the magic to fade.

2:47 p.m.

The mall is absolutely packed, but that doesn't prevent us from running into Lucifer herself, i.e., Carlie.

Carlie is out shopping with her mom, who is also a very tall, very redheaded woman with perfectly clear skin and perfect white teeth. Their perfection is almost blinding without adequate eye protection. I require one of those welder masks to deal with the sheer absurdity of their beauty.

"Hey," Carlie says to all three of us, taking a slurp of her beet-purple smoothie in a plastic take-out cup, looking every inch the Abercrombie model. I say all three of us—she mainly looks at Ajita as though Danny and I are transparent poltergeists. "What's up, girl?"

Girl. Singular. As though I am not present. A bubble of anger pops in my belly.

"Just picking out a dress for tonight," Ajita explains, gesturing to the shopping bags Danny is carrying on her behalf. "Are you going to Baxter's party later?"

"Totally! It's going to be super fun."

Ajita smiles. "You say this now, but I fully intend to take you down on the Ping-Pong table. You may run rings around me on a real tennis court, but the table is my domain."

"We'll see," replies Carlie, with a girlish giggle, pouting her berry-stained lips and taking another sip of smoothie.

If you ask me, this is an incredibly dull comeback. I almost fall asleep with sheer boredom.

"Okay, well, see you later, I guess?" Ajita says, after a beat that lasts slightly too long. Why does this feel so awkward? Whatever the cause, I'm incredibly relieved when we part ways, Carlie's mom giving us a formal nod as they head in the opposite direction.

Throughout the entire five-second conversation, Carlie's eyes do not stray from Ajita's. It's genuinely like Danny and I aren't there. Maybe she's not into our weird sense of humor, or the way we, as a group, gently bully each other. [You know, in a funny way.] Or maybe, as a jock who looks like *that*, she's ashamed to be seen with us. We're hardly the most popular kids in school.

Either way, it's kind of rude. She doesn't even try to be polite even after we invited her to join us at the diner. She couldn't possibly make it any clearer that she wouldn't hang out with us if it weren't for our marginally cooler best friend. This irritates me, and does nothing to dissipate the devil horns I imagine on her.

For the rest of the afternoon, I keep secretly hoping we'll bump into Carson and Co. There's a group of basketball dudes hanging out at the wishing fountain, laughing raucously at something on one of their phones, but Carson isn't among them. In fact, on second glance, I'm not even sure they go to our school. By the time we finally sit down for hot pretzels, I'm pretty sure I've given myself repetitive strain injury in my neck.

I guess it's a good thing we don't see Carson, since Danny might just explode in sheer fury if we did. Though to be fair to him, he's acting pretty normal today. Making witty observations about dumb fashion trends and such. Long may it last, I say.

Still, thinking of what Betty told me about his parents, while Ajita's ordering our sodas and pretzels I nudge him on the shoulder.

"Hey, everything okay at home?" I say, quietly enough so the table of snooty-faced soccer moms next to us don't hear, but loud enough that it's not weird or conspiratorial.

Regardless of my volume policing, he immediately tenses. "Why wouldn't it be?" He sweeps stray salt granules off the table with his hoodie sleeve, then rubs at a dried condensation ring with his thumb.

Message received. "No reason. Forget I asked. Hey, what noise do llamas even make?"

3:17 p.m.

The plan for tonight is to get ready at Ajita's, as her house is a stupidly beautiful mansion and also just around the corner from Baxter's place. Her parents are super rich neurosurgeon geniuses who fully expect Ajita to follow in their footsteps, which is hilarious because Ajita has flunked every science class we've taken over the last two years. Not because she's dumb [she isn't], but because Danny and I are terrible human beings who lead her astray on a daily basis, like annoying parrots sitting on her shoulder and chirping in her ear about how much more fun it is to perform a silent film for our classmates than it is to learn about plant cell structure. Besides, I have it on good authority that in the real world, nobody will ever question you on the function of the mito-chondria [THE POWERHOUSE OF THE CELL! See, I know things] or the vacuole [nah I got nothing]. By good authority I obviously mean my grandma.

Thankfully, Ajita herself has little to no interest in enter-ing the medical field. I just hope I'm not there when she decides to finally tell her parents.

Then, armed with our crates of beer [Capri Sun], we'll get a lift to Baxter's empty house at like 7:30 this evening. The party starts at eight, and I know it is borderline tragic to arrive so early, but you know how I told you I need to know everyone's drama and business? Yeah, I have FOMO when I miss a significant portion of a social event. Ajita does too. So we just sit in a corner watching everyone and eating popcorn, like it's *Big Brother* but more intrusive.

6:24 p.m.

Writing this from Ajita's bathroom, because DANNYYYY.

So after I've dragged a brush through my scarecrow hair and done my makeup to the best of my ability [smoky charcoal eyes and nude lipstick, if you're interested], I pull my party attire out of my duffel bag and start to get changed in front of Ajita and Danny, as I have a hundred million times before. Seriously, they have both seen me in so many different stages of undress that they could probably do a pretty accurate life drawing of my naked body, with freckle location accuracy down to a fraction of a millimeter. Since I'm not body conscious, and because we've all known each other for so long, I've never felt weird getting changed in front of them. It just wasn't a thing. Before tonight.

Ajita's sitting at her vanity, trying and failing to get fake eyelashes to stay on her face, and has accidentally glued one eye shut as a result, while Danny's sitting on the edge of her bed and flipping through his phone. Honestly, he's barely even paying attention to either me or Ajita. I kinda get the feeling he'd rather be playing video games with Prajesh, but Ajita's prodigy of a brother is away at some sadistic weekend cross-country meet in another state.

I whip my tee off so I'm just standing in jeans and a bra, *as I have a hundred million times before*, and before I can put my fancy Armani shirt on, Danny groans, covers his eyes emphatically with his hands, and says, "Do you have to do that here?"

Ajita's glued eye pings open in shock. "What are you

talking about, dude? You've seen her shirtless before. Hell, you saw *me* shirtless about ten seconds ago. What's the big deal?"

He drops his hands into his lap and stares at his grubby fingernails, cheeks burning as fuchsia as Betty's nail polish. But before he has to reply, I save his awkward ass.

"S'all right," I say quickly. "I'll go next door."

He shoots me a grateful look that fills my stomach with dread. Because . . . what if this *doesn't* just go away on its own? What the hell do I do then?

10:53 p.m.

Update from the front line: Danny is off chatting up one of the cheerleaders, who looks like Malia Obama's twin, but he keeps glancing over at me to make sure I am witnessing his superb flirtation skills. I just nod encouragingly, trying to ignore the fact that to the untrained eye I look like a creepy uncle lurking on the edge of the dance floor and supporting his lecherous nephew's efforts to get laid for the first time.

Forreal, though, I'm super relieved he's trying to hook up with another girl. It takes the pressure off me for a while.

Ajita and I are chilling on a lime-green sofa in the living room. The house is crammed with sweaty teenage bodies. The lighting is low and the music is loud, and everyone's drinking beer out of plastic cups, spilling it all over the wooden floorboards. That's gonna stink in the morning.

My best friend, bless her heart, is completely unperturbed by the fact that I'm updating my blog while at a party.

At this point in our friendship she's pretty used to me tapping furiously on my phone's touch screen as she chugs her beer and observes the drama unfolding around us.

Baxter's house is actually super nice, probably because his mom launched this tech start-up a couple years back and it's really taken off. They used to live in a low-income housing community like mine, with metal bars over the windows to prevent break-ins, but now they're firmly in the fancy part of town, where every mansion has at least three cars in the driveway. One of which is usually a Range Rover, let's be real.

"Beer pong?" I ask Ajita, who's curled into the corner of the sofa with her shoes kicked off, hugging a black-and-white chevron-print cushion. She's pretty buzzed after just two beers, on account of her severe tininess.

"Nah, that requires moving," she practically yawns. She's a sleepy drunk.

"Good point," I concede. "In that case, can I get you another bottle?"

"Now you're talkin'." She winks at me like some sort of gangster. I mean, gangsters probably don't wink at each other all that much. But you know what I mean.

Oh god, Vaughan just arrived with his oily entourage. His hair is slicked back and his Abercrombie shirt is way too tight, and he has a swastika tattooed on his exposed chest. [I made that last bit up as I have a tendency to do. But his dad is, as previously stated, a notorious racist. So you can never be too sure.]

And now he's scanning the room, probably scoping me out like those birds that hover in the air above their prey until they're ready to strike. I don't really know what kind of bird this is but I swear I saw it on some nature documentary, or in real life, or on one of the rare occasions I was paying attention in class. It's hard to distinguish at this point. Anyway the analogy made perfect sense when I started typing, and I've committed now so I'll stick to it.

I'm a worm. Or something. A drunk little worm trying to wriggle away from its gross predator.

Brb, off to dig a hole in the dirt and stay there until he goes away.

11:48 p.m.
Yeah, I slept with Vaughan.

SUNDAY, SEPTEMBER 18

9:18 a.m.
Last night went up in flames. Seriously, I make such unbelievably bad life choices. Can I blame this on the tragic orphan thing again? No?

Sigh. Here we go.

Vaughan eventually tracks me down in my little wormhole, aka the sofa, because I am not sufficiently committed to my role as a creature of the dirt, and offers to get me a drink. By this point Satan— i.e., Carlie—has joined Ajita and me on the couch, and is once again behaving as though I am not present, so I accept Vaughan's proposal on account of the fact Satan's sickly sweet perfume is giving me a headache, and our crate of beer is running low, and I'm losing my buzz quite rapidly, and I think we have established at this point that I am utterly shameless in an impressive variety of ways.

En route to the fridge, he makes some actually rather astute observations about our surroundings, such as: "Wow, there are like so many people here" and "Baxter is an embarrassment at beer pong" and "If Kenan Mitchell were green he would basically be Shrek." I agree good-naturedly because I am very thirsty. [Not like that. Stop snickering.]

Of course my respiratory system chooses this precise moment to start evicting a metric fuck-ton of phlegm from my body, and I cough like a maniac for several decades. Vaughan says, "Yeah, it's really smoky in here, let's get some fresh air." Literally not one individual is smoking a cigarette or any other substance in our immediate proximity, which does seem statistically unlikely and yet is true at this precise moment, but like an idiot I follow him outside anyway because 1) he is carrying my beer and 2) fresh air doesn't actually sound too horrible thanks to the general scent of teenage boy in the living room.

Also, the Shrek thing did make me laugh. Is it possible Vaughan does, in fact, possess a sense of humor? There's only one way to find out.

We sit on one of those fancy swinging bench things only rich people ever have. The yard is pitch black, meaning I don't have to look at his overgelled hair, which is perhaps why I temporarily forget I'm talking to Zachary Vaughan. [Don't call him Zach, he gets upset for reasons I cannot begin to understand.] I half expect there to be long stretches of awkward silence, but he just hands me my beer and asks me a nice question about my grandma. This is one of many signs that I have somehow fallen through a wormhole and landed in an alternate universe, and thus cannot be held responsible for my own actions. Or something.

"So how's your dad's campaign going?" I ask him, once

I've finished telling him about how when Dumbledore the Dog dies, we're going to get another dachshund and call it Voldemort, and pretend to our house guests that the Dark Lord has risen once again and killed all our other pets, including Luna and Neville the goldfish and Hermione the hamster, none of which ever existed but the story works best if Voldemort commits mass homicide. Betty and I both feel this is exactly what Dumbledore the Dog would want. Vaughan appears completely unperturbed by this idea, which you sort of have to admire.

But at the mention of his dad, he immediately stiffens. [Again, not like that. What's wrong with you?]

"Do we have to talk about it?" he mutters, swigging from his plastic cup. We can almost hear the babble of laughter and the low pounding of house music, but the thick walls are doing a pretty good job of keeping the yard quiet. Which is unfortunate, because right now I could really do with something cutting through the awkward silence.

Hastily I explain how I don't give one singular shit about his father's campaign and only brought it up because conversational protocol dictates that I ask him a question, and I know absolutely nothing else about him.

"You're cute when you babble," he says to my total horror and disgust, because unlike the popular aughts rock band, cute is never what I aim for.

"So tell me something about yourself that has zero to do with your family's controversial political stances," I say. I regret adding the word "controversial" but he lets it go.

"All right. I'm the oldest of four siblings. I want to go to law school, preferably as far away from here as possible."

"That's cool," I say. "Have you always wanted to be a lawyer?"

"No," he admits. "It's just what my parents want me to do. They're both defense attorneys. Or they were, until my dad got into politics. God, why does every conversation always swing back around to my dad?" This last sentence is laced with a bitterness I wasn't expecting.

As we sit in silence, a rare profound thought enters my brain. What might *my* life be like if I had parents to compare myself to?

Before they died, my dad was a car mechanic and my mom worked in a convenience store. How different would my childhood have been if I'd spent weekends watching my dad fix up an old secondhand car until the engine purred into life? Or helped my mom unload candy deliveries at the convenience store, sneaking packs of fruity bubble gum into my pockets? How different would my life have been if they'd survived to see me grow up? How different would *I* be?

The thoughts are painful and unwelcome. I know I'm supposed to pity Vaughan for his douchebag father, but I don't. I'm jealous. I'm so jealous it makes me sick to my stomach.

"Um. Right. So. Here's a question," I mumble, in a desperate bid to change the topic from parents. "What's your patronus?"

This is in fact a test disguised as an interesting point of

conversation. If he doesn't know what a patronus is, I know immediately that there is no reason to proceed with the swing-based festivities.

But without even hesitating, he just replies simply, "A duck-billed platypus."

I'm pretty taken aback by this. It's not at all the answer I was expecting. Most dudes go with something obvious like a lion, but this is super original. "Oh, really? Why's that?"

He swigs his beer again. Despite the speed of his drinking, he still seems pretty sober. "They're just awesome and unique. Like, did you know they're the only mammal that has a sense of electroreception? They hunt their prey by detecting the electric fields generated by muscular contractions. So basically they're super smart, but in their own way." He shrugs, like he can relate. "And they're the only venomous mammal on earth. I like that they can strike back and defend themselves if they have to."

What. The. Hell. He's genuinely given this some thought. If there is any surefire way to win my respect, this is it.

I smile, observing his silhouetted profile. He's really not terrible to look at—one of those cute dimpled chins and a ski-slope nose that tilts up at the end. His father may be a fascist, but he obviously has good genes.

"What about yours?" Vaughan asks.

I've had my answer prepared for over a decade. "A sloth."

He spits beer everywhere as he laughs. "That's hilarious.

It's so perfect. Cute and sleepy and highly entertaining. Yep . . . you're a sloth, Izzy O'Neill."

I grin. I can't help it.

"Okay . . . what else can I tell you about myself?" he muses, looking around the yard as though waiting for divine inspiration to strike. He clocks the creepy gnomes hanging out by the pond, and looks suitably perturbed.

Then, borderline surprised like it's the first time the thought has ever crossed his mind, he goes with: "Oh, I know. I am a virgin, ha ha ha."

???

[Yeah. Not what I was expecting either. I'll give you a few minutes to process this. You good? Okay, so you recovered faster than I did.]

I have zip/zilch/zero/nada/nil problem with the fact that he's a virgin, I just was not anticipating this plot twist in the slightest.

So, very supportively and insightfully, I say: "Oh."

Then the awkward silence kicks in. And all I can think to add is, "Why are you telling *me* this, of all people? We've never spoken before tonight, even if we do know each other's patronuses now. How do you know you can trust me? I mean, I assume this is a secret."

He shrugs and says, "I like you, Izzy. You're funny and stuff." Another shrug. "And . . . I don't know. I know you probably think I'm a jerk, like everyone else in school does. Because of my dad and all. So I thought if I was honest with you about something really personal . . . I don't know. Maybe I thought you wouldn't think that anymore."

Now, I personally find this logic quite flawed, because I could very easily have turned out to be a vindictive psychopath and leaked this information everywhere. Obviously this is not the course of action I actually choose to take, but really, how did he know I'm not fundamentally awful? Also, being a virgin and being a jerk are not mutually exclusive, so the whole thing is quite hard to wrap my head around.

This isn't going the way I expected it to. In a good way, mostly. Like, if I had put any thought into what we would talk about when we got out here I probably would have guessed he'd start praising travel bans and walls on the Mexican border, or he'd say something creepy and inappropriate, or I'd just generally feel gross sitting so close to him, because seriously, his father is not an awesome guy. But in the end, none of those things happen. Vaughan has already made me laugh, made me think, and let me see his vulnerable side. And I'm enjoying myself. Genuinely.

Don't get me wrong, it's not like we're going to get married and have babies and all that. Can you even imagine Ted Vaughan and Betty O'Neill sitting around the same table at Thanksgiving? No. It would be absurd. Betty would probably offer to carve the turkey but then let loose on Ted's balding head with the serrated knife instead. Suffice to say, it would be carnage.

But right now, I've had a few drinks, and I feel warm and fuzzy, and Vaughan is actually an okay guy, and also

I have that high sex drive that's always getting me into trouble.

And also . . . I feel kind of vulnerable. Thinking about my parents, and what my life would be like if they were around, has cracked something buried deep inside me open. It's just a small crack, letting in a tiny sliver of light, but even that small amount of light is too much. Too exposing.

My chest twists. I don't want to feel these feelings. They hurt too much. I need a distraction.

So I down the rest of my beer and then instantly start kissing Vaughan. Which is a mistake, because if you've ever downed three-quarters of a can of fizzy liquid in six seconds, you know what happens next.

burp

Fuuuuuuuuuuccccccckkkkkkkkkkkk—

My cheeks start to burn like the fiery magma of Mount Etna as I pull away, mortified.

Next plot twist: he is not an asshole about this horrifying bodily development. He just laughs and says, "I guess now we both know something embarrassing about each other."

Then I get all serious, which shockingly I am capable of on occasion. "Being a virgin is not embarrassing, Vaughan. You know that, don't you?"

"Try telling that to the rest of the basketball team."

And then he's kissing me again, and it's actually not terrible, actually it's really good, like really good, and he smells like fresh laundry, and his lips are so soft, and sweet Jesus of Nazareth—

You know what happens next. Yes, I take his virginity on the porch swing.

Izzy O'Neill: keeping it classy since never.

12:42 p.m.

Betty just came knocking on my door with a bacon, egg, and cheese sandwich and a glass of extra pulpy OJ like the true hero she is, and demanded to know everything. I told her the abridged version. She laughed so hard at the burping incident she almost gave herself a hernia.

[Most of you probably find it really odd that I tell my grandmother about my sexual conquests, but she's just . . . never been weird about it. She doesn't treat sex like it's dirty or taboo, and as long as I'm keeping myself safe, she really doesn't mind that I treat it as an extracurricular activity. Plus she's of the general opinion that my mom (her daughter) led the life of a saint and she still ended up dead at the age of twenty-four, so I may as well enjoy myself because this could all be taken away at any moment, and do I really want to be at heaven's gates/hell's trapdoor thinking about all the things (read: people) I wish I'd done?]

Speaking of enjoying myself. Remember Carson Manning? Hot-yet-unintimidating, class clown, alpaca doodler? Yeah, him.

Vaughan and I come in from outside, and it isn't like in those clichéd movies where people who've just had sex look very obviously like they just had sex. There are no tree branches in my hair, for example, or dirt on my knees.

I have that relaxed and happy post-sex feeling I always get after a hookup. Honestly, I haven't had that many bad sexual encounters. Every teenage boy I've ever banged has been so enthusiastic that it makes up for any logistical difficulties we stumble upon. I really don't get why sex is considered such a big deal. It's just . . . it's fun, and it feels good. And so I do it on a regular basis, whether alone or with a friend. [I know you're going to want me to talk numbers here, but really you're just being nosy. It's somewhere between two and two hundred. Happy? And yes, I always use protection. My life is enough of a train wreck without having syphilis to contend with.]

Anyway, we come back inside, and much like Vaughan thirty seconds ago, the party seems to be reaching its climax. There are several people passed out in corners, several people making out against kitchen counters, and the music is now some sort of soft remixed reggae I don't actually hate. The windows are now steamed up with sweaty condensation, which is pretty gross, and there are plastic cups scattered all over the floor.

I disappear to find Danny [oh shit, Danny!!] and Ajita, leaving Vaughan in the kitchen with Baxter and some of the other basketball guys. Vaughan doesn't do anything gross, like squeeze my ass as I walk away, which I appreciate because catcalling-construction-worker-style romance is not really my idea of a good time. I know some of you may find this unreasonable and absurd, but it's true.

Ajita is in exactly the same spot on the sofa, playing on her phone and looking generally bored.

"Hey, where'd Sa—I mean Carlie go?" I ask, plonking myself next to her.

Ajita shrugs and nods toward the corner of the room. Carlie is playing some kind of unhygienic drinking game that involves people passing a Ping-Pong ball to each other via their mouths. As we watch, Carlie has the ball perched between her lips, and passes it to Baxter so intimately it looks like they're kissing. Baxter drops it, so he has to down a bottle of beer.

Meanwhile, Carlie and the girl next to her—an athletic-looking blonde in a sundress—giggle and nudge each other playfully. Wait, no, not playfully. They're flirting. My suspicions are confirmed when Athletic Blonde tucks a lock of Carlie's hair behind her ear and whispers something softly. They're way too close to just be friends, Carlie's hand resting on Athletic Blonde's waist.

I turn back to Ajita, who looks a little bummed out. "You okay, friend?"

"Yeah, just . . ." She trails off, then shrugs. "Carlie didn't even ask me to play. She just disappeared and left me sitting here alone like a loser."

I remember the way Carlie seemed embarrassed to be seen associating with Danny and me in the mall earlier, and the way she ditched us as soon as the cheerleaders walked into the diner, and this behavior doesn't surprise me in the slightest. Carlie seems like the type who picks who she hangs out with carefully, assessing her company according to social hierarchy. And even though Ajita is definitely cooler and more popular than Danny and me, she's still not *popular*. So Carlie ditched her for rich jock Baxter and Athletic Surfer Blonde. Ugh.

Maybe my assertions that the girl is Satan personified weren't just a product of friend jealousy. My instincts were actually correct, for once.

"Where's Danny?" I ask, only mildly terrified of the answer. What if he saw Vaughan and me on the swing?

She cocks an eyebrow knowingly, like Buddha or some other wise religious figure, and points.

Huzzah! Danny is playing tonsil tennis with Malia Obama's twin! This is excellent news. He can no longer go all Judge Judy on me for my romantic escapades. He's moving on from his crush on me. I celebrate with another beer. To distract her from Carlie's betrayal, Ajita and I play a game of Shut Uppa Yo Face, whereby we watch other people's conversations from a distance and improvise what we think they're saying, each of us taking a character. The loser is the one who can't think of anything to say and stalls, ultimately conceding with the words "shut uppa yo face." I will admit this is a very niche game and not suitable for most social situations.

We're right in the middle of an epic duologue—a big-issue argument over whether shredded cheese tastes different from its blockier counterparts [obviously I prefer shredded because of my fundamental laziness]—when Carson approaches us. As Ajita and I are both deeply competitive souls, neither of us wants to lose, so we just keep going and going and going, debating heatedly about the merits of grated cheddar. Carson does not contribute to the conversation, given he has no idea it is part of an elaborate improvisation contest. Or maybe he just doesn't have strong opinions about cheese, which I have difficulty wrapping my head around.

Eventually I lose the game, because my beer-marinated banter is not on top form by this stage. Ajita politely excuses herself, disappearing in the direction of Baxter's hotel-like bathroom.

"O'Neill," Carson says. His voice is amazing, all warm and gravelly. "Can I sit?"

I resist the temptation to jokingly reject him and say, "Sure."

He seems genuinely pleased as he sinks into the sofa next to me. He's close enough that his arm is pressed against mine, and I can feel his muscles bulging. The smell of his cologne makes me want to lean in even closer, but I manage to control myself for once. The soft remixed reggae continues to play in the background.

"This music's pretty cool," I say, bobbing along idiotically to the laid-back beat. I wish I could stop myself from looking like such a moron at all times, but alas I cannot. I'm actually pretty nervous, though I hate to admit it. The doodle hilarity has me all kinds of intrigued, and I find myself actually wanting to get to know Carson better. It's rare for me to like someone for more than sex—I'm no virgin, but

I've never been in a long-term relationship. Or, you know. A relationship period.

"Thanks!" he grins. "It's actually my playlist." Again, he looks genuinely pleased with the compliment. He's peeling away the label on his beer bottle and not actually looking at me, though, which makes me think maybe he's feeling the same nerves as I am. I hope.

My memory of most of our conversation is a little fuzzy, but what I do remember is . . .

"So, hey," he says, slurring his words slightly. "I found your blog."

Anyone who keeps an online journal will understand the sheer horror and humiliation associated with this sentence. It is the stuff of nightmares. It is legitimately enough reason to load yourself into a cannon and fire yourself into the ocean clutching your laptop to your lifeless chest.

I start scanning my mental archives for any and all mentions of a) periods, b) other bodily functions, or c) Carson himself. Ding ding ding. Pretty sure I've covered all the important shame bases with my now-not-so-hilarious anecdotes. I'm about to excuse myself to go and immediately change my URL and install a password [which you will be relieved to know I have now done] when he adds: "So you like me, huh?"

"No," I say matter-of-factly. "I just think you're hot in a sexy-yet-unintimidating way."

He grins wolfishly. "Always the goal."

I think I might as well just tattoo a perma-blush to my face at this point because of the amount of time I've spent in a state of embarrassment tonight. Fortunately for my shame-addled voice box, Carson picks up the conversational baton once again.

"And I think you're hot too. In an entirely intimidating way."

Then he kisses me!!!

Lest you think I am an even worse homo sapien than you already do, let me just say that I am fully aware of how inappropriate this is. I can't even enjoy the moment I've fantasized about endlessly through classes on trigonometry, because I'm scanning the room for Danny and/or Vaughan through the corners of my eyes. For a minute I wonder why I am so concerned about Vaughan. It's not just that I don't want him to tell people about my gas problems. I think it's maybe the fact that I've recently learned he's not a grade-A asshole and actually has a soul? Who knows.

Clearly I am not ashamed enough to stop the Carson-kissing and such, but just so you know, I do have a conscience, although it is perpetually buried under several gallons of beer and aforementioned high sex drive.

The music is very loud and most people are very drunk, and I'm very dizzy like I've spun around in circles for eleven days, so eventually I just relax and let myself enjoy it. Surprisingly Carson is not as good a kisser as Vaughan—too much Dorito-flavored saliva for my personal taste, although I am sure others are into that particular sensation—but he's kinda cute in the way he keeps pulling away and smiling bashfully before diving in for another round of tongue hockey. Don't worry, he won't read this review of his make-out technique. Like I say, I've password-protected my blog now. [Which should have really been my first move upon its creation, but you live and learn.]

I'm in a slight quandary.

Part of me—the biggest part—wants to get it on with Carson. He's cute and funny and, well, I want to, which should not be too hard for you to grasp.

Then there's the annoying, niggling part of me that worries what people will think of me if I do. If the school population discovers I banged two dudes in one night, the girls will call me a bitch and a slut, and the guys will high-five and call me easy while flinging their own feces at each other.

Anyway, due to that abnormally high sex drive I'm always mentioning, I'm soon following him upstairs to Baxter's parents' room, where we proceed to have a lovely time. 10/10 would recommend having sex with Carson Manning. You can do it at least three times in one commercial break, and I sometimes think brevity is an underrated quality in coitus. I'd rather have short and sweet than cross over into slightly-boring-and-chafey territory.

So, to summarize: two guys, one night, both highly enjoyable. Is there a TripAdvisor for one-night stands? If there was, I would definitely recommend both gentlemen to a friend.

[I know you're probably reading this thinking, "Oh my god, what an unbelievable whore!" even though you generally consider yourself to be fairly progressive, but that's really on you. I'm having a good time and I'm not hurting anybody. What's the problem?]

MONDAY, SEPTEMBER 19

5:47 a.m.

I know! Look at that time stamp! While I am generally of the opinion that one should not rise before the sun unless one has been roused by a swarm of locusts, I can't sleep. Not only because I find out whether I've made it to the next round of the screenplay competition this week—have already refreshed emails six thousand times this morning—but also because even more shit went down last night, and my metaphorical tail is well and truly between my legs. I did a Really Bad Thing. I'm too ashamed to even tell Betty, which gives you some indication of its magnitude.

After I finish typing out the full recap of the party yesterday afternoon, Ajita texts our group chat and invites Danny and me over for a full debrief and twelve tons of extra-jalapeño nachos. This makes me slightly nervous because I'm not sure how much Danny already knows about my sexploits at this point. By slightly nervous I mean a herd of rhinos are stampeding my guts. But like the brave soul I am, I abandon my physics homework and head over on my rusty death trap of a bicycle.

Five treacherous miles later I arrive at Ajita's, and Prajesh greets me at the door with a berry and spinach smoothie. Because he's one of those student athlete types, he's always talking about The Daily Grind, and also lecturing me about the fact that I'm probably vitamin deficient in basically everything. [Do not fear, I did not have sex with him, for he is fourteen and even I draw a line somewhere.]

"Hey, Praj," I say as warmly and big-sisterly as I can. "How you doing?"

He zips up his hoodie. "Yeah, I'm cool. You?"

I want to ask him how school's going, but at the same time I don't want him to feel crappy about the fact that we've been discussing his lack of friends behind his back. So instead I say, "All fine and dandy. I hear you've been hanging out with Danny. Playing video games and such."

He nods. "Yeah. He's a cool guy."

There's a weird silence I've never really experienced with Praj before. He's definitely going through an awkward adolescent phase. His voice broke over the summer, and he still looks uncomfortable with the way it sounds.

I take a sip of the smoothie to be polite, and even though it resembles sludge it tastes pretty good. I thank him for looking out for my arteries and wave him off as he heads to practice.

Heading down to the basement, I spot Danny's sneakers by the door, and the nerves begin to multiply in my large intestine. Logically I know I don't owe him a damn thing, but guilt's a funny and unpredictable beast. Ajita's curled up in the armchair like a python, leaving Danny and me to sit up close and personal on the two-seater sofa.

My first clue that Danny knows ALL THE THINGS is that he doesn't look up when I "accidentally" trip down the last three stairs in a bid to make them laugh. Ajita snorts like a wild boar. Danny sits rigidly. I flump into the seat next to him.

"What's up, guys?" I ask, cheerier than Mrs. Cheery during National Cheeriness Week, helping myself to a handful of nachos from the table. They've barely touched them, which is another sign that it's not just my imagination— there is definitely An Atmosphere.

Ajita eyeballs me, which I think translates to: tread carefully, he's pissed. Which makes me pissed, to be honest, as he does not have ownership of my vagina. What right does he have to make me feel like shit for acting on said vagina's natural urges?

So I throw him a trademark Izzy O'Neill curveball. "How was Malia?" I ask, grinning and nudging him in an old-buddy-old-pal kind of manner.

I feel like this is a strong tactic, focusing the attention on his behavior rather than my own, until he mutters, "How were Vaughan and Carson and the rest of the basketball team?"

As I flinch, Ajita says, "I'll be upstairs," which surprises me because usually she thrives on this quite rare level of severe awkwardness. Even more upsettingly, she takes the nachos with her, and I feel their absence deep in my soul.

The door at the top of the stairs bangs shut behind her, and I immediately start smirking. I don't know what it is. Sometimes I think our bodies are hardwired to respond to extreme tension with uncontrollable laughter. It's that thing where your teacher tells you to stop giggling and it just makes you giggle even more and then you get sent out of the room to calm down, and you think you've managed it but then as soon as you come back in you collapse into another fit of hysteria. Yeah, that.

"It's not funny, Izzy," Danny snaps.

The TV flashes silently in the corner, illuminating the purple velvet on the pool table. There's an abandoned game still set up from before I arrived.

"Why isn't it?" I ask, sincerely wanting to know the answer.

"Do you really want that kind of reputation?" His voice is colder than the North Pole pre–climate change.

Suddenly I'm not laughing. "What's it to you?"

"I care about you, Izzy. I don't like seeing you make a fool of yourself." He's fidgeting with his man jewelry—a leather-strapped watch from some vintage shop downtown, a shark tooth surfer bracelet that doesn't suit him in the slightest, and a festival wristband from the summer, which has all the ink rubbed off so it's basically just a fraying bit of plastic.

"I had a good time, Danny. I don't see how that makes

me a fool. Would you judge one of the guys for sleeping with two girls in one night?"

Now he looks up at me, aghast. "You slept with them both? I thought you just kissed Vaughan! Jesus, Izzy. What's wrong with you?"

I'm getting mad, but am trying desperately to swallow it so I don't drive a wedge even further between us. "Nothing is fucking wrong with me."

"They're both just using you." He looks so sad, and guilt starts building inside me, even though I know it's illogical and futile to regret anything. Actually, I know I don't regret anything. I just don't want to hurt him more than I already have.

I soften my voice. "So? I'm using them too, Danny. It's not like I'm gonna marry either of them. I'm young. I'm allowed to have fun."

He sighs, still staring at his ragged festival wristband. Pushes his glasses up on his nose. "Wouldn't you rather sleep with someone who actually cares about you? Who'll still want to know you the next day? Who likes you for you, not just your body?"

I bite my lip, which is chapped as hell from hangover dehydration. "And who would that someone be, Danny?"

He finally meets my eyes, and the look on his face tells me everything I need to know. This isn't just some crush he's going to snap out of any day now. He has it bad.

Finally, because I am so articulate, I manage to say, "Oh. I'm sorry."

Then I lean over to give him a hug—I mean, what else do you do when your best friend is sad?—and he hugs me back so tenderly and affectionately that The Atmosphere is amplified tenfold. His heart beats against my shoulder, and he's so warm, unlike most skinny people. Something tickles my neck, and at first I think it's his hair but it's his soft breath, and then my chest starts pounding too.

What's going on? Betty convinced me I didn't want this but right now my traitorous body is telling me otherwise. But I can't. I can't. The dude's in love with me! I can't lead him on like this! Stop, Izzy. Stop.

No! Now I seem to have pressed my face into his neck too, and oh man he smells good—not like cologne but just clean, you know, like he uses really good soap probably stolen from a fancy hotel—and WHAT THE HELL, THIS IS DANNY! DANNY! Remember Danny? He's seen you cry snotty tears when you broke your wrist playing hopscotch on the playground, and he's seen you make a complete dick of yourself doing your Arnold Schwarzenegger impression, and he's seen you eat an entire sharing platter by yourself at TGI Fridays, and . . .

Wait, why did I ever think that was a bad thing? Isn't it nice that he knows everything and still wants to kiss you? Oh! Now I see what he was getting at. It's deeper, and it feels nice, like home, and even though somewhere in the back of my mind I know it's not what I want, that voice is getting quieter and quieter, and so when he pulls away just a few inches and our mouths are almost touching, I don't move a muscle, and I let his lips brush mine, and I shiver, and then . . .

Then we're kissing and it's not awful and everything I thought I knew is blown out of the water.

Cue my mind becoming stuck on an eternal loop of this-is-wrong-no-it's-right-no-it's-wrong-but-doesn't-it-feel-good? I can't recall ever having thought so much during kissing in my entire life, and I have done a lot of kissing, and also a lot of thinking, just never quite at the same time.

Danny's not a bad kisser. Better than Carson, worse than Vaughan. Is that a really cruel thing to do? Pitting these dudes against each other in some sort of kissing league bracket? Ooooh, maybe I could create some kind of anonymous online voting system where students give feedback on their best and worst kissing experiences, except the results would only be visible to me so I could make smart future smooching choices and nobody's feelings would get hurt.

This is totally going to become the new Facebook. Maybe I should just sell the idea to Mark Zuckerberg so I don't actually have to do any of the work, like coding or design or general administration. He probably has teams to deal with that kind of thing. Or maybe . . .

Christ on a bike, O'Neill. STOP. THINKING.

His hands move down to my waist, then the tops of my thighs, then along the waistband of my jeans, and that's when it starts to feel a bit wrong. I think I have cognitive dissonance when it comes to kissing. I honestly believe there are not many people on this planet that I would not kiss. It's just not a big deal to me. But even I find sex stuff more intimate and personal, and Danny's adventuring hands are giving me the willies.

There's a weird expression on his face. Urgent yet tentative, like he knows I will realize this is a huge mistake at any second, and the primal part of him wants to capitalize on the situation before that happens, while the best friend and good guy part wants to make sure I'm ready.

But it just doesn't feel right. It doesn't. Not at all. He's all sharp angles and translucent skin [I apologize if this is offensive to a) angular people or b) vampires]. And I always knew those things, of course I did, but I've never been so intimately aware of them before. There's always been a distance, and now that it's being closed, it's uncomfortable and I want it to stop. And as soon as I realize this, the guilt is crushing; I've made a mistake, I've led him on, and all I can think about is how I'm going to have to let him down.

Hopefulness is written all over his face, and I hate it. Because I can tell this moment has confirmed something for him too.

That's why, midkiss, I start to cry. It starts as a single whimper, and quickly escalates into pathetic sniffles, shortly followed by racking sobs. All the good stuff.

He knows why. He knows me too well, so there's no point in lying to him. He knows what it means, and seeing the moment it registers, seeing the moment his hopes come crashing down, is like being slammed in the chest with the butt of a gun.

"I'm s-sorry," I stammer.

And then, like the coward I am, I run.

I keep crying as I slam out the front door, and I keep crying as I mount my bike and start pedaling home. The streets are pretty empty, thank god, because I have mascara all over my dried-out face and a stream of snot running down my nose.

Why why why why whyyyyyy—

But I know why. I know exactly why. Such a huge part of me was hoping that I'd kiss him and feel the same way he does. That I'd realize it was right, and that Danny and I should be together, and that I love him too. If it worked out that way, it'd be so much easier than having to tell him no, having to let him down, having to hurt him in a way you never want to hurt your best friend. But instead I've made it so much worse. So, so much worse.

6:24 a.m.

I can't sleep and my alarm is going to go off soon anyway, so I'm rereading texts from last night. I haven't responded to any.

Ajita:

Babe, Danny told me what happened. Can you call me so I know you're okay and not in a ditch somewhere? I'm worried. Love you xo

I'm getting pissed at you. You know when I'm worried my body temperature escalates, and then I start to sweat, and then I inevitably break out in zits for at least a week. So: fuck you! Love from Ajita's epidermis xo (I do love you though. And you are not a bad person. Stalin was a bad person. You are lovely. See you tomorrow. xo)

Danny:

I'm sorry, Iz :(

I thought it's what you wanted. I never would've done it if I didn't.

Please, don't let this ruin our friendship. You're too important to me.

Ajita again:

lots of phallic vegetable emojis

I hate them both, and I love them both. And now I'm crying again.

Maybe if we all put our heads together, we can invent a Ctrl+Z option for horrible life decisions?

9:17 a.m.

After about seven seconds of sleep, I go to school looking like something out of a zombie movie. Throughout history and economics, which I have without Ajita and Danny, my gut twists so severely I think I might actually have developed bowel disease over the last few hours.

In my head I play out a number of detailed scenarios in which Danny a) burns me at the stake b) designs some actually rather impressive posters featuring *Sim*-like versions of us mating on the couch and plasters them all over the school, and c) makes human nachos by covering me in cheese, salsa, and sour cream, then baking me in the oven like some kind of Mexican Hansel and Gretel.

Judging by these worryingly elaborate hallucinations, it is possible that lack of sleep and severe emotional trauma have rendered me delusional and insane.

I mean, I've always been an overthinker. I even sometimes imagine full-blown confrontations with people, even though they haven't actually done anything wrong and are entirely unaware that we fell out inside my head. This usually occurs in the shower, for lack of anything better to do. So I'm no stranger to having fantasy arguments. But the human nacho thing is a bit far-fetched, even for me.

On the plus side, once third period has come around and it's time to face the music, it's clear that no matter how terribly it goes, it cannot be as messed up as my daydreams.

Because economics is on the other side of campus, it takes me so long to get to biology that class has already started by the time I flump into the seat behind him.

Danny doesn't turn around, but Ajita does, and winks at me to let me know she's not mad at me for potentially smashing our friendship group into smithereens. To be fair, she does have an impressive cluster of zits forming on her chin, and I make a mental note to buy her some peanut butter cups to apologize to her ravaged epidermis.

I then proceed to stare at the back of Danny's head for

forty-five minutes. Again, maybe it's the lack of sleep, but it feels like I'm looking at a stranger's neck; like our kiss somehow transformed his body into something I no longer recognize. His pale skin, covered in a thin layer of peach fuzz and tiny moles, is strange and unfamiliar.

Guilt presses in on me from all angles, and I'm in real danger of bursting into tears all over again. I can barely think about Carson or Vaughan, neither of whom I've bumped into yet. All I can do is obsess over the way I hurt my best friend.

The bell rings and it reverberates right through my skull, and the shuffling of bags and squeaking of chairs over the linoleum sparks a fresh wave of anxiety. When he turns to me, I plaster the most absurd grin on my face.

He looks tired as hell. Forget bags under his eyes, they're damn shopping carts, and they're indisputable evidence that he's been obsessing just as hard as I have.

"Iz." He shuffles from one foot to the other, rubbing the back of his stranger's neck.

"Hey." And right then my unfaltering situational judgment kicks in, and I know this is not the place to have it out, so I add, maintaining the ludicrous ax-murderer smile, "Let's talk at lunch?"

He smiles back, probably relieved not to have to spill his guts all over room 506B. Ajita sees the temporary truce and moseys over to us.

"Hey, kids. Wanna run lines on the way to drama?"

We then skip [sort of] to the theater side by side, reading from our *Great Gatsby* scripts and obnoxiously crashing into lockers/students/water fountains/Mr. Rosenqvist as we channel our Academy Award–worthy thespian technique. It's insane, really, and I know I've taken it too far when I add a Russian accent, but it makes them laugh and honestly, that's the only thing in the world I care about right now.

Like Carson Manning, lunch comes too fast.

Ajita grabs our usual table and enough fries for an entire battalion, then sends us outside to talk it out. At first I feel bad for leaving her alone, but before we've even left the cafeteria, Carlie has plonked herself down next to Ajita, obligatory salad on her tray and a self-satisfied expression on her beautiful/demonic face. Of course.

There are some woods behind the gym, and in our bid to get far enough into them that nobody will hear us, Danny and I pass a few fourteen-year-olds smoking a squashed pack of cigarettes, as well as our phys ed teacher jumping through the trees like a chimp to build his functional fitness. I think he's one of those CrossFit douchebags, I don't know.

Eventually we stop in a little clearing, and I'm so exhausted I just flop to the ground and lean back against a tree trunk. "Did you sleep as terribly as I did last night?"

He smiles despite the fact that this situation could not be any less funny. "If by terribly you mean not at all, then yeah."

I sigh and let my eyes flutter closed, partly because looking at him is guilt-inducing, and partly because I'm hoping I can squeeze in a little nap between now and the next sentence.

"Danny, I'm so sorry. I thought I wanted . . ."

"I thought you did too. Otherwise I wouldn't have . . ."

I grimace. "Our sentence-finishing abilities never cease to amaze me."

He sits down next to me, and flashbacks from last night play in my mind. He tugs a handful of long grass from the ground and starts tearing it to shreds. The earth smells damp around us, and the only nearby sound is the phys ed dude grunting maniacally as he does chin-ups like his life depends on it. Maybe it does. I don't know his circumstances.

"Hey," he says. "Remember when we were kids and we used to find hours of entertainment with just a pack of white chalk?"

I smile despite the situation, tilting my head back so it's leaning against the tree trunk. "We'd go out onto the sidewalk and draw miniature towns on the concrete."

"Yup. Then populate them with completely bonkers characters, and act out full-blown soap opera scenes." A funny little snort. "I'll never forget the misogynistic old shopkeeper you role-played all the time."

"That guy was a dick," I reply, indignant. "He thought all women owed him something. I'll never forgive him for how he treated his imaginary wife."

We both sit silently for a moment, reliving our screwed-up childhood. Well, mine was screwed up. I just dragged Danny along for the ride.

Weighing his words carefully, he adds, "You're like a sister to me, Iz. Always have been. Which is what makes this so confusing."

"I know," I say. "I'm sorry." And I am. Not for sleeping with people who aren't him, but for the fact that we're not in the same place. We might never be again. Maybe there will just always be this imbalance now, in every conversation, in every joke and every moment of silence. Maybe things will be off-kilter forever. The thought is devastating.

His throat sounds thick as he says, "You know how I feel about you."

"Yes," I whisper. A strange, sad hollowness blooms in my chest. I hate that a relationship that's brought Danny so much joy for so many years is now causing him pain. And most of all, I hate the fact I can't do a damn thing to fix it.

"I didn't want to pressure you."

"You didn't." I mean it, too. I knew exactly what I was doing, and need to own my share of the responsibility. I can scarcely ask the next question, but I know I have to. "What now?"

He runs his hands through his ridiculous hair. I want so badly to hug him, but I can't tell whether that'd make it worse.

Quietly, he mumbles, "I know how I feel, but I also know how you feel. And that's okay. I didn't plan for this to happen, and I won't let it ruin our friendship. It's only a matter of time before you do something disgusting and ruin it for me. It'll pass, I'm sure. Like a kidney stone. Might be painful, but it will pass." Another smile, but there's not much strength behind it.

We stand up, and we hug, and we let thousands of

unspoken words flow between us. And then we do the only thing we can do: we move on.

With Carlie long gone, Ajita is relieved as hell when we make it back with both of us tear-free and relatively unscathed. "Oh, thank god. For a moment I was genuinely concerned our tripod was about to lose a leg. Now please, eat some cheese fries. Drink some soda. It's going to be A-OK."

TUESDAY, SEPTEMBER 20

<u>4:41 p.m.</u>
The life-changing email comes through in the last period of the day, and I squeal like a pig having a bikini wax. [Do pigs even have pubes? These are the important questions, folks.]

The teacher doesn't notice, but Ajita looks at me quizzically, which is fair given that I do not normally sound like a barn animal maintaining its hair removal regimen. So I fire off a text riddled with excitement-induced punctuation discrepancies.

I made the screenplay competition longlist!!1!!1!!11!!!!

Seeing her little face light up across the room is the best feeling ever. I did that! My accomplishment made another human being happy!

Shut the front door! Dude!! I am so proud of you. That is not something I ever thought possible, because you are a mess and a joke in every facet of existence, but it's true. I'm proud. xo

I'm grinning harder than a grinning machine in turbo mode at this point.

Who'd've thunk! My dumb sense of humor is actually translatable to real marketable screenplays!

Ajita smirks as she's typing her scathing response.

It definitely would not have even crossed my mind to thunk. In fact your terrible sense of humor has rendered me completely unable to thunk in any way whatsoever. You are the single least funny person in the northern hemisphere. xo

This may sound horrible and not supportive at all, but our century of friendship has taught me that she makes very little sense when happy and excited. Her confusing usage of the incorrect past participle of the verb "to think" leads me to believe that actually, she might not hate me as much as she says she does. Bless her heart.

Celebratory beveraginos tonight?

A split second later:

Hell yeah. xo

As soon as the final bell goes, I practically sprint [well, jog, because I think my legs might just eject themselves from my body in sheer shock if I attempted to sprint] to the teachers' lounge and knock on the door.

Mr. Davies, our math teacher, answers. "Miss O'Neill. How can I help you?"

I'm ready to burst with excitement. "Is Mrs. Crannon around?"

A few seconds later she appears at the door, wrapped up

in a raincoat and clearly ready to rock and roll her way out of the building.

Breathless, I manage to say, "I made the longlist!"

"Izzy! That's wonderful!" She throws her arms around me, which teachers are absolutely not supposed to do nowadays for fear of being accused of sexual assault, but neither of us particularly care in that instant because we're just so goddamn happy that something in the world is going well.

It feels good. It feels really, really good.

7:18 p.m.

Betty gives us the green light to have a few tipples at mine, which might sound like lax parenting but you forget that I am a tragic orphan, so Ajita and Danny traipse over at around eight and we merrily crack open a couple of beers and toast my completely unexpected and quite frankly baffling career success.

We're all piled onto our mangled couch, Ajita in between Danny and me to prevent any awkward bodily contact, and sharing a bag of chips. I've been chewing the skin around my nails too much—nervous habit—and the salt and vinegar flavoring makes the broken skin sting like nothing else, so my chip consumption is nowhere near as formidable as usual.

Licking her fingers with her freak tongue, Ajita sighs, "I wish I knew what I wanted to do in life. You're so ahead of everyone else, Iz. It's awesome. But I'm kinda jealous." She sighs again, rummaging in the bottom of the bag of chips. "I just don't understand. How the hell are we supposed to have it all figured out by the age of eighteen? We don't even know who we are yet, and still we're expected to choose what we want to do with the next fifty years. It's madness."

Danny shifts on the sofa, and the whole thing groans despite his meager body mass. "We'll figure it out, though. All of us. We have each other's backs, right? Jeets, if you wanna hash out some career ideas sometime, I'm all ears." I smile. I haven't heard him call her Jeets, her old nickname, in forever. "I know your parents pressure you and Praj like hell, but there's gotta be something you love doing just for you. We can build on that, okay?"

Danny has always been a sweetheart when it comes to encouraging Ajita and me. Even though his complex feelings toward me have somewhat changed the dynamic between us, it's good to see this version of him resurface. Maybe hanging out with Praj has been good for him—he doesn't have many other guy friends.

"Thanks, D," Ajita says. "There are a couple of things I think I want to look into, but I think if I told my parents I might want to go into fashion, they'd just expire there and then." A sad sort of smile. "Anyway, maybe we won't have to do anything for ourselves," she adds. "Izzy's gonna be so rich she'll buy us a mansion each."

While Ajita is mid-rant about the potential benefits of having a world-famous comedienne as a best friend, most of which involve her getting free stuff, my phone bleeps with a text message from an unknown number.

Hey Izzy, it's Vaughan. Heard about your script-writing
thing. Congrats! Remember me when you're famous.

Slyly, so that Danny does not see me engage with his
sworn enemy, I reply:

Thanks! Word travels fast. Hope everything's good
with you!

Two seconds later, *bzz bzz*.

Things are awesome, thanks. Can't stop thinking about
last weekend . . .

AND HE ATTACHES A DICK PIC. I shit you not. An
actual photograph of his erect penis. I nearly drop the phone
in horror and disgust. All right, you nosy bastards. It's above
average in length, below average in girth, and bends slightly
to the left. Are you happy now??

I honestly do not know why guys think unsolicited dick
pics are a turn-on. Like, have they ever seen a penis? Do
they really look at their own genitals and think, "Yeah, that
looks *good*"? No. Exactly.

At first I think Danny picks up on my absolute revulsion
because something odd flickers across his face, but thankfully he and Ajita have moved on from the mild success of
their sex-crazed best friend and are now discussing a sketch
idea based on a surfing shark who's terrified of humans. So
I'm guessing they don't notice me turn a delightful shade of
salmon.

It takes a few seconds to regain composure, but before
I've even mustered a halfway humorous response, he messages me again.

Your turn ;)

Like I know triple-texting is an accepted thing now, which I am very glad about due to my incredibly needy nature, but surely when one of those texts is a photograph of a penis, we should reevaluate protocol?

I am slightly buzzed from the couple of beers but my inhibitions have not been adequately lowered as of yet. So I simply say:

Thank you for the splendid dick show. Really. You should start charging admission to this world-class event! I confess this would price me out of action due to the fact that I am a poverty-stricken orphan, but as your business adviser, this is a risk I am willing to take.

Not sure what possesses me to go all Richard Branson on him, but I'm not in the habit of questioning where my "jokes" come from, and I am not about to start while embroiled in a disturbing dick pic fiasco.

God, you're weird. But also very hot. Just one pic? ;)

Then three milliseconds later:

I'll make it worth your while...

Teenage boys really do have precisely zero chill when it comes to nudes.

I leave him hanging for a little while, because I'm very evil and enjoy the idea of him sitting on the couch next to his Republican senator of a father, indiscreetly checking his phone five times a minute, and trying to disguise his lop-sided boner with a goose-feather cushion, or whatever rich people use to shield their aroused penises from each other.

But then, once Ajita and Danny have stumbled out the front door like moderately intoxicated baby deer, I look at the nude picture again, and this time it doesn't invoke quite as much nausea. Maybe because I've had a couple of drinks, or maybe because now that I'm alone I don't have to worry about anyone [i.e., Danny] peering over my shoulder, or because suddenly I'm remembering how much fun we had on the porch swing.

I've never sexted before, believe it or not, but suddenly I really, really want to. Knowing Vaughan was a virgin before me, and that he probably hasn't done this before either, makes me feel way more comfortable. This could be fun.

And so I retire to my bedroom, whip off my clothes, and take the damn picture, hitting send before I have time to talk myself out of it.

[Yes, gasp, sigh. But are you even surprised at this point?]

WEDNESDAY, SEPTEMBER 21

7:20 a.m.

I fall asleep before Vaughan replies, but it's no great loss because he only manages to say "fuck" before I assume making a mess of the goose-feather cushion. And that's that.

12:57 p.m.

Lunch break is spent trying not to get kicked outside by the power-hungry hall monitors who take their jobs as school police more seriously than the actual US police force. We have to go outside and get fresh air after we eat, for no other reason than the school authorities want us to be miserable. Fresh air is number three on my top ten list of overrated things in life, which, although constantly evolving, currently looks like this:

1. Sliced bread. It's undeserving of its eponymous cliché, "the best thing since sliced bread." Give me a crusty baguette any day. Maybe the cliché-makers chose sliced bread because "the best thing since a French stick" sounds vaguely sexual.

2. The Super Bowl. Its only redeeming quality is the way we, as a nation, come together to eat chicken wings and yell at the TV, but you can do that any day of the week without the inconvenience of having to watch sports, or as I call it, Sportsball™.

3. Fresh air. Outside = weather, insects, and the chance that at any given moment, you may be hit by a car. I also think people who love camping should never be trusted.

4. Shower sex. A logistical nightmare from start to finish.

5. Smoking. At some point it became synonymous with cool. Why? It tastes gross. It makes you smell gross. It coats your lungs in ash. [I'm not sure if that's medically correct. Remind me to ask Ajita.]

6. Reading in the bath. You have to dry your hands every thirty milliseconds in order to turn the page, and you live in constant fear of dropping the book spine-first on your bare foofer.

7. Shakespeare. It's like he made a point of writing sentences that would be impossible for high school students to decipher hundreds of years later. Dude totally thinks he's better than us.

8. TV talent shows. But maybe I'm just bitter about having a face for radio.

9. Yoga. Specifically the way in which it is marketed as a relaxing pastime. There is nothing relaxing about twisting yourself into a pretzel and saying "om" a lot.

10. Dubstep. I don't feel this requires further explanation.

Thankfully, word doesn't seem to have gotten out about my controversial sexcapades this past weekend. Sexmageddon remains a secret.

But of course, the universe is a hormonal son of a preacher man at times, and I'm well overdue a generous helping of bad karma, so inevitably I meet both Vaughan and Carson in the hall at the same time on my way to fourth period. They're strolling along together, probably chatting about defense tactics or some other Sportsball™-related subject I have no hope of understanding.

Despite the flurry of activity around the lockers, they both clock me burying my face into my upside-down copy of *Wuthering Heights*. Ajita smirks dirtily in their direction, which is almost definitely a fireable offense as my supposed best friend, but at this point I just have to be thankful that Danny has double AP chemistry this morning and isn't here to witness such an unfortunate coincidence.

I mean, they *are* on the same basketball team, so I should really have anticipated this kind of hideous confrontation, but thankfully it doesn't seem like either of them are aware that I banged the other. These are their reactions to seeing their latest conquest out in the wild:

Carson: playful grin, trademark swagger, "Izzz-zaaaayyyyyyy."

Vaughan: fierce blushing, frenzied throat-clearing, not

a word. [Probably picturing the goose-feather cushion and getting aroused all over again.]

"Hello, gentlemen," I say ever-so-calmly, despite the voice inside my head screaming ABORT ABORT ABORT. Remember how I love all drama except my own? This definitely falls under the category of drama I do not love.

Ajita grins ecstatically next to me, probably wishing she had a bucket of popcorn and some 3D glasses. Her mocking gaze flits between us all in turn, waiting for someone to break the ice. For a minute there's just the sound of freshmen giggling nearby, and Vaughan flipping awkwardly through his history textbook as though his life depends on it, then:

"So—"

"D'you—"

Carson and I both start to speak at the same time, then both immediately stop when the other makes a sound, gesturing vaguely to continue, which neither of us do.

Thankfully Vaughan mutters something inaudible and excuses himself, disappearing in the direction of the chemistry labs. With his history textbook. Very good.

Ajita senses the opportunity for me to chat with Carson and follow through on my teeny tiny crush, so reluctantly says, "I'll see you in English, Iz." She disappears swiftly, giving my elbow a supportive squeeze on the way.

"So I heard your good news," Carson says, shifting the backpack from one shoulder to the other. "Nice one. Always knew you were funny as hell."

Those last three words have the same effect on me as a certain other three words would have on most normal people. It turns me to mush. Especially when uttered in that ridiculously attractive voice of his.

"Thanks, man," I manage to reply, immediately regretting calling him "man."

"No problem. Long as I can be your arm candy when your movie premieres." He winks, slowly and exaggeratedly, in a way that lets me know he's mainly joking but also a little bit serious.

I play ball. "What's in it for me?"

He strokes his freshly shaven chin, pretending to consider the options. "Don't suppose the pleasure of my company would cut it?"

"Hard pass," I answer matter-of-factly. "I've gotta get to class, but lemme know if you come up with anything worth my while."

Carson's smile is so massive I can practically see his tonsils, and, to be fair, he has got that movie-star charisma that'd probably make him right at home on the red carpet.

"Will do, O'Neill. Will do."

3:20 p.m.
Holy hell. So we're leaving the classroom after a snooze-worthy session on some idiots called Cathy and Heathcliff, ready to meet Danny outside so we can walk home together, when Ajita stops talking abruptly. She's seen something, or someone, that I haven't. I follow her gaze.

Carson is leaning back against a row of lockers, bouncing a basketball up and down. He must feel our eyes on him, because he stops dribbling immediately—and doesn't pick the ball back up, just leaves it mid-bounce and strolls over.

"Hey," he says, not even registering Ajita's presence because he's looking at me so intensely. He smiles another huge smile. "So I thought of something that might convince you to let me be your red carpet date."

I smirk. He has specks of red and white paint on his shirt, and the palms of his hands are stained blue. He must've come from art class, which is unexpected in itself. "Oh yeah? What's tha—"

But before I can even finish my sentence, HE KISSES ME!! Right there in the hallway!

He tastes fresh and awesome, like spearmint, and his technique is much better than it was that night at the party. It's not a full-blown tongues affair; more soft and gentle. I like it. I like it a lot. I drop my copy of *Wuthering Heights* and let my hands rest on his chest.

When he pulls away, still somehow maintaining his cartoonish grin, I half expect Ajita to give us a round of applause. Instead, she just says in a strange voice, "Izzy . . ."

She's wincing, looking just over my shoulder. I turn around, hands still on Carson.

Danny is standing on the opposite side of the corridor, watching. When I meet his eye, he shakes his head sadly and storms off toward the fire exit.

"Crap," Carson says, big smile fully disappeared. "I didn't mean to get in the middle of anything. Are you guys—"

"No," I say quickly. "Not at all. It's . . . complicated."

Carson looks relieved, but not altogether convinced. He rubs the back of his head, uncertain. "All right. Well, I guess I'll catch you later then?"

Somewhat deflated, he picks up his ball and walks away. I turn helplessly to Ajita, who for once does not seem to be enjoying the show.

"It's not your fault," she murmurs, grabbing my book off the floor for me. "Really. Danny's the one who has to find a way to get over this. Don't feel bad, okay?"

"Okay," I lie, knowing perfectly well I'm going to agonize over this for several hours.

Still, even the guilt isn't enough to suppress the butterflies lingering in my tummy from the first sober kiss of my life.

THURSDAY, SEPTEMBER 22

7:56 p.m.

Being an astonishing success story is really quite time-consuming. Ajita invites me over to film a sketch, but I decide to do one last read-through of my script before sending the full thing to the judges, so I make myself a giant mug of hot cocoa with extra mini-marshmallows and get to work.

Yes! Me! Working! It's absurd at the face of it. But it's weird. When you enjoy what you're doing, it doesn't really feel like work at all. It's difficult, sure, but it's still fun. What a revelation. I've never once felt this way about school assignments. I get into a rhythm with my Sharpie and actually find myself enjoying doing something other than being an unbelievable waste of space.

In the back of my mind while I edit is Carson's kiss. I remember the smallest details—the tingling mint on his lips, the vague scent of paint on his hands, the shape of his chest beneath my hands. The fluttering in my belly.

Like I say, it was the first kiss I've ever had while not under the influence of alcohol. It's not that I haven't wanted to do it sober, more that the opportunity has never really arisen. I've never had a boyfriend, and I've never gotten close enough to anyone to want to make out with them outside of a party setting.

[Also *whispers* maybe I'm not as confident as I pretend to be, and I just need the wonderful inhibition-lowering qualities of Capri Sun to take the edge off—and remove that layer of fear Ajita is always trying to get me to defy.]

Anyway, all I know is that despite the obvious Danny issues, I really, *really* enjoyed it. And would very much like to repeat it in the not-so-distant future.

But back to business. While I'm editing, a few things trip me up, like whether the love interest's career obsession makes her cold or unrelatable, so I start a list of things to discuss with Mrs. Crannon when I next see her.

It's all going pretty well until my phone bleeps.

I half expect it to be Vaughan with another close-up of his genitals, or Danny proposing, but it's my main squeeze Ajita.

Um. Iz. I dunno how to tell you this, so I'm not going to. But . . . well. Xo

And there's a link attached:

http://izzyoneillworldclasswhore.com

What. The. Eff?

Frowning, I open a new browser window and type in the URL. And instantly regret it.

Someone made a blog. With the title "Izzy O'Neill:

118

World Class Whore." The first post, date stamped yesterday and posted by the site owner, is a picture from the party of me straddling Vaughan on the porch swing—judging by the angle, it was taken from the kitchen. You can't see any willies or va-jay-jays, but it's pretty clear we're having sex.

Bile rises in my throat.

After that, there are pages and pages and pages of posts about how much of a slut I am. They've all been uploaded in the last few hours, and all from different user accounts. I recognize a couple of names from school, including a sophomore girl I beat out of the lead part in our school play last year.

How has this spiraled so fast? It must have been shared around social media like wildfire.

Hands shaking like crazy, I scroll through all the selfies I've taken over the past year—each with a dick photoshopped into my mouth.

I scroll through anonymous "confessions" about all of the hideous sexual acts I've apparently engaged in.

I scroll through a detailed account of last Saturday night, i.e., sexmageddon. My encounters with both Vaughan and Carson are on display for the whole world to read. I mean, I know I hardly kept my sexual encounters particularly hidden at the party. But . . . fuck.

My blood runs cold. I don't know whether to laugh or cry or throw up all over my stack of Post-it notes.

Who would do this to me? Who hates me this much?

My privacy has somehow been violated, but I can't even process the logistics right now. All I feel is a repeated stabbing pain in my chest, like palpitations but ten times as vicious.

I might put on a tough exterior, but . . . nobody likes to be hated.

Ajita texts me again.

Have you looked? Are you okay? xo

It takes me several attempts to type out my response.

No, Ajita. I'm not. I'm the exact opposite of okay.

FRIDAY, SEPTEMBER 23

9:04 a.m.
Overnight, the site continues to snowball out of control. People share it on social media, mass email the link to every kid in school, add even more content than before. I feel cold and numb, like I'm in a nightmare. Surely this can't be real. This stuff doesn't happen in real life.

I've been here less than twenty minutes and school is already a second circle of humiliation hell. Everyone stares.

I walk down the hallway to a chorus of mutterings and whisperings, like I'm the subject of some kind of medieval shaming ritual. I feel like I should be wearing a dramatic hooded cloak and carrying an ancient torch.

I'm a performer. I'm used to people watching me. But this feels different, you know? At least when I'm onstage, or cracking a dirty joke, I want to be watched. I want to be laughed at.

But this?

Nothing about this is on my terms.

The low murmuring and conspiratorial giggles make

me want to cut someone. Ajita tries her damn best to cheer me up, though it's hard to focus on anything she's saying. There's a high-pitched ringing in my head, and the horrible comments play on a loop. *Slut. Whore. Bitch. Ugly. C***.*

Worst of all is the picture of me straddling Vaughan like something out of a cheap porno. You can't see my face, but still. Everyone who was at that party knows it was me.

As we walk, the hallway around me whooshes and swirls. It feels a little like an out-of-body experience, which I've always dismissed as melodramatic until now. I have to snap out of this. I can't let cyberbullies win. So I plaster a smile on my face and pretend not to care.

Besides, it could be worse, I suppose. It could always be worse. I am not quite sure how, exactly, but thanks to my handy habit of shielding my true emotions from the world, Betty often says I am so optimistic it borders on the sociopathic, and now is as good a time as any to look on the bright side. I've been through the death of both parents on the same day. I won't let the words of a pathetic bully leave a scar.

So, like the disturbingly chirpy individual I am, I whistle cheerily as I stroll down the hallway, completely ignoring the hordes of people staring me down. Unfortunately I cannot whistle, so really I'm just blowing silently [behave yourselves], but the effect on my mood is positive all the same.

But then, when I walk into second period, there's a group of girls crowded around a desk, staring at a phone and whispering stuff like "Oh my god, what a slut!" and "Fucking whore" and "If I was her, there'd be no way I could show my face around here."

They shut up when they see me, but it's too late. I already heard.

2:34 p.m.

Of course. Of course today is the day we have a mandatory sex ed lecture in the gym. Of course it is.

Hundreds of us pile into the hall, taking up seats on the rows of bleachers. There was a basketball game last night, and there are still plastic bottles and wads of tickets stuffed underneath the benches.

Ajita sits protectively next to me, with Danny on her other side. Other than "I'm sorry, Iz" he hasn't really said all that much about the website, which is probably justified. It can't be nice looking at pictures of the girl you love having al fresco intercourse with the guy you hate.

The whole way through the talk, I feel everyone staring at me. Not all at once, but in turn. As soon as one person looks away, another chances a sneaky glance in my direction. It's a constant stream of staring I can't escape from.

For some reason, our Bible-thumping English teacher and all-around abstinence champion Miss Castillo is the one delivering the talk. Because obviously in America the only thing we should be teaching our teens about sex is that they shouldn't do it. Don't have sex because you will get pregnant and die. That sort of thing. It's working out soooo well for us.

So instead of informing us about contraception and such, she goes on an epic rant about the will of god and how virginity should be preserved until marriage. This works well for her in theory, because by the time we are all married, we'll be long gone from Edgewood High and she won't have to do any awkward banana demonstrations. I'm pretty sure this is the main reason she preaches abstinence. Banana aversion tactics. [And also it's the law.]

Then come the questions. Oh, the questions. Here's what never to ask a crowd of two hundred horny teenagers: "Do you have anything you'd like to ask about sex?"

A football jock pipes up first. "Is it normal to masturbate over fifty times a week?"

Everyone laughs. Castillo blushes furiously, smoothing down nonexistent creases in her pussy-bow blouse. "I—I . . . masturbation is impure, Jackson, and—"

Another dude from the basketball team interrupts. "Is it normal to have sex dreams about your teachers?" Then he winks at Castillo. She looks like she wants to die.

Amanda Bateman, who has a stellar reputation as a lover of third base, chirps up next. "Is it true guys don't like hand jobs because they can do it better themselves? So there's no point in anything but a blow job?"

Castillo cringes so severely it looks like she's giving birth in a similar manner to that scene from *Alien*. "I really wouldn't know, Amanda, but—"

"Maybe you should ask Izzy O'Neill," someone shouts, and everyone cackles. "She's a bit of an expert."

The mention of my name is like an electric shock as adrenaline spikes unpleasantly in my system.

That picture.

My cheeks burn. Then the jeering starts. Another girl yells, "Yeah, how many guys is it now, O'Neill? Or did you lose count at a hundred?"

"And that's just on Saturday night!" another dude shouts.

Never one to cower in the corner, Ajita has my back as usual. She yells, "You're just mad you didn't make the cut. A hundred guys and she still won't sleep with you! Gotta hurt."

I steer into the joke. "You don't even make the top thousand, buddy!" I disguise the shaking in my voice as best I can. I don't regret anything I did. It's the world that has the problem, not me. I let that conviction steady me.

Castillo toughens up a little at this point, and leaps to my defense. "That's enough! Out. All of you. Class dismissed."

I think she has a soft spot for me, which is extremely baffling on account of my poor moral compass and alleged Sexual Centurion. But I am grateful all the same.

We all stand up at the same time, and conversation erupts everywhere. No prizes for guessing the topic on everyone's lips.

The muttering and giggling as we file out of the gym isn't about Castillo's cringeworthy delivery. It's all for me. From behind me, Danny squeezes my elbow, which I massively appreciate. Focusing on breathing as steadily as I can, I steel myself as much as possible. I can break down later, in the privacy of my own home.

8:17 p.m.

By the end of school I'm super miserable, despite my best efforts to power through, so I head over to the Dutta residence for an evening of tomfoolery with my pals.

I meet Mr. and Mrs. Dutta at the door—they're heading out for a Vinayaka Chaturthi feast. Mrs. Dutta proudly tells me about the holiday's origins, explaining how it's a ten-day Hindu festival honoring the elephant-headed god Ganesha's birthday. Mr. Dutta watches her talk as though hearing the story for the first time, completely enraptured by his wife's gift for storytelling.

I love listening to Mrs. Dutta talk about her culture; her face lights up, and her voice fills with passion. Ajita doesn't talk about this stuff much, even though I try to ask her about it, so it's cool getting to hear about all these traditions and celebrations from her folks.

Once her parents have left, Ajita throws an impromptu "would you rather" party in her basement for our tripod. This basically consists of us taking turns in asking each other impossibly difficult "would you rather" questions, such as "Would you rather have teeth for pubes or pubes for teeth?" and then heartily debating the answers like we're members of the UN.

Prajesh joins us for a while, but as the questions become increasingly rude, he starts to get more and more uncomfortable hearing his big sister talk about sex so openly. He excuses himself with the general expression of someone who's trying very hard not to be sick.

When he leaves, he gives Danny this weird fist bump and says, "We still cool to hang out after I finish at the meet tomorrow?"

"'Course, bro," Danny replies. It's incredibly cringe-worthy hearing him call anyone bro, but nevertheless, Ajita nudges his shoulder and flashes him a grateful look.

After an hour or so, with the aid of a metric crap-ton of nachos, I'm slowly coming back to life and laughing hysterically while listening to Danny justify why he'd rather have penises for arms than a vagina for a mouth. Ajita is insisting that this just is not practical because a) penises can't grip things, and b) there would simply be no hiding your arousal. You would just be walking around the supermarket with your arms in the air, knocking boxes of cereal off the shelves, trying to convince the shop assistant that you aren't sexually attracted to Cap'n Crunch.

The website thing is actually falling to the back of my mind, until Ajita asks me: "Would you rather sit on a cake and eat dick, or sit on a dick and eat cake?"

Clearly, because unlike the pube-teeth debacle there is only one correct answer, I reply, "The latter, definitely. In fact there is literally not any situation I would enjoy more."

Danny then scoffs and mutters, "Jesus. Are you ever *not* thinking about sex?"

I'm kind of caught off guard by his tone, which is nothing short of scathing, but like the talented improv actor I am,

I bounce back. "No. One time I thought I might be thinking about the Chinese inflation rate, but I was, in fact, thinking about forking."

Really I should snap back at him way harder than this, but I'm honestly just not in the mood for a fight, and in fact I feel like I could burst into tears at any moment, so I just say, "Next question, please."

It's only when I'm leaving Ajita's that the darkly impossible thought emerges. Maybe *Danny* uploaded that porch swing picture in a fit of rage, angry over being kissed then rejected, and then it spiraled out of control. After all, the site went live just a few hours after Danny saw me kiss Carson in the hallway. The timing works out.

Oh god. Is it possible? Would my best friend really do that to me?

11:13 p.m.
The thought alone feels like a betrayal. My cheeks burn with the shame of even considering it. Am I a shitty person for doubting him?

11:24 p.m.
I'm going on a mini internet hiatus this weekend. I need to clear my noggin, and also some time and space away from the place where a full-blown character assassination of me is taking place.

Have also told Ajita not to expect hearty contributions to

our group chats for the foreseeable future, and like the horrid creature she is, she informed me that my contributions are not particularly valued anyway, so I would not be greatly missed.

On that note: so long, farewell, auf Wiedersehen, good night, or however that preposterous song goes.

MONDAY, SEPTEMBER 26

<u>6:14 a.m.</u>

Have spent the entire weekend moping, walking Dumbledore a combined total of forty-two yards, and attempting to figure out how to confront Danny about his potential involvement in the Izzy O'Neill: World Class Whore blog.

In a feat of willpower one could accurately label superhuman, I've managed to steer clear of the blog itself. In fact I have become quite content in my vacuum of ignorance, to the extent that I have not even told Betty about this unfortunate development. Not just because the idea of showing her a picture of me having sex on a porch swing is both horrifying and disturbing, but also because I don't want to worry her. While I often share the whimsical and occasionally explicit details of my love life with my aging grandma, somehow telling her about the accompanying shame and fear feels a little too personal. [I know. I'm all kinds of messed up.]

Ugh, shame? Where did that come from? I've never, ever felt ashamed of my sex life before. I refuse to let those internet trolls do this to me. I refuse.

What I want to know more than anything is the who and the why. And I've been obsessing pretty hardcore over whether or not to believe Danny is behind it.

Here are the facts:

I kissed him and led him on.

Then rejected him and broke his heart.

Mere days later, he saw Carson kiss me in the hallway.

This is Danny we're talking about.

Danny!

Suspecting him feels like a huge betrayal. We've had such a kind, loyal friendship for so many years. Every time I consider the idea that he'd willfully hurt me, my subconscious throws up another example of a time he was an amazing friend. Last year, he helped me plan a big surprise birthday party for Betty at his parents' house. He even paid for a fancy buffet and everything. Betty got so drunk on mimosas that she mounted the replica Roman gladiator statue [no really] in their hallway and proceeded to dry hump the leg of a Spartan warrior, who looked the furthest thing from impressed.

Yet everything that's happened in the last couple weeks makes me think I'd be an idiot *not* to suspect Danny. After all, it feels like every time there's a school shooting, it's only a matter of time before it emerges that the guy who "finally snapped" had been rejected by a girl. Guys who seem harmless until someone tells them no.

This is my best friend. I don't *want* to believe that he

could be one of those people who can't deal with being rejected. And yet I genuinely think I'd be a naive moron not to consider it as a possibility. I hurt him. Is it too much of a stretch to say he wanted to hurt me back?

In any case, if these last few weeks have taught me anything, it's that it's better to talk about things openly and honestly, as opposed to letting them simmer beneath the surface until everything bubbles over and the damage is ten times worse than it would've been otherwise. Which is why I plan to ask him, plain and simple, whether he had anything to do with it.

Anyway, it's not the kind of accusation I can make lightly, and I'm pretty sure that no matter what happens, he will hog-tie me and roast me over a campfire for even daring to ask the question. But I have to know.

The thought of returning to school, and having to face not only the relentless abuse of my peers but also the potential wrath of my best friend, is giving me Nervous Belly. Hardcore. Basically it's D-Day, only I'm fairly sure the troops landing in Normandy were a bit more relaxed than I am at present.

[You may be thinking at this point, wow, Izzy O'Neill is such an inspiration for maintaining her sense of humor and wit at a time like this, but honestly it's more that I just don't have the mental capacity to process serious situations. Rest assured, the inevitable apocalyptic breakdown is imminent. Can I just take this opportunity to state: THIS APPROACH

IS NOT ADVISABLE. I would love to be your poster girl for squeaky clean mental health but unfortunately I am not that chick.]

My stomach cramps painfully. More than anything in the world, I hope Danny has nothing to do with this blog. I don't know how I'd survive this if he did.

7:13 a.m.

To kill time before school, and to use up some of my nervous energy, I pluck my eyebrows. Unfortunately for me and others around me, I get a bit overzealous with the tweezers and remove a significant portion of my left brow. This is not great.

7:16 a.m.

Don't have an eyebrow pencil, but managed to find a box of crayons. Have filled in the patch of hairless brow with Burnt Umber. The finish is a little waxy for my taste, but that's all the rage nowadays, isn't it? People stupidly pay for two separate products, both powder and wax, and yet they really need look no further than their average arts and crafts box.

7:17 a.m.

Had to wash the crayon off. Think I might be slightly allergic as my entire forehead is now mottled with charming red pinpricks. I'm so glad Danny will be able to take me seriously as I accuse him of ruining my life.

10:32 a.m.

As I walk down the corridor toward math class, a gaggle of fourteen-year-olds point and laugh. News spreads fast.

I almost flip them off, but the idea that they've all seen a picture of me having sex, and that they all probably buy into the notion that I am a whore of unparalleled proportions, makes me feel hot and exposed under the harsh strip lighting.

It's a horrible dynamic flip, suddenly having a group of younger kids feel like they have emotional power over you.

1:34 p.m.

Disappointingly my eyebrow does not magically grow back before lunch, which is unfortunate as I was hoping for at least a little five o'clock shadow by now. The look of shock on Danny's face as I approach him in the cafeteria is cartoonish and hilarious.

He's lining up for chili fries, so while my audience is captive, I mutter, "Heycanwetalk?"

He looks up and says, "What about?"

I force myself to meet his eye. His gaze keeps floating up to my speckled forehead. Like, can you not? I'm aware I look like a dermatology inpatient. There is no need to draw constant attention to the situation.

Anyway, we arrange to meet in the woods after school. I briefly consider burning the woods down but decide against it.

Well, that could've been worse. Such as if the dinosaurs had roused from extinction and ravaged the entire school campus.

It's pretty cold in the woods, even though it's still early fall, and I shiver as I pluck up the courage to say what's on my mind. Danny shuffles awkwardly, kicking at a pine cone with the rubber toe of his sneaker.

"So this website thing," I start incredibly tactfully and eloquently, trying not to meet the gaze of the gym teacher who is pole vaulting with a long tree branch just ten feet to my left. [Not really. He's doing push-ups. But you know I have a penchant for exaggeration.]

"Yeah. Sorry, Iz. Sucks."

At this point we have both established it sucks. I can't even be bothered to make a joke about two-way sucking and/ or 69s, which is how you know I'm in a poor emotional state.

"I just kind of wondered whether . . . you might know anything about who's behind it?"

Obviously at this point I do not expect him to say, "Yes of course, Izzy, it was I, jilted man friend and all-round Nice Guy, forsooth how doth thine know?" [There I go again with my unconvincing usage of medieval lingo.] But I am studying his reaction pretty intensely for flushed cheeks or averted gazes.

He just shrugs nonchalantly. "I dunno." Then, realizing his performance is lackluster at best, he tries to inject some anger. "But if I ever find out who did this, so help me god I will—"

"As much as I enjoy the 'Prince Charming to the rescue' routine," I interrupt, only half-jokingly, "I don't need you defending my honor. I can look after myself."

"Clearly," he mutters. The two syllables drip with sarcasm.

Snapping back, I say, "What's that supposed to mean?"

He looks conflicted, like part of him wants to backtrack, but he knows I'm stubborn and won't let that comment slide. So he just mumbles, "Never mind."

I cross my arms and fix a firm look on my face. This is difficult, because I have the opposite of Resting Bitch Face. My round cheeks, big eyes, and docile demeanor often encourage conversation from strangers at bus stops, which sounds pleasant but has in fact made me consider an acid attack on myself on more than one occasion.

"Look, Danny," I say, eager to get to the actual point of this confrontation. "All I know is you weren't that happy with me after the whole two-one-night-stands scenario. That's all."

In the silence that follows, branches crack and snap, and the gym teacher pants nearby.

Danny peers at me with an expression I can't read. Anger, I'd guess, but laced with something else. "What are you accusing me of?"

"Nothing." Everything. My heart hammers against my rib cage. A thousand cruel comments repeat on a loop in my head. *Slut. Whore. Ugly bitch.* "I just want to figure out who's behind it all. Because you know my motto: do no harm, but take no shit. And this right here is shit I am categorically unwilling to receive."

He shakes his head slowly, narrowing his eyes. "I can't believe this. I genuinely thought that when you asked to talk to me, you'd had a change of heart. About . . . us. I thought . . ." He swallows whatever he was about to say next. Then: "But no. You're *actually* accusing me of setting up that blog."

The awkwardness-averse cringe-phobe inside me desperately wants to backtrack, to insist I'm not accusing him of anything, but I'm too upset. I won't back down.

I'll never forget the quiet venom in his next words.

"Fuck you, Izzy O'Neill."

6:00 p.m.

So he lost his shit? xo

Ajita, texting, obviously.

Ajita, I don't think Danny has been in full possession of his shit since 2011. But yep. Totally lost it.

This can't be an easy situation for her to be in, stuck between the two of us. [Actually, who am I kidding. She loves the drama. She feeds on it like a reality TV–addicted leech.]

You still think he's behind it? xo

I have no idea. In fact it is frightening how few ideas I have. What do you think?

A pause.

I think the boy is stupidly in love with you on account

137

of his terrible taste in women. But no. I don't think he did it. xo

It's at this point I realize I really should've spoken to Ajita before confronting Danny. Despite her insistence that she cares little about either of us, I know she probably hates seeing us both hurting like this. And she really does have both of our best interests at heart. I make a mental note to be less impulsive in the future, and actually discuss stuff with her before leaping in feetfirst. Neither of us loves talking about feelings and emotions, because ARGHHHH DISCOMFORT, but I know some things are too important to gloss over.

In fairness, I am starting to feel a little bit bad for asking him in the first place. We've been best friends for so long, and yes, he's harboring an inconvenient crush on me for reasons I cannot begin to understand, and yes, I did accidentally kiss him that one time, and yes, he did see me kiss Carson just a few days later. But surely I know him better than that. Surely he would never set out to hurt me that way.

Doubt creeps in. Did I do the wrong thing in confronting him?

7:56 p.m.
And if Danny really didn't do it . . . who the hell did?

11:04 p.m.
In all the self-loathing and furor, I almost forgot that two other people were sort of dragged down with me on the

blog—Vaughan and Carson were collateral damage. Of course, they are not generally subjected to the same level of sexual scrutiny due to their Y chromosomes, but still.

I am essentially a Mother Teresa meets Dalai Lama type figure, so I take it upon myself to reach out to these poor fuckboys and make sure they're okay. I know, I know. Fully anticipating the Nobel Peace Prize any day now. I mean, anyone can get shot in the head by the Taliban but it takes a really big person to text a fuckboy. [I am 113 percent being sarcastic here. I firmly believe Malala should be leader of the free world, and also CEO of Hershey's because I swear to god peanut butter cups are getting smaller, which is an act of terrorism in itself.]

Text to Vaughan:

Hey. Assume you've seen the blog. I have no idea
how the person who made it knows so much about
what happened that night, but I can only apologize—
obviously this is the last thing I wanted to happen.
Well, not the LAST. The zombie apocalypse would be
worse I think. Anyway. Hope you're all right.

Facebook message to Carson:

Hey. Assume you've seen the blog. I have no idea
how the person who made it knows so much about
what happened that night, but I can only apologize—
obviously this is the last thing I wanted to happen.
Well, not the LAST. The zombie apocalypse would be
worse I think. So would a ruptured butthole. Anyway.
Hope you're all right.

As you can see I utilized the copy-paste function on my phone very well [adding the butthole comment for the second text because I know Carson's sense of humor is even more vile and misguided than my own]. You know by now that I am a fan of a shortcut, such as when shaving your legs [nobody cares about anything above your knees], or while performing any other sort of body hair admin. In fact I think cutting corners is advisable in almost every physical situation, with the exception of maybe brain surgery.

Because he is by far the superior human being, Carson is the only one who replies.

Hey, what's up? I'm cool. This kinda thing doesn't really bother me. Are you ok, though? Pretty brutal stuff on there, bro. Sorry you gotta deal with it. Lemme know if you need anything.

I am quite touched by this, to the extent that I am willing to overlook him calling me bro.

I'm doing ok. Trying not to let it get to me. Thanks for being awesome about it.

Against all the odds, I go to bed in good snuff. [This is a seventeenth-century term for "happy," which I firmly believe should be reinstated in the modern vernacular. See, I do pay attention in school when it suits me, such as for picking up entertaining slang.]

TUESDAY, SEPTEMBER 27

10:34 a.m.

Aforementioned good snuffery does not last as long as one might have hoped.

For one thing, we have math first period. Honestly, what was that Pythagoras dude's problem? Why did he have to ruin the simple triangle for everyone? It's just downright inconsiderate, is what it is.

I think it is perhaps the repeated usage of the word "hypotenuse" that sends most of the class into a state of deep boredom that can only be relieved by shit-talking. Of course that someone is me on this occasion, due to my unashamed sexploits and generally ludicrous nature that invites shit-talking in all its forms. Thus my new nickname becomes Herpes McWartface. Kids really are not very inventive with their mockery these days.

As a rule I tend to lean into jokes at my expense, like how you're supposed to steer into the swerve when you're driving and lose control, so I marked my homework "H McW" yesterday and promptly forgot all about it. So when Mr. Davies hands us the homework back, he frowns and says, "Who is H McW? Do we have a new student?"

The whole class erupts. Because I am sick in the head, I enjoy the laughs. As a comedian I am perfectly willing to throw my dignity under the bus if it means getting a giggle.

But Mr. Davies won't let it drop, and insists I explain the new initials to him. He's the sort of teacher who thinks of himself as someone who's pals with his students, but he doesn't really pull it off because he is fundamentally not a cool person.

Always coming to my rescue, Ajita chimes in with, "Sir, I believe it is an allusion to the sexually transmitted diseases my friend here may or may not have contracted according to the website Izzy O'Neill: World Class Whore. Anonymous source. Would you like my bibliography in the MLA format, or will footnotes suffice?"

Even I crack up at this point. People all around me are just dying, like actually expiring with the utter hilarity of the situation, and Mr. Davies tries his very best to muster an "I'm with you, comrades" sort of grin despite the fact he's so disgusted he might possibly shit himself right here and now.

The only guy in the entire room whose face looks like a smacked fish? Danny. He glares straight ahead and grits his teeth.

And just like that I'm back to feeling like dirt.

11:15 a.m.
Instead of actually paying attention in class, I spend the

whole morning obsessing over who else hates me enough to do this, but since I generally fly below the radar most of the time, it's pretty difficult to come up with any realistic options. Nobody really knows who I am. At least, they didn't until very recently. So why would they bother making a website with the sole intent of shaming me?

For a brief moment I wonder whether someone from theater wanted to punish me for always landing the lead role despite my lackadaisical attitude to line-learning, but that seems pretty tenuous.

Okay, so it stands to reason that whoever did this was at the party. They had to be, in order to take that picture. And yet when I run through the faces I remember seeing that night, none jump out as potential suspects.

I mean, it's possible that someone has a secret vendetta against me. You know, one of those random dislikes you know is irrational. I have a petty hatred of Adam Silverstein, because back in kindergarten he lifted my skirt up and showed the class my Disney underwear. Over a decade later he's turned into a pretty decent guy, by all accounts, but I'll never be able to forget his one moment of indecency as a five-year-old.

Is that it? Did I embarrass someone as an infant? Have they been biding their time to finally seek revenge?

What is this villain's origin story?

1:04 p.m.

By lunchtime the mockery begins to focus specifically on

the porch swing picture. You know, the picture in which I am *literally having sex on a porch swing*. Wunderbar. Gone are the glory days of flying below the radar with every single thing I do or say.

We're in the cafeteria, which is actually pretty quiet because the entire sophomore class is off at some careers fair in the city. It's spaghetti and meatballs day, and the kitchen obviously forgot about the mass sophomore absence, so those of us still in school are enjoying mammoth bowls of the stuff.

A guy I half recognize as a member of the cross-country team [which is how I immediately know he is some form of psychopath, as any person who voluntarily runs without a gun pointing at his head is] approaches the bench I'm sitting at with Ajita. She is mid-rant about our absurd two-party political system and its failings, so is quite annoyed at the interruption.

"Hey, Izzy," Psychopath Runner says, a nauseating grin combined with a strange fake-concerned expression on his face. "Are you all right? Would you like me to fetch the first aid kit from the nurse's office?"

I sigh. "All right, I'll play along. Why would I require the first aid kit?"

He's beside himself with excitement at being granted the opportunity to recite his punch line. "Well, you're bound to have splinters from rubbing your knees back and forth on that porch swing. And back. And forth. And back. And—"

"Yes, yes, very good, thank you," Ajita says, slurping her Capri Sun. [It actually is Capri Sun, for once. Even Ajita

144

does not drink beer at school. Yet. Give it time.] "Goodbye now."

He disappears, receiving a multitude of fist bumps from his fellow cross-country psychopaths.

Ajita finishes her juice pouch and scrunches it up. "Hey, I made you something."

She attempts to toss the pouch in the nearby trash can, missing entirely, then starts digging around in her backpack until she triumphantly pulls out a glossy postcard.

It's a printout of the porch swing pic, but she's turned it into a work of art! I think she's probably just applied one of those Photoshop filters that makes it look like stained glass, but still. It is funny and very Ajita.

I squeeze her hand. "Thank you. For . . . y'know."

Standing by me. Making me laugh. Allowing me to feel like I might actually survive this ordeal, even though I'm too proud to ever dream of asking for help.

She squeezes mine back. "I know. You're welcome."

4:23 p.m.

A girl I vaguely recognize from math class comes up to me in the hallway before last period. She's in a wheelchair and has mousy brown hair and round little glasses and I think her name is Meg.

"Izzy?"

I try very hard to maintain an air of detachedness, since there's at least a 95 percent chance she's about to mock me. "Yes, Meg? May I help you?"

"Um, I . . ."

"If you're here to crack any sort of porch swing–based joke, please do it in the next five seconds because I am going to be late for geography, and Lord knows rock formations are the number one thing on my mind right now. The last lesson ended on quite a cliff-hanger." [Geddit? Cliff-hanger! Rock formations! The best jokes are the ones you have to explain.]

She shakes her head vehemently. "No! I wasn't going to . . . I just wanted . . . well, I wanted to say that I think you're really cool. And funny. You really made me laugh in math this morning. With the H McW thing. I wish I could be as funny as you." She's blushing furiously at this point.

A huge grin breaks out across my face. I can't help it. The unexpected sweetness catches me so off guard that I completely forget the aloof vibe I was aiming for. "That's such a nice thing to say, Meg! You should totally come and hang out with me and Ajita sometime. We make excellent nachos."

"Ohmygosh, really?" she beams. "I would *love* that!"

I scribble down my phone digits for her and head to geography class feeling very grateful for the few remaining nice people in the world.

5:16 p.m.

Wtf. Danny turns up to *Great Gatsby* rehearsals carrying a bunch of tulips and a box of my favorite chocolates [Ferrero Rocher. Yes, my taste in candy is unreasonably pretentious given my financial situation]. Bearing in mind the last thing he said to me was fuck you, at first I foolishly think this is but a simple apology. Alas, that is not how the following events transpire.

He waltzes down the aisle between rows of seats. Everyone turns to stare. We're about to start blocking the opening scene so everyone is onstage, and when he walks down, face completely obscured by the obnoxiously large bunch of flowers, an eerie silence falls over us.

Mrs. Crannon absolutely does not know how to proceed. So I just slip off the stage and run over to Danny, hissing, "Please tell me these are not for me," silently praying that they are lest I look like a self-absorbed loon.

An innocent frown. "I thought tulips and fancy Nutella balls were your favorites?"

"They are. But . . . why?" Here's where I'm hoping he'll acknowledge he was a giant dickwad and will apologize accordingly.

He thrusts the gifts into my arms and awkwardly shoves his hands into his pockets. "Just because. I want to start fresh. Forget the last few weeks, you know?" When I don't say anything in response, he adds, "And . . . well, I wanted to show you how great it could be. If we were together."

And that's when I realize. It's not an apology. It's a bribe. Here, have some gifts. Please be my girlfriend and blow my mind with your sexual prowess. That sort of thing.

"Oh," I say. "Thanks. I guess."

I mean, what else could I say with a whole room of

extravagant drama types watching? Besides, I'm still all kinds of hurt that he said "fuck you" in such a vile way.

Danny smiles awkwardly. "You're welcome. I'm going to win you over. You'll see."

One slow clap from Evan Maclin turns into a hearty round of applause. I can see why, to the innocent onlooker, this might seem sort of sweet, but it leaves me feeling kind of uneasy. I don't know why. Maybe because his words are so unambiguous, and remove the possibility that I might say no. "I'm *going* to win you over." I feel . . . trapped, I guess?

Maybe I'm being too hard on him. Danny's fundamentally a decent person. We grew up together, and it must be tough for him to develop unrequited romantic feelings. I should cut him some slack. I probably wouldn't handle it all that well either.

I don't bother going backstage, where I've left my purse, phone, and other worldly possessions. Instead I dump my "gifts" on the front row seats and retake my place onstage, stomach twisting uncomfortably. Danny's got an awful bashful-but-also-proud-of-himself face on, accepting the "awwww"s from girls and shoulder jostles from guys.

And yet for the rest of the rehearsal, I can't shake the discomfort his proclamation has caused me. It squirms and writhes through my veins, but I still can't pin it down, still can't identify why it feels so toxic.

Eventually, after I've spaced out countless times onstage and had to mumble my apologies, it hits me. This wasn't a display of romance and affection. It was a categoric ultimate rejection of his place in the Friend Zone. A thinly veiled assertion of male dominance. A statement: that his feelings and desires are more important than mine.

It's like he's saying: "I don't respect your decision not to want to fuck me, and I will manipulate the hell out of your emotions until you change your mind."

Argh. I've told him I don't want a romantic relationship. Why isn't that enough?

8:02 p.m.

By the time rehearsals are over I just want to get home to leftover mac and cheese and a gallon of hot chocolate. But no! That would be too simple! Teenage boys always have other ideas.

Vaughan is waiting for me by the parking lot, shifting on his feet like a rookie drug dealer. I'm about to inform him that I'm all set for horse tranquilizers when he grabs my arm, hard enough that it's painful, and mutters, "Can we talk in the woods?"

Carrying Danny's obscene gifts in my arms, I follow him until we reach a clearing. "If any detectives happen to be tailing us, this definitely looks like a botched drug deal type situation," I say. He looks at me like I have all of a sudden grown an extra nose. I pat my face just to make sure.

Vaughan grits his teeth. I honestly don't know why his default facial expression is a poor imitation of beef cattle. I would bring it up but he already looks so unimpressed by my character as a whole. "It's not funny. Stop making jokes."

"I'm sorry. It's because of who I am as a person. What'd you want to talk about?"

"I just wondered if you knew which asshole was behind that web—"

Both of our phones bleep at exactly the same time, mine with a text message, his with a notification. This does not sound particularly impressive but seriously, how often do phones make the same tone in perfect synchrony? Am I just easily pleased? [My sexual track record would suggest yes.]

The joy and merriment of the ringtone situation quickly evaporates when I see the message from Ajita.

My nude picture has been leaked.

The one I sent Vaughan.

Every single inch of me. Plastered all over the internet for the whole world to see.

No no no no no no no no no please no.

Whoever posted it has dragged Vaughan down with me, because his name shows up at the top of the conversation.

Which means it's a screenshot. Which means it was taken from my phone, because my messages are in blue bubbles. His replies have been uploaded too—the begging and the dick pic and everything. But all I see is my own naked body.

Shit shit shit shit shit shit nooooooooo.

[Sorry for the expletives but I cannot muster anything more articulate right now.]

My boobs and va-jay-jay are out there in the world. I feel disgusting and violated and bare.

Oh my god. I just noticed the name of the person who uploaded it to the World Class Whore website: Izzy O'Neill. Someone did it directly from my phone. I left it backstage during rehearsals. Oh god. Oh no. Please no.

Twisting uncomfortably in my chest, my heart sinks. This absolutely cannot be happening. I'm shaking so hard it's probably measuring on the Richter scale.

Vaughan slams his palm against a tree trunk. He's definitely going to regret that tonight when he can't rage-masturbate.

"*You* leaked them. Thought it'd be good publicity for your little screenplay? Nothing launches a career quite like a sex scandal, does it?"

"I guarantee I am not that intelligent," I say numbly.

A crazed grin splits his face in half. [Not literally.] "Do you know what my father is going to do when he finds out about this? Kill me. He's going to kill me." He looks like he might genuinely cry. "How do we make this go away? How do I make *you* go away?" He practically spits this last part.

He then grabs Danny's tulips from my hands, hurls them to the ground, and starts stomping on them like he's trying to kill a cockroach. He does this for at least thirty seconds before I ask, "What are you trying to achieve, exactly?"

Vaughan stops abruptly. "Do you have any idea what kind of pressure I'm under? To support my father, to go to law school, to be successful? To be the perfect fucking model son with the perfect fucking grades and the perfect fucking life?"

"No, I don't," I say matter-of-factly. "Because my parents are dead." Adrenaline is ringing in my ears. "I'm going to walk away now because you're pissing me off. Come and talk to me when you've calmed down and we'll figure out how to fix this mess. I will either be here or in Mexico. It is really anyone's guess at this point."

Right now I'm thinking, okay, new plan: go home, talk to Betty about my disastrous existence, maybe purchase and consume a vegetable because on top of everything else, I'm probably at real risk of developing scurvy.

However, Betty's pretty weary after a double shift at the diner, and to be honest she smells like old french fry grease, but I still hug her super tight the minute she walks in the door. She's damp from the rain outside, which is nice because when I cry silently all over her woolly yellow cardigan, she barely notices.

"Kiddo! What's all this about?" she asks. We're standing in the doorway, her sodden umbrella dumped next to the shoe rack, me clinging to her like a limpet to a rockpool. "Don't get me wrong, I enjoy sudden and alarming displays of affection as much as the next girl. But this isn't usually your style."

"Sorry," I sniffle, finally pulling away. Betty pushes the door shut, locking and chaining it while still looking at me with deep concern.

Her glasses are spotted with rain, but instead of wiping them dry she just peers at me through the kaleidoscopic droplets. "Rough day?"

"You could say that."

She ushers me into the kitchen and immediately gets to work filling the kettle. It's one of those unnecessarily heavy beasts that she inherited from *her* grandma, and she can barely lift it despite the Popeye arms she's developed over decades of manual labor.

Once it's simmering away on the stove, she takes a seat at the table with me. It's still covered in crumbs from our breakfast sandwiches this morning. I fill Betty in on the Danny situation, but somehow, when I come to tell her about the leaked nudes, the words get stuck in my throat.

"That's sweet of Danny to buy you flowers," Betty says, missing the point entirely.

"No, it's not."

The kettle whistles on the stove and Betty goes to get up, but I gesture for her to stay seated. She's been on her feet all day. I busy myself making tea in the biggest mugs I can find.

"Why isn't it?" Betty asks, propping her feet up on the chair I left empty.

Stirring milk and a third spoonful of sugar into each cup, I sigh. "He's not respecting my decision not to have sex and/or partake in a romantic relationship with him. Did you not read that Feminism 101 book I got you for Christmas?"

"I don't think this exact scenario was in there."

I bring the tea over to the table and take a seat, propping Betty's feet up into my lap. Dumbledore sniffles around the floor, hoping for some rogue bacon grease or even a mini-marshmallow from last night's hot cocoa, even though he's probably checked this exact spot a hundred times today. I scoop him up onto my lap too, so he can act as a foot warmer for Betty. He wiggles uncomfortably at first, but soon settles into the strange sort of cuddle, accepting my gentle strokes of his soft brown fur.

"Anyway, the hows and the whys are sort of beside the point," I say. "I'm just feeling kind of exhausted by it all. School. Danny. And . . . some other stuff." I trail off vaguely.

I'm not sure why I don't want to tell Betty about the website, or the nudes. Mainly I don't want to worry her, especially when she's so damn exhausted herself. In fact I feel kind of guilty about complaining, given all the sacrifices she makes just to keep me alive and in full-time education.

But it seems like she's not really listening. She traces a wrinkly thumb around the rim of the tea cup, staring intently at the steam. It looks like she wants to say something heartfelt, but she often needs to give herself a pep talk before spouting a sentence containing actual emotion, so I give her the space she needs to build up to it.

"Listen, kiddo," she starts, throat hoarse like it so often is at the end of a long shift. "I wish your mom was here to see you now." Her voice catches. "You know your own mind, and you're not afraid to speak it, you know? She'd be so proud of you."

Tears press heavily against my eyes.

No she wouldn't, I want to scream. If my parents were here, they'd see nude pictures of me all over the internet!

I can't talk about this. I can't. And from the tension on Betty's face, she's too exhausted to handle me launching into a conversation about being branded the school slut. So I shut it down.

"Anyway," I say, swallowing my comparatively meager pain. "How was your day?"

10:01 p.m.
Once I'm alone, I take a deep breath and find the link to the World Class Whore blog. Not in a self-flagellatory way; I just want to wrap my head around what's happening, and the way it went down with Vaughan in the woods made it hard to do that. As much as I'm an insane extrovert and love being around people, when something major happens I need time to process it alone.

I wash my face and brush my teeth, change into prehistoric pj's, switch the lights off in my room, and climb into bed. I then proceed to create a cocoon-type setup with the duvet and some pillows, pulling the covers all the way over my head and curling up into the fetal position. I'm not sure what it is about this maneuver that feels so comforting. If I was in any way academic, I'd probably posit that it's something to do with re-creating the atmosphere of the womb. But alas, I am not in any way academic. Remind me to ask Ajita.

The website takes a few seconds to load on my phone screen, but it's still not long enough. Even though I know exactly what I'm about to see, it's still like a punch to the gut when the screenshot flashes up.

My boobs and my va-jay-jay, on show to the world. Just under the pic of Vaughan's above-average length, below-average girth, bending-slightly-to-the-left penis. For which I'm 104 percent sure he will not receive anywhere near as much criticism as me.

I stare and stare and stare at the photo of me, gut churning uncomfortably. It's not that I'm body conscious or anything. I'm not. But I am old-fashioned in the sense that I like to give people individual permission to view my boobs and other parts, rather than allowing blanket access to seven billion internet users. That may seem unreasonable, but it's true.

Oh my god oh my god oh my god. This feeling of violation is skin-crawlingly terrible. It feels like being on the criminal side of a police mirror, where everyone can see you but you can't see them. I am an exhibit, laid bare before every single kid in my school—hell, probably my town. And I feel so exposed.

Again, I'm not body conscious. But your private parts are just so . . . intimate. I have a hard enough time showing them to my doctor. A couple of years ago I had a weird lump on one boob, and even though it turned out to be nothing, I still think about the embarrassment of being fondled by a middle-aged male doctor with stale coffee breath, while I tried and failed to make conversation about the strength of the dollar.

Now that mortification is multiplied a thousandfold. And I still don't know anything about currency depreciation.

1:02 a.m.

Who could do this? Seriously, who is heartless enough to want to expose me in such a brutal way? I'm just a girl. A teenage girl. How could anyone do this?

1:14 a.m.

Fuck. What am I going to do?

WEDNESDAY, SEPTEMBER 28

<u>8:05 a.m.</u>
Feel beyond anxious at the thought of going to school today. I woke up stupidly early again this morning, so decided to write a sketch about a senator and his son who get stuck in a waste incinerator like that hugely traumatic scene in *Toy Story 3*. Not that I am harboring any violent feelings toward the Vaughan family or anything.

At least there is slight progress on the eyebrow front. Ajita lent me her pencil, which is a good five shades too dark for me, and I attempted to fill in the little gap. Because of the mismatched hue, I then had to even up the same spot on other side. So I have a very attractive ombré caterpillar type situation on my forehead, a look that I am sure we can all agree will hit beauty bloggers' screens any time now.

I'm too scared to look at the online reaction to the nudes. The mid-sex porch swing pic was one thing, but this is so . . . explicit. Every time I remember they're out there, which is roughly every 2.3 milliseconds, I get a horrible sinking sensation in my belly, like when you go over a speed bump too fast. I obsess over who might be looking at these pictures of me—bare, exposed, eighteen—and judging me for them. Judging my body; my choices; my life.

I know this will blow over eventually. But until then, it's going to be hell.

8:47 a.m.

Who did this, who did this, WHO THE HELL DID THIS?

9:01 a.m.

Ajita, Danny, and I arrive at school to find a cluster of freshmen armed with smartphone cameras pointed straight at me. As soon as I get within twenty feet of them, they start to snap pics and hit record, and I hear a couple of them narrating my humiliating entrance to their bazillion followers live on social media. Danny wraps an arm protectively around my shoulders, and I don't really know how to take it in the context of everything else that's happened between us, but in the moment I'm just grateful for the support, both emotional and physical. It steadies me.

Then someone shouts, "Jeez, O'Neill, have you banged Wells too?"

It is at this point that Ajita delves into her backpack, pulls out some overripe kiwi fruits, and hurls them straight at the freshman scum. Green pulp explodes everywhere. It's fantastic to behold. Then she yanks my arm and hauls me and Danny past them without looking back.

When I look at the kiwi juice all over her hands quizzically, she simply says, "We were out of eggs."

"And you knew this was going to happen when you left the house this morning? That I was going to be harassed by the entire world?"

She sighs. "No, I brought them to snack on, then improvised. Must you kill the triumph of the moment with your incessant questions?"

9:14 a.m.

In the last thirteen minutes, I have been sarcastically told "nice tits" in excess of 587 times.

9:37 a.m.

Oh shit and merde and scheiß and every other linguistic variable on the word. Danny found the mashed-up tulips in the woods. Of course he did! Why would anything run smoothly! I'm a writer. I should've known the tulips were some sort of Chekhov's gun and were doomed to go off in the third act. [I know this is still only the second act but who are you, the story structure police?]

He found them all muddy and smooshed before first period. He just went out to get some fresh air [I have tried to explain to him why this is so overrated but he won't listen. In conclusion, if people just listened to me a bit more we'd find ourselves in far fewer upsetting situations]. To clear his head. And boom, he walks straight into the mangled flower carcasses.

Because he is a highly dramatic individual, instead of just leaving the flowers there and letting me off the hook, he gathers them up in a paper bag, brings them back into school, and dumps them on my desk just before chemistry is about to start.

"You left these behind last night."

It is such a petty move but I'm struggling to be mad due to lack of energy and enthusiasm, and the fact that the only thing I'm capable of thinking about right now is the nude photograph of me on the internet.

"It wasn't me," I explain feebly.

Danny shakes his head at me and flumps dejectedly into the seat in front of me.

Yeah. Like *he's* the one who should be feeling sorry for himself right about now. You'd think he'd be concerned about the emotional stability of his best friend, who's just been exposed in all her naked glory to the entire world, and maybe, just maybe, put his own feelings aside for once.

But no. This is all about him, like it always is. He's incapable of imagining how situations affect other people, and thinks solely of his own feelings. That's what the flowers symbolize: he was hurt that I rejected him, so he set out to fix it. To make himself feel better. Never mind how *I* felt; that I was content with my decision to stay friends.

He's always been like this. Only Child Syndrome to the extreme. As a fellow only child, I feel qualified to diagnose this.

I want to call him out. I do. Unfortunately, right now I need all the friends I can get.

3:56 p.m.
So the entire school has now seen my lady parts. And holy backlash, Batman.

The rest of my day at school is an unmitigated nightmare. Everywhere I go, kids of all ages and social standings point, whisper, and laugh, the words "slut" and "whore" and "legend" echoing around the corridor. The latter is in reference to the two dudes who bedded me, as that is the way of high school and also the entire world. At one point I pass Prajesh in the hallway. He's by himself, but he doesn't say hey to me. He just tucks his chin to his chest and barrels past as though I'm not there.

I get it. I do. If he's already feeling like a bit of a pariah, the last thing he wants to do is associate with an *actual* pariah and alienate himself even further. But it still stings.

Vaughan's dad arrives at lunchtime and practically drags his son out of school, probably to prepare his press statement about how Vaughan is an innocent party in this debacle, and the rumors surrounding his involvement are nothing more than high school hearsay. Honestly, after his flower-stomping and woe-is-me performance I'd be quite glad not to be sexually associated with him.

It is vaguely concerning that actual adults are now aware of the website, but I'm hoping Ted only knows about it because his son makes an appearance on it. Not because every adult in the state knows about it too. That's just too horrifying to contemplate.

Anyway, I was sort of hoping a bunch of other girls in school might rally around me in a show of feminist support, but alas, this is not what happens.

When I'm using the bathroom just after lunch, some horrid creature with an incredibly unoriginal sense of humor says loudly to her pal: "No wonder she's peeing. Being pregnant makes you pee a lot. Ha ha ha!" Seriously. How is *anyone* so unfunny? It is truly beyond me.

To be fair, her friend promptly fact-checks this lackadaisical attempt at humor and says, "I don't think she's pregnant. She's just a whore. With lopsided boobs and love handles." More giggles.

Delightful.

In all seriousness, I don't really blame the other kids for their reactions. After all, it's human nature to experience a kind of dark thrill whenever Something Happens. It's like me and my love of other people's drama. I think anything that helps pass the time in a slightly more interesting manner is always going to become a topic of conversation. So yeah, I don't blame them for their fascination in this whole nude picture situation. It breaks up the monotony of human existence. Hell, it's probably why someone created World Class Whore to begin with. Restlessness.

Speaking of which, I still have no idea who could be behind the website, and my paranoid brain is beginning to attach suspicion to every face I see. Every giggling freshman in the restroom, every guffawing jock in the hallway, every sneaky-faced stranger who casts a glance my way. They all become the villain in my head. It's exhausting.

I know I need to find out who really launched the blog, but it's an overwhelming prospect. Where would I even start? I don't have the technological savvy to determine the site's IP origins, nor do I have the Sherlock-style intelligence needed to apply the art of deduction to the problem. And do I even want to bury myself neck-deep in finding out who did this? Isn't it best to try to forget about it and move on? There's no right answer. Both options suck.

Anyway, I'm hanging out with Ajita and Danny tonight. I wonder just how mad he is about the flower thing. Maybe witnessing my brutal public shaming will have made him feel a tad sorry for me. Usually my toes would curl at the idea of such sympathy, but like I say, right now I'll take any kindness I can get.

4:08 p.m.
Text from Carson.

Hey, Iz. Sorry for dropping off the radar lately—family stuff. Anyway, if you wanna meet up and chat about anything that's going on, give me a call. Playing b-ball this afternoon but free all day tomorrow. Let me know.

C

Why is my chest fluttering like some sort of lovesick teenager? Seriously. This is Carson Manning we're talking about. Class clown! Brisk fornicator! Why is my ridiculous crush on him escalating despite everything that's going on?

There's another part of me that's relieved. After the debacle with Danny seeing us kiss and storming off, and then the sudden appearance of the WCW website, and *then* the leakage of my nude photo, an insecure part of me wondered if Carson would tap out of . . . whatever he and I are. It's a lot of drama to be willfully associated with.

6:21 p.m.
After school we go to Ajita's to film a sketch or two. And, you know, generally take my mind off the hideous state of affairs plaguing my existence.

Our last YouTube upload racked up a dizzying 418 views, so we're feeling quite high on our success and just the right amount of cocky to capitalize on it. We've roped in our fellow theater nerd Sharon, a Chinese American girl with literally the best deadpanning skills you've ever seen in your life, to help out with a sketch I wrote before all the screenplay competition stuff kicked off. It's a piece of satire about a kooky old grandmother who moonlights as a stripper in a very niche establishment where saggy boobs are not only celebrated but also fetishized. I got the idea when Betty told me she wanted to moonlight as a stripper in a very niche establishment where saggy boobs are not only celebrated but also fetishized.

It actually feels pretty good to do something comedy and writing related in the midst of all the chaos. It kind of . . . centers me, if that makes sense. I know who I am when I'm writing and filming and telling jokes. And it's always nice to have people laughing with you, not at you.

Danny isn't here yet, so I run through lines with Sharon while Ajita messes with lighting—a very professional and advanced combination of desk lamps, overhead chandeliers, and one lonely light reflector. Once the set is all sorted out, we just have to wait for Danny to arrive with his camera and mics.

Ajita's phone buzzes and she looks at the name on her screen discreetly. I wonder if it's Carlie. Carlie, who has pretty much disappeared off the burgeoning friendship radar since my nude picture leaked. As a new girl at Edgewood, I can see why she wouldn't want to be associated with me. Moving schools is hard enough as it is without hitching your wagon to the most widely mocked student on campus. But still, it kind of sucks.

I wonder if she and Ajita still communicate on the sly. I wonder how much I'd care if they did. On my list of things to be upset about, Carlie's opinion of me is not high.

Eventually Danny arrives, flustered from hauling the tripod on foot, and barely looks at me as we fumble with the equipment. That's when I remember how pissed off he is about the mangled flower fiasco. Should I mention it to him? Should I brush it under the rug? Should I leave for Mexico sooner than first anticipated? There is just no right answer.

Maturely I decide to crack a relentless stream of "your mom" jokes at him until he softens [not like that, stop it]. The genius thing about this tactic is he really cannot crack any back on account of the fact that my mom is dead, so it would just be unnecessarily cruel and harsh.

However, the only effect this has is making Ajita laugh so hard a little bit of pee comes out, and she has to go for a shower to sort her life out. Thus leaving Danny and me making small talk with Sharon, who is lovely but deadpan in real life too, so it's hard to tell what she's thinking. It could just as easily be "wow my new friends are so cool and original" as it could "what a bunch of morons." There is just no way of knowing.

While Ajita's showering and Sharon is changing into costume, I take the opportunity to ask Danny, "How's Praj doing? Anything we need to worry about?"

Danny tinkers with a mic. "He seems okay. Focusing on his next track meet. Still seems kinda lonely, though. I'm hanging out with him at some point next week, which is helping, I think, but I still want him to make some friends his own age, you know?"

"I do. You're a good friend, looking out for him," I say, and I mean it. There aren't many eighteen-year-old dudes who'd hang out with their best friend's little brother just to make sure he's doing okay. It reminds me why I'm friends with Danny despite the recent melodrama.

Part of me suspects Danny enjoys being around Praj too. Like I say, he doesn't have many guy friends, and if things are rough at home it's probably serving as a nice distraction. And he *really* loves Mario Kart.

"Hey, important question," I say. "What character does he play on Mario Kart?"

"Donkey Kong, like some kind of amateur," Danny grins. "Everyone knows it's all about Toad."

"False. Team Bowser, forever and always."

Danny snorts. "Aaaaand that's why I always kick your ass on Rainbow Road." I return his grin, relieved that we've managed to have a normal conversation for the first time in too long.

Once Ajita has washed away her rogue urine and hopefully found a diaper to wear, I call action. Although I love to perform, I also secretly love to direct, even though I have a tendency to whine about having to do it. I think it's because I enjoy bossing people around, but there is also something so satisfying about seeing your creation come to life on screen. I get a strange little flutter of excitement at the idea of doing this as a career.

I check my emails for the millionth time today, hoping for news about the screenplay comp despite the fact that it's only been a few days since I sent back my revised script. Nothing.

Then it hits me. What if the judges have seen the nudes?

8:50 p.m.
Honestly, what a self-obsessed drama queen I am. Why would hotshot comedy producers and a panel of professional

screenwriting judges be scouring the internet in pursuit of teen nudes? If that were the case, surely they're the ones who should be embarrassed, not me.

Get a grip, O'Neill.

10:14 p.m.
Danny and I cycle back from Ajita's together. Our neighborhoods are pretty close, even though his is so much more expensive it might as well be another world.

We're at the junction and about to part ways when he says, "Hey, why don't you come to my house for a bit? My mom's been nagging me to invite you over for months. It's been so long."

To be 100 percent honest, I'm super tired and just want to get home to Betty, Dumbledore, and my cozy bed, but it's been kinda nice to hang out with Danny today. Plus I remember what Betty told me about his parents' rocky marriage, and the way he dismissed me when I probed him about it. Inviting me back to his house is a big show of trust—one our friendship definitely needs right now. And it *would* be nice to see his mom, Miranda. She was my mom's best friend, and she always has the most awesome stories about her.

Which is how, nine minutes later, I'm sitting in the living room of their fancy four-bedroom house, making polite conversation and wishing I were in the comfort of my own home.

Their living room is super formal. It has stiff chesterfield sofas with tiny, firm cushions, and the floor is pale marble topped with a giant Persian rug. The fireplace itself is bare and unused, but the mantelpiece bears an antique clock and several miniature statues of Jesus and his disciples.

It's the total opposite of Ajita's house. Her parents are rich too, but their home is warm and inviting, just like they are. Nepalese rugs, dancing shiva statues, a roaring fireplace in winter. I've spent so many evenings in that cozy living room, eating Mrs. Dutta's delicious homemade milk balls and chatting about the weird and wonderful medical cases she's treated in her decades as a neurosurgeon. Mr. Dutta is cool too—the very definition of a goofy dad. His jokes are as heartwarming as they are cringeworthy.

In contrast, Miranda Wells is beautiful, but in a plastic surgery kind of way. Her forehead's a little too tight and her lips are a little too plump, but she's always impeccably dressed. It's hard to imagine her and my mom being best friends in college. My mom was apparently a total hippie type, by all accounts, all tie-dye and weed and protests. Maybe Miranda used to be too, but she's been the way she is now for as long as I can remember.

"So, Izzy, how's school going?" she asks, folding one leg tightly over the other and taking a sip of chilled white wine. "Have you figured out which colleges you're going to apply to yet?"

Here we go again. "Actually, I—"

Danny butts in. "Izzy's decided she doesn't need to go to college."

Sure. It's because I don't *need* to go. I press my lips

170

together. "I just don't think it's the best option for me right now."

Miranda looks like she might be trying to raise her eyebrows, but it's impossible to be sure through all the Botox. "But, Izzy, darling! It's so important to get a good education. I know it's what your parents would've wanted, especially your mom. Did you know she graduated summa cum laude? Political science major." [This comes across badly in writing, but I know her heart's in the right place.]

Eager to move on, I change the subject. "So, Mrs. Wells, are you going back to Lake Michigan for Thanksgiving this year?"

"Actually, I was thinking of visiting my sister and brother-in-law in Europe," she replies. She sways slightly. I wonder how many glasses of wine she's had. Or where Mr. Wells is at ten thirty on a Wednesday night. She thinks I don't see her checking her watch every few seconds, but I do. "I haven't seen them in so long."

There's something oddly sad and vacant about Miranda tonight. It makes me think that things really are that bad between her and Mr. Wells. I feel bad for her, I really do. She might be a bit cold sometimes, but she's always been there for me. And she was important to my mom, so she's important to me too.

"What?" Danny snaps, catching both Miranda and me off guard. "When were you planning on telling me? You know I love going to Lake Michigan for the holidays."

It's been so long since I've been to his house that I've

forgotten how spoiled Danny can be sometimes. He doesn't always react well when he doesn't get what he wants. I mean, sure, we're all different around our parents or various legal guardians. But still, I would think Danny's attitude was messed up even if I hadn't seen the hurt flit across his mother's face when he snapped at her.

Suddenly the weight of everything hits me. I'm just so tired that I can't bear to be here a second longer. "Mrs. Wells, I better be taking off," I say, rising from the sofa. "It's been good to see you. I won't leave it so long next time."

With a slight wobble, Miranda stands up too, setting her glass of wine down on the coffee table a bit too hard. Unexpectedly, she throws her arms around me. She smells of expensive perfume and sauvignon blanc. "You take care of yourself, Izzy. And you always know where I am if you need anything." It's not a maternal gesture, and for once I don't feel like there are thirty years between us. It just feels like one struggling woman hugging another. Like we're peers.

I smile warmly, giving her a reassuring squeeze. "Right back at you."

After a slightly awkward goodbye hug with Danny, I walk through the hallway and toward the front door right at the same time Mr. Wells is returning home from . . . wherever. Judging by the smell of Scotch, he's been in some kind of bar.

He clumsily removes his coat and hangs it on the umbrella stand beside the door. I'm surprised by the swollen belly hanging over his suit pants—it's grown a lot since I last saw him.

Only when he turns around does he finally see me. A sloppy grin registers on his face. "Izzy! Great to see you. Been too long."

I'm about to cheerfully reply, and ask him about work, and tell him about the screenwriting competition, when a wave of fear reaches a crescendo in my chest.

What if he's seen the nudes? What if this guy who's like a father to me has seen the most intimate parts of my body, has looked at pictures of me having sex on a porch swing? The thought is so awful it knocks the wind from my lungs, and suddenly I can't even look at him. I can't be here. I can't do any of it.

As I push past him into the dark night, sobbing into my fist, I feel disgusting. Like my childhood is vanishing before my eyes. Like I'm being forced to grow up too fast.

THURSDAY, SEPTEMBER 29

9:07 a.m.
The entire way through geography class, Carson doodles caricatures of Peruvian animals and passes them to me. The especially thoughtful part is that none of them have eyes, so none of them have seen me naked. Which is always a victory, in my book.

A+ cheering up, 13/10 would recommend being consoled by Carson Manning.

1:35 p.m.
Some delightful human has printed off and photocopied hundreds and hundreds and hundreds of my nudes and stacked them in neat piles all over campus like some sort of visitor information leaflet. They're all grainy and grayscale, but the quality of the printing is not the issue here. The issue is that everywhere I look, the photo is tucked into binders and journals and shirt pockets and uuurgggghhhhhhh.

As I walk down the gap between benches in the cafeteria,

several gorilla boys from the soccer team fling paper airplanes made from the nude printouts at me. Ajita bats them out of the way with her palm like she's merely swatting away flies. One stabs me in the elephant ear. Everyone laughs.

And it occurs to me that the vast majority of these people have also contributed to the website. Sure, the creator posted the original porch swing pic, but there have been so many comments and insults since then.

God, it would be so easy to spiral right now, thinking about just how little my peers think of me. How willing they are to go public with their contempt. Maybe it's mob mentality, I don't know. Maybe they really do want to hurt me. Maybe they're high on the power dynamic of slut-shaming, maybe they love the way the control feels in their hands. Either way, it hurts like a bitch.

But Ajita just sits me down at our usual table, sweeps away a fleet of origami boats also made from the photocopies, and launches into a monologue about the livelihood of barley farmers in Ethiopia. I mean, I wasn't really listening, so it might not have been about that, but let's give her the benefit of the doubt.

At this point I am so ridiculously grateful for Ajita Dutta. If it weren't for her, I'd definitely be spending my lunchtimes holed up in a toilet cubicle or hiding up a tree trying desperately to avoid branch-swinging Tarzan wannabes practicing their muscle-ups.

Unbelievable. Danny has bought me another gift to apologize for freaking out over the destruction of his previous gift. I just want to scream at him "I don't need gifts! I just need you to stop being a grade A bucket of dicks!" but I don't think that would go down very well.

Anyway, as we're all walking home together after school—celebrating the slightly cold breeze—he makes the following announcement: "So . . . what are you guys doing on the first weekend in December? Oh, I know! You're going to see Coldplay live at the arena!"

Oh, wonderful. My inner cynic suspects he probably just wants to sing along to "Fix You" while crying and staring poignantly at me.

Ajita squeals and throws her arms around him. "Danny! That's so awesome. Thank you! I can't even think of anything horrible or sarcastic to say right now."

I attempt to muster some gratitude and deliver a well-intended-but-somewhat-lackluster high five. Lackluster due to my emotional exhaustion and general wariness toward the behavior of Mr. Wells.

He purses his lips, clearly put out by my lack of enthusiasm. In his defense, they must have set him back a buck or two of his parents' cash, since the gig has been sold out for months.

Again, it kind of rubs me the wrong way, this pattern that's emerging. It feels like every time he wants me to feel a certain way, he throws money at the situation. Milk shakes, tulips, Ferrero Rocher, concert tickets. Almost as if he thinks he can buy my love.

I wanted to show you how great it could be. If we were to-gether.

Maybe I'm overreacting. The Coldplay tickets are kinda sweet, I suppose. Danny knows Ajita and I love them, and despite the fact that he himself is too hipster to allow himself to enjoy their "overrated drivel," he's a big enough person to swallow his own taste in pretentious hipster music and attend the concert with us. He is trying to be a good friend, at least. In his own way.

I just can't figure him out at the moment. One minute he's looking after Ajita and Prajesh like they're his own family, and the next he's snapping at his actual family for no reason. There must be some serious shit going down chez Wells. The thought alone makes me feel bad enough to over-look his weird behavior.

Plus, things are crappy enough in my life right now. And I have the option to forgive Danny's relentless stream of weapons-grade douchebaggery, and try to rebuild our fractured friendship. All I want is for things to go back to normal, and this seems as good a place to start as any.

So I say "thank you" and hug him too.

6:28 p.m.
We've been playing Ping-Pong in Ajita's basement for around eleven minutes, deftly avoiding the nude elephant in the room, when my phone vibrates. Message.

Since I'm in the throes of a heated tie break with Ajita, Danny inexplicably picks it up and reads before I can even stop him. "It's from Carson," he says flatly. "He wants to see you."

Shit! I forgot to reply to Carson's last text!

Shit! Why did Danny read it!

"Oh. Right," I respond, carefully avoiding Danny's stare. He wants to gauge my reaction, obviously, and I want to deprive him of that luxury. I pick up the ball to serve, facial expression set to intense mode as though winning this match means more to me than anything in the entire world, even awesome basketball-playing boys who look like movie stars and make me laugh and don't judge me for screwing up.

I try to serve, but miss the table entirely. The score's now 22–22.

Danny goes bright red, shoves his feet into his beat-up sneakers, and mutters something about seeing us later, which I silently pray does not come to fruition. Within three seconds he's gone.

I'm so stunned at his departure I allow Ajita to ace me: 22–23. "What. The. Actual. Hell."

She shakes her head. "I get it. The guy's hopelessly in love with you. And he knows he's taken up permanent residence in the Friend Zone."

"Oh, right," I snap. "And because he's spent enough money and inserted enough friendship tokens, the offer of sex and/or marriage should just fall out any time now?"

Sighing, she bounces the ball up and down, waiting for me to regain sporting composure. "I know. It's male-entitlement bullshit."

"But?"

"Still can't be nice reading that message."

"Oh yes. Poor Danny. He is absolutely the one we should feel sorry for in this scenario. Did I ask him to read it? No. I know I am sadistic at times, but masochistic I am not. And this hurts me as much as it does him."

"Does it really?" she asks pointedly.

"Really what?"

"Hurt you." She lays her paddle down on the table, perceptively realizing I shall not be calming down anytime soon, and takes a swig of soda. "You seem to be taking all of this in stride. The website, the nudes, the whispers in the hallway. Vaughan. Danny. I know you're a tough cookie, and you'd rather impale yourself on a garden rake than ask for help or show emotion of any kind, but you're allowed to freak out, you know?"

I'm not taking it in stride! I want to scream. It's absolutely killing me!

And yet, as self-aware as I am when it comes to my own bullshit, the thought of opening up to Ajita makes my chest tighten, makes my throat dry up. The words are on the tip of my tongue, the words about how disgusting I feel all the time, how vulnerable and exposed, and how much it sucks that Danny is trying to manipulate my pain so that I'll fall into his arms and finally let myself cry and/or kiss him.

Because it truly seems like he doesn't care which, just as long as I fall into his arms.

But I can't. I can't do it. And I have no idea why.

Instead I say: "Have you ever considered a career in the counseling profession? That garden rake image in particular is very vivid."

She sighs. "You know what I mean. You don't have to be unflappable all the time. And you're allowed to ask for help."

I do appreciate her trying to talk to me semi-sensibly for once, but honestly, I am just so over Danny's self-pitying martyrdom that I cannot face it. So I shoot her a smirk. "Can we talk about something else, like how you pissed yourself yesterday?"

An old episode of *Scrubs* starts in the background, with that irritatingly catchy theme tune: "I can't do this all on my own, no I know, I'm no superman." Or whatever.

Obviously Ajita has no self-control and cannot help herself. "You are no superman, Izzy. And you can't do it all on your own."

Like I say, I'm not in the mood, so I nip this conversation in the bud. "Good talk, coach."

She finally gives up. I feel kind of bad because I know how painful she finds it trying to be a decent human being, but what can I even say? That all of this is like some kind of nightmare, where I'm paralyzed and can't do anything but sit and watch?

7:04 p.m.

So a thing happened. A small thing, and yet possibly a big thing. All I know for sure is that it's definitely A Thing.

The garden rake image gave me an idea for a new sketch, set in a dystopian society in which garden rakes are literally used for psychotherapy [I'm aware this sounds incredibly unfunny but that is beside the point of this tale]. While the idea is fresh in my mind, I ask Ajita if I can borrow her laptop to start typing it up.

"Sure thing." She tosses me her sleek MacBook, which makes my decrepit laptop with the "H" key missing look like some sort of prehistoric tombstone.

She's not looking at what I'm doing when I open it up, which is good. Because as soon as I do, the first thing I see is an open Facebook tab.

The last thing Ajita looked at online was a photo of Carlie on a beach in a tiny bikini.

Kissing a girl.

7:36 p.m.

I knew Carlie was gay. But is it possible Ajita is too?

How have I never considered this before? Yeah, we've gossiped about guys for god knows how long, but looking back . . . is it always just *my* drama we're analyzing? Does she ever discuss guys she likes? I'm actually not sure she ever has—at least not in a romantic way. I rack my mind for the last crush she told me about, but I come up empty. I always thought she was a virgin just because she was waiting for the right guy, but what if there *is* no right guy?

God, I'm a self-involved mess of a friend. I mean, I'm never going to be a detective, but my lack of observational skills is truly astounding, especially when confronted by something so significant in my best friend's world. What else have I missed?

Back on the day Carlie was first introduced to us, I remember the intense way Ajita was looking at her. I remember how surprised I was that Ajita hadn't mentioned her new friend to me until that moment. Was that because she's not just a friend?

Then there was that day in the diner, back when Carlie first told us about her dying grandmother, about how the cancer-stricken old lady was deeply religious and didn't agree with Carlie's sexual orientation. What facial expressions was Ajita making? I can't remember. I wasn't paying enough attention. But I do remember how crestfallen Ajita looked when Carlie ditched us for the cheerleaders.

Oh, and the way Carlie was around Danny and me. Like we weren't there. That day in the mall, when we bumped into Carlie and her mom, she barely registered our presence. I distinctly remember feeling like a transparent poltergeist. What if she wasn't just being a stuck-up jock, or trying to preserve her reputation? Maybe all she saw was Ajita because Ajita is the girl she cares most about seeing.

And at the party, when Carlie played the mouth-to-mouth Ping-Pong ball game, then blatantly flirted with

Athletic Blonde. I'd thought Ajita was sad because she wasn't invited to play too, because she thought she wasn't cool enough for her new friend, but in hindsight, it's possible she was sad because the girl she liked was flirting with someone else right in front of her.

Ajita. Sweet Ajita. Her words from a few weeks ago float into my mind. "How the hell are we supposed to have it all figured out by the age of eighteen? We don't even know who we are yet, and still we're expected to choose what we want to do with the next fifty years." The way she said "who we are" makes me wonder whether she was thinking not of her career, but of her sexuality.

Or am I reading too much into this? Was Ajita casually flicking through Carlie's Cancún photo album and just happened to land on that particular picture before I arrived?

But I have a gut feeling that it's more than that.

If Ajita *is* gay, what's she going through right now? How long has she known? Is she terrified to come out because of what her family and friends will think? I remember the fallout in their traditional Hindu community when Ajita's second cousin came out as bi last year. It makes sense that Ajita would be scared of rocking the boat again.

Or is she afraid of what *I'll* think? Of course I would be nothing but proud of her, and happy that she's embracing her sexuality, and I hope she knows that. But still, it can't be easy having to guess how people will react. To gauge responses before they even happen.

All I want is to be there for her, but I don't know how

best to do that. I keep thinking about what I would want if the situations were reversed. I'd probably wish she would sit me down and be like, dude, I know what's going on and it's fine, I still love you, okay? I'll keep this a secret for as long as you need me to.

But no matter how close we are, Ajita and I are different people, and I can't treat her the way *I'd* want to be treated—I have to treat her how *she* wants to be treated. It's an important distinction. What's best for one person is another person's worst nightmare. And right now, it seems like she'd rather keep this all quiet while she figures it out. You know, if there's even anything to figure out.

Riddle me this. How doth one ask one's best friend if they're gay when said best friend clearly isn't ready for one to know?

8:14 p.m.

Brain still whirring after the discovery on my best friend's laptop, I head down to the outdoor basketball courts after eating five portions of Betty's iconic mac and cheese. Don't tell her I told you, but the secret is she crushes up salt and vinegar chips and mixes the crumbs with the grated cheese topping to make a crunchy crust thing that is basically better than sex, and I should know, because I have had a lot of both.

Anyway, Carson and I have been texting for a couple days—mainly lighthearted banter with a strong emphasis on a) our favorite cheeses and b) South American wildlife—and this evening he told me I should come see him by the river courts. He has the night off work and wanted to get some solo shooting practice in before this weekend's game.

Because the universe clearly felt bad for leaving me in this cesspool of a situation, Carson is shirtless. Seriously, what have I done to deserve this good karma? Absolutely nothing, that's what.

It's still light outside, but the sky has that kind of late-summer dusty quality, with tiny flies and a slight haze hanging on the air.

Carson stops dribbling when he sees me lurking on the bleachers. I wave awkwardly, i.e., the way I do absolutely everything ever. He slowly makes his way over to me, buff chest rising and falling rapidly from the exertion. Oh, flash-backs.

Flumping down onto the bench in front of me, he grins. "Izzzaaayyyy."

My eyes follow his dark happy trail, disappearing into the waistband of his yellow basketball shorts. "Ummm."

He winks. He's so beautiful, seriously. "Super glad you came. I had a lot of fun with you at the party. You're a lot of fun."

Now I'm grinning too. Stop, Izzy! Do not engage with flirtatious banter! I repeat, do not engage!

"Thanks, Carson. If only the entire world did not equate harmless fun with whoredom of the highest order."

His face kinda drops, and I feel bad for ruining the mood so soon. I didn't mean to bring up my woeful personal life, but bam, there you go. I fidget with my key ring—an Indian elephant wearing a top hat. Ajita got me it when she went to Delhi with her family back in tenth grade. She said it reminded her of my ears. Bless her heart.

"Yeah." He nods, wincing. "Sorry, dude. It sucks, the way people are treating you. Like they ain't ever seen titties before."

"To be fair, most of them haven't."

"Yeah." A sarcastic eye roll as he spins a ball on his index finger. "Virgins."

I'm not sure what point he is trying to make here, but he says the word "virgins" with such vitriol I don't bother questioning it. Boys are weird.

"You got any idea who's behind it all?" he asks as I try to fail to look him in the eye. [Not because I am ashamed, but because his torso is just so appealing.] "The website. The leaked photo. All that."

"Nah." I shrug, pretending to be nonchalant when in reality my heart rate is roughly one ninety-two. "Whoever it was had my phone at one point, though. I leave it backstage in the theater all the time. So it could've been anyone who took the screenshot and uploaded it to the site from my phone."

He stares at me, utterly aghast, as though I have just announced my candidacy for prime minister of Uzbekistan. "You gotta be the only person in the Northern Hemisphere not to have a passcode on your phone, dude."

I shrug again, because apparently I am incapable of doing anything else. "I can barely remember my home address. Or the fact that I have to brush my teeth in the morning. The last thing I need is something else to forget."

A cheeky grin, which does flippy things to my insides. "Well, I don't think I'll be forgetting that photo anytime soon."

Ugh. This does not sit right with me, and I guess my face shows it, because he hurriedly adds, "Because you're so hot. Not because, you know. You should be embarrassed or anything. 'Cause you shouldn't. Not at all."

But I don't know. Making that kind of comment about naked pictures I did not want to be shared just feels kinda skeevy. I mean, he's a teenage boy. They're generally skeevy by nature. But . . . ugh.

Is this just my life now? Fielding skeevy remarks because I dared to send a naked picture? Will the world now just assume I'll give it away for free all the time, because I did it once?

Do people feel like they own a piece of me; like I'm public property?

I don't think Carson is like that. Not at all. But this whole thing has made me paranoid as hell, and now I have no idea who to trust.

Right then, my phone bleeps. A text message from a number I don't recognize.

Fucking whore.

My heart sinks, I swear to god. Actually sinks. Heat prickles behind my eyes. I don't know why. I don't know why, out of all the abuse and all the public shaming, this is the thing that gets to me. I hate myself for being pathetic, because I pride myself on being anything *but* pathetic.

All I want to do is cry. The need is so sudden and overwhelming that I simply choke out:

"Sorry, Carson. I gotta go."

Almost as soon as I turn on my heel, the tears start to come.

I'm not sure why it's an anonymous message that breaks me. Maybe because it reminds me just how many people have now seen me naked. Maybe it's because it perpetuates that uncomfortable sensation of being watched and judged by a faceless entity. Maybe it's because I'm tired and overwhelmed and it's the straw that broke the camel's back. Maybe it's because, even though being hated by people you know is infinitely worse than being loathed by strangers, the combination of both is just agonizing on every single level.

Carson calls after me, but I barely hear.

9:48 p.m.

Back in my bedroom, I pull out my phone and stare and stare and stare at the nude picture of myself until it's burned into my retinas forever.

I look at it in the way a stranger might, picking out the imperfections and flaws and telltale signs that I'm still just a scared teenage girl. I look at the soft belly I've never hated until now. I look at my boobs, one bigger than the other, one nipple pierced on a reckless whim last summer. I look at my short legs, one crossed in front of the other as I stand in front of a dusty mirror and try to angle myself in a flattering way. I look at my va-jay-jay and want to die, knowing how many people have now seen it too.

I look at a happy, naive kid who has no idea how much she'll come to regret taking that naked picture in a moment of carefree spontaneity. That it'll make her question every single man in her life and his intentions. That, above all, it'll make her question herself.

Betty hears me sobbing and taps softly at the door. I don't reply, so she lets herself in.

"Sweet girl," she murmurs, voice raspy from her illness. "What's wrong?"

I sniffle and press my face into the pillow before handing her my phone.

"Please don't hate me."

FRIDAY, SEPTEMBER 30

<u>8:47 a.m.</u>

I wait for twenty minutes, but Danny never arrives.

<u>10:05 a.m.</u>

Ajita is shocked to see me in school after I told Betty what happened. Her parents would make her come to school even if her arms had fallen off in the night, but she knows Betty is a bit of a soft touch. She once let me stay home because of a paper cut. To be fair, it was in the webbing between my fingers and thus a deeply traumatic experience. But still.

Thing is, Betty is generally in tune with what I need. She's amazing like that, like some sort of psychic presence. Such as the paper cut thing—we both knew I was actually having a horrible day. I'd gotten my first period the week before, and even though my grandma was great, I really felt my mother's absence that whole week. It just felt like the kind of thing she should've been there for, like riding my bike for the first time, or accidentally getting stoned on pot brownies and breaking into the old folks' home. And so the paper cut became a scapegoat for my grief, and Betty let me stay home.

On the same level, she also knew that what I needed today was not to stay at home obsessing about a nude picture on the internet. So she sent me to school.

I somehow make it through first period without having a breakdown, then Ajita grabs me and hauls me into an empty classroom near the cafeteria.

Leaving the lights off, we close the door, dump our stuff on the teacher's desk, and slip into a few chairs near the back of the classroom. The sky outside is overcast, and after the bright strip lighting of the corridor, it takes a while for my eyes to adjust to the dimness.

Ajita's face is covered in zits. She's obviously been stressed about my situation. "Dude, what did Betty-O say?"

[We love calling her Betty-O. It makes her sound like a low-end cereal brand.]

I sigh and rub my eyes. They sting from tears and sleep deprivation. "She was actually really great. I expected her to nail me to a cross and force me to drink vinegar—"

"Stop with the jokes, for once in your life. I need real deets. What did the old girl say?"

Even though the door to the classroom is shut, some scumbag sophomores have gathered behind the glass, staring at us agog. Without hesitation, Ajita strides up to the window, pounds it with her fist—causing several of them to flinch—then hastily wrenches down the blind that usually stays up until the end of the day. She rejoins me in our seats as though the last ten seconds never happened. Maybe they didn't. Like I say, I'm pretty sleep deprived at this point.

"Honestly, Betty was awesome. For one thing she did not bring up my lopsided boobs, which I appreciate. Some grandmothers would express concern at my lack of aesthetic perfection and haul me straight to the plastic surgeon, but not Betty." I know Ajita told me to stop cracking jokes, but it's not that easy to break the habit of a lifetime.

Ajita frowns. "I don't think I know any grandmothers who would take that course of action."

"Ajita, will you please stop taking everything I say so literally. Never in your life have you taken me seriously, why doth thine haben started now?" [Oh wonderful, now I'm throwing random German infinitives into my bastardized medieval sentences. Things just keep getting better and better on the intelligence front. I think my brain cells might just be falling out of my ears in the night. Remind me to buy plugs.]

Before she can interrupt with another painfully literal interpretation of my strange answers, I add, "No, really. She was all kinds of amazing. At first she was super mad, but not at me, just at the scumbag who made the website and at all the other scumbag minions who do things like make paper airplanes out of my nudes."

"Then?"

"Then she told me to stay calm, hold my head up, all that clichéd crap . . . and she'll figure out what to do next. Whether that's go to the principal, or to the police, since it's harassment and all that, or string every guy on the basketball team up on her washing line by the balls."

"Hopefully a combination of all three."

"My thoughts exactly, Ajita. My thoughts exactly."

She smiles sympathetically. "Hey, so, um . . . guess what?"

"What?"

Her perfect little face lights up. "I made the tennis team! Turns out my hand-eye coordination is actually pretty good thanks to a decade of Ping-Pong and video games. Who knew?"

"Oh my god! Dude!" I consider giving her a hug, but decide against it because unsolicited bodily contact gives her the willies, and even though I'm like a puppy who likes to be touching people at any given opportunity, I have to respect her wishes. "That's awesome. I'm so fricking proud of you."

And I mean it. I'm really happy for her.

But even though this latest plot twist is giving me the perfect opening, I can't bring myself to ask her about her sexuality, or her relationship with Carlie. It's sheer cowardice, really, but I don't trust myself to broach the subject without upsetting her. Because in reality, she doesn't know I found that bikini pic on her laptop, and she maybe isn't aware of the blatant attraction floating between her and the redheaded Victoria's Secret angel whenever they're together. I don't want to burst her bubble and force her to confront something she might not be ready to confront just yet.

I wish I was better at this stuff. I can crack jokes and tell stories and make my best friend laugh until the cows come home, but I seem to be missing that innate ability to emotionally support someone through something tough. I really need to work on this, because it's not okay. Is there some sort of course I can take? A diploma in being a certified good pal? Remind me to look into it.

As she skips off to meet Carlie before lunchtime practice, I can't help feeling slightly abandoned. I know that sounds so selfish, and I hate myself for being this petty, but without her by my side, everything just feels so much more overwhelming.

Like I say. I really need to be a better friend. She deserves so much more.

6:58 p.m.

I hang out with Carson at the basketball courts again after school. We shoot some hoops together, even though I have the sporting ability of a concussed hippopotamus, as I fill him in on the latest developments. This time I manage to avoid a full-scale breakdown, which is good for maintaining the illusion that I am not certifiably unstable. Anyway, he seems genuinely concerned about my well-being, which is all new one-night-stand territory. He is like a pioneer. A beautiful, beautiful pioneer whose bones I'm in mortal peril of jumping at any given moment.

"Anything I can do?" he asks. "To help y'all, I mean. You and Betty." It's such a small thing, but the fact that he remembers my grandma's name warms my heart.

Barely even looking where he's aiming, he gracefully tosses the ball in the direction of the hoop. It makes a perfect arc, then slides straight through the net, not even skimming the rim. Even as a non-Sportsball™ lover, I have to admit it's impressive.

He hands me the ball. I bounce it a couple of times, pretending to know what I'm doing, and say, "Nah. Don't worry about us. Everybody has shit to deal with, you know? Even you, I'd imagine, despite your hot-yet-unintimidating demeanor." He grins at this, and I grin back, before adding, "So I'm not in the habit of off-loading mine. It isn't fair."

Clearly picking up on the fact that I have no idea what I'm doing with a basketball in my hands, Carson comes up behind me and places his hands on my hips, tilting them toward the hoop. My pulse quickens as he angles my body perfectly to make a winning shot, even taking the time to rearrange my feet. I'm not sure why this feels so intimate, given that we've already had sex. But I like it. I really, really like it.

As he works, he says, "Okay, I'll off-load some of mine to level the playing field. You know I have four brothers and sisters?"

He's back upright now, still behind me, a hand on each of my arms. I focus on steadying my breathing. "Wow. That's a lot."

"Yeah."

I consider this as he runs his hands slowly down my arms until his hands are cupping mine. "You probably know I am an only child, and an orphan, and an all-around disaster," I say.

He nods. "Yeah." I wait for him to continue. I get the impression he's been thinking about this for a while, and as usual I am ruining his flow by stating obvious tragic details about myself. But when he doesn't, I say, "So you have family trouble too?"

"Yup." Both of us holding the ball, Carson takes aim. I can feel his heart beating against my back, even through my woolly sweater. Like he's working a bow and arrow, he gently guides my arms back, then flicks the ball deftly up toward the hoop.

Again, it slides straight through the net.

I whoop, then turn to face him, grinning. He matches my smile. "You're a natural."

See? He is a good guy. Which is very different from being a Nice Guy à la Danny Wells.

Also, for some reason, I don't feel the need to constantly crack jokes and prove how funny I am when I'm around Carson. At first I thought this was a bad thing—like, shouldn't I be bouncing off him and being hilarious?—but it's actually nice to just relax and have a normal chat like normal people. So it's weird.

Our faces are so close together that for a moment I think he might kiss me. Wow, he has such long eyelashes. [Good grief, I really need to stop objectifying this poor boy, it is very unfeminist of me.] But after a tantalizing moment, he skips off to retrieve the ball.

I take the opportunity to continue the conversation. "So is everything okay at home? You mentioned family issues. I mean, you don't have to talk about it. But you can if you want."

He grins again, bounding back over to me. He really is cute with a capital "C." Huge smile, smooth brown skin, symmetrical features, striking eyes like Michael B. Jordan's. "Nah, it's a'ight. My mom's partner of eight years left us a few weeks back. Really screwed us over financially. Five mouths to feed and all. So I've been picking up extra shifts at the pizza place downtown."

"That is unbelievably crappy. I'm sorry."

"Nah, don't be. I get free pizza."

I gasp exaggeratedly. "That is the holy grail of job perks. I love pizza more than most things, including oxygen."

He drops his eyes to the ground. [Again, not literally. That would be deeply uncomfortable for him. Nobody wants gravel in their corneas.]

Biting his lip, he finally says, "Then, uh, maybe we should get pizza together sometime."

Something in my chest, something I worried the nude picture scandal might have damaged irreparably, glows with warmth. It's the same feeling you get when thinking about a favorite memory, or thinking about exciting things in the future. It's halfway between happiness and hope, and it feels good. It feels really, really good.

I smile. "Yeah. Maybe we should."

After we've finished shooting hoops, Carson offers to

walk me home, which I happily accept. There's something about being around him that just makes me feel calm and level, despite everything going on, but also tingly and excited. And that's a sensation I appreciate now more than ever. I can't get enough.

We walk and chat as the sun is setting, casting a warm glow over the town. Carson and I live in the same neighborhood, so I don't have to be embarrassed as we stroll past the beat-up cars and overflowing dumpsters and stray dogs scavenging for food. To be honest, the only time I ever properly see those things is through other people's eyes. Danny's and Ajita's, mainly, and even though I know they never judge me, it's kinda nice to be with someone who lives in the same world. It's just . . . easier.

On one street I've walked down a thousand times, a woman I recognize sits on her doorstep, smoking a roll-up cigarette as two toddlers run around her ankles. She berates the little boy for pushing the girl a bit too hard, even though the girl looks totally unfazed.

The woman is big and beautiful. Her black hair is swept up into a bright yellow headscarf, and her lips are painted purple. When she sees Carson, her eyes light up.

"Hey, Mom," Carson says, in the same relaxed tone he uses with me. I blink in surprise, but it also makes perfect sense. The woman's skin is the same perfectly smooth brown as Carson's, and she has the same wide smile. "This is Izzy. I was just walking her home. Izzy, this is my mom, Annaliese."

I smile, and I'm about to call her Ms. Manning when I realize I have no idea whether she and Carson share a last name. So I settle for, "Pleasure to meet you, Ms. Annaliese."

His mom blows one last puff of smoke through her lips, then buries the cigarette in a terra-cotta plant pot next to the doorstep. Dusting her hands off on her patterned dress, she stands up and gives me a warm hug.

"Carson's told me a lot about you." Her eyes are mischievous, and I know what she's trying to communicate: he's told me a lot of *good* things. I grin conspiratorially.

"Chill, Mom," Carson jokes, but his voice is light. Nothing like Danny's when he speaks to Miranda. "Everything cool?"

His mom nods. "Yeah. Mike was gonna come by, but he didn't show."

I guess they're talking about the partner who left recently, leaving them in the shit with money.

Carson grabs the little girl by the ankles and lifts her up. She squeals with delight as he dangles her at shoulder height. "It's gonna be a'ight. I picked up some extra shifts this weekend." He places the giggling girl down again and turns his attention to the boy—his brother? "Looks like someone's getting pizza for dinner again. PIIIZZZAAAAAAA!!" He growls this last bit like a pizza monster, chasing the kid a short way down the street. "GRRRRRR!"

His mom and I are both laughing too. Then she says, "Cool it, pizza monster. Time for your prey to go shower."

"Yeah, he's pretty stinky," Carson says, fanning his nose extravagantly to illustrate his point. His prey laughs hysterically. "Want me to do it?"

"Nah, it's cool," Annaliese says. "You walk Izzy home. I got it."

Despite the crappy situation she's in, she's all twinkly at the sight of me and Carson together.

As we walk back to my house, I don't have to force conversation. It just flows. "So is your coach cool with you skipping practice to work at the pizza place?" I ask.

"Nah, he's a dick about it," he replies. He works a thumb into the back of his shoulder to dig out a knot, wincing a little as he does so. "But what's he gonna do? Cut me from the team? Pfft. I'd like to see 'em win a game without me."

His confidence is nice. It's not arrogant. It comes with a cheeky grin and a jesting tone, rather than a condescending sneer.

"You must be pretty good then, huh?" I ask. "I mean, I've seen you play, and it looks impressive. But I know more about algebra than I do about sports, and that is saying something."

He laughs. "Yeah, I'm not bad. Not like I'm gonna be one of the greats, though."

"No?"

"Nah. For one thing, I'm too short." I shoot him an unconvinced look. He's well over six feet tall. He shrugs. "Hey, I don't make the rules. I'm short as hell compared to the NBA all-stars. So yeah, not tall enough, or committed enough. Or interested enough, to be honest."

This last one catches me off guard. "Really? I thought you loved basketball."

"I do, man, I do. But you can love a thing without necessarily dedicating your life to it, y'know?"

The profoundness of this statement leaves me slightly breathless. I feel like it might apply to my situation, to the pressure I'm putting on myself to succeed in this screenplay competition. I tuck that thought away in the back of my mind to revisit later.

"So do you wanna do the whole college thing?" I ask. As much as I like Carson the class clown, I am enjoying getting to know this side of him.

He shrugs noncommittally. "I dunno. I figure I'd enjoy it, but am I willing to get into that much debt just to check a box?" Another shrug. "Right now, I don't think so. I'd rather stay home and support my family. Leave my passions as hobbies. Play when I wanna play, read what I wanna read. That'd be enough for me, I think."

I smile, another warm feeling spreading through my chest. Carson's on my wavelength. He genuinely understands that following your wildest dreams isn't the best option for a lot of people. And he's made his peace with it, but not in a depressing way. He's happy. And for the thousandth time since we started talking, I feel refreshed by him. By his personality, his kindness, his outlook.

Uh-oh. I'm in trouble.

"So what other passions do you have? Besides basketball."

I find myself actually caring about the answer, rather than just thinking about the next thing I'm going to say. As a nervous conversationalist, this is something of a breakthrough.

"I like to paint. Not, like, hills and trees and shit. More like art as activism. Art that says something about the world." His hand finds mine, but not awkwardly like some teenage boys would do it. Just relaxed and nice. "I never told anyone that before."

I remember how good his alpaca sketch was, and the blue, white, and red paint the first time we kissed in the hallway. "Art as activism. Like Banksy?"

"Man, Banksy's white ass is on some bullshit. Sorry," he apologizes hastily, as though he might've offended my white-ass feelings.

I nudge his shoulder playfully, trying to show he doesn't even a little bit have to worry about that. "Why's that?" I ask. He still looks wary. "I genuinely want to know," I add, squeezing his hand.

"A'ight, so the dude flew out to Gaza to spray-paint a kitten on a house that'd been destroyed in an air strike. Like, who the fuck does that? Talk about insensitive. Just like a typical white savior, he has the audacity to call it art, to demand folks listen to *his* views on the atrocities of war, rather than the Palestinians who gotta live through it." He shakes his head, his hand tensing and untensing in mine. "Sorry. That kinda shit drives me crazy sometimes."

"Don't apologize," I insist. "I love listening to you. And

you're right. That's some white-ass bullshit."

He laughs. "You're cool, O'Neill. Maybe I'll show you my work sometime."

"I'd like that." I smile back.

Strolling past the dusk-lit windows on Carson's street, I catch our reflections in the glass. We do look kinda cute together.

No wonder Annaliese's eyes were twinkling. Mine are too.

10:37 p.m.

Once I'm safely back in my own house, I wave hello to Betty, then shut myself in the bathroom and start running a hot shower. Slowly, I step out of my clothes and into the red-hot steam, letting it scald my skin and clear my mind.

As much fun as it was spending the evening with Carson, something about it has left me feeling raw. At first, I think it's because of the Ajita/Carlie thing. Because I'm an actual child, I'm a little sad that Ajita making the tennis team is going to mean losing her to practice and matches. Our best friend time is going to get way more limited. Plus I feel kind of terrible for not addressing the possible Carlie romance with Ajita herself. I mean, yeah, maybe she's not ready to talk about it, and that conversation should totally happen on her own terms. But still, I should say *something*, right? She's been so great with me over the last few weeks, and I should repay the favor. I make a mental note to check in with her next time we're alone, even though it might be kinda uncomfortable for both of us. Emotional conversations are not our strong suit.

But even after I make this decision, I still feel off. Exposed, in a different way from the nude photo. Vulnerable.

Not because of anything Carson said or did, but because seeing him with his mom, interacting so effortlessly and lovingly, has deepened the crack in the buried part of me that first splintered back on that porch swing with Vaughan. The part that wonders how different my life would be if my parents were still around. How different I would be.

As I rub soap into every nook and cranny, one hot tear slides down my cheek, then another.

I'll never be able to bring a guy home to meet my parents for the first time. I'll never watch Carson make awkward small talk with my dad about cars and basketball and his intentions for dating me. I'll never watch Mom feed him pot roast from an old family recipe, or have her wink at me behind his back when she's sure nobody else will see. I will never see my parents eyes' sparkle the way Annaliese's did tonight.

Never. And never is a hard word to bear.

10:42 p.m.
Just received a Facebook message from Danny.

Hey, so I just found this cool Getting Into Screenwriting masterclass you can do online. It's with some prolific writing duo I've heard you talk about before.

And he attaches the link. But before I can even click it, another message comes through.

I know you'll probably freak out that it's $120, but I don't mind paying for it. You deserve a break :)

The order of my reactions are as follows:

Heart-stopping nausea at the sight of the $120. I've had this knee-jerk reaction to large monetary values for as long as I can remember.

Disbelief that Danny would offer to pay.

Cautious gratitude.

Temptation to take him up on the offer.

Remembrance that Danny is in love with me.

Guilt.

Disconcerting feeling that he's still trying to buy my affection.

Concern that I'm thinking too much into it.

The familiar sensation of unspecific discomfort starts prickling in my veins once again, like it did after the flower-giving ceremony in the theater. I can't pinpoint it. I don't know why this nice gesture feels so manipulative. Why it makes me feel two inches tall.

He's never made me feel like I'm any different, not once in our thirteen years of friendship. Never made me feel like he's rich and I'm poor. Not until now.

Too drained from my shower-crying fest to argue, I type out what I consider to be a diplomatic response.

Thanks for thinking of me! This sounds like a cool opportunity, but I'd never take money from you. I don't want to feel like some kind of charity case, you know?

The three dots showing he's typing a response appear almost immediately.

Don't worry, I get it. Just thought I'd offer :)

I'm about to thank him for understanding when he sends another message:

You know what, Izzy? I'm just trying to help. You always talk about how unfair the movie industry is, how disadvantaged kids with no connections can't get a foot in the door. Like I say, just trying to help.

His tone reads as passive aggressive, but I wonder if I'm just misunderstanding. It often happens via text, because you can't gauge someone's mood or expression. Taking a deep, steadying breath, I reply:

When I complain about how the movie industry prices poor people out, it doesn't mean I want a rich person to buy me in. It means I wish the barrier to entry didn't exist at all. Does that make sense?

Two seconds later . . .

Perfect sense. Sorry for bothering you.

For a while after the conversation ends, I sit very quietly and try to unpack why it's left me so low. Am I still emotionally raw from thinking about my parents? Or is this genuinely upsetting me? I think it's the latter.

Up until super recently, Danny never bought me a thing, and I liked it that way. It made me feel like we were equal. And now he does it regularly, buying me milk shakes and flowers and Coldplay tickets and offering to fork out an eye-watering sum of money in order for me to advance my career.

Did he maybe learn this strategy from watching his dad buy his mom's affection instead of earning it? The Lake Michigan lake house was bought right after the news of Mr. Wells's affair came out, back when Danny and I were still in grade school. I was too young to fully grasp what was going on, but looking back it seems like Danny's dad used money to fix a grave mistake, rather than actually repairing the emotional damage.

11:07 p.m.

Texting Carson. You know, an actual decent guy, who has never once tried to bribe me into having sex with him. What a revelation! He messages me first, which is nice, because although I do not subscribe to the sexist notion that girls should wait for potential suitors to make the first move in a heterosexual relationship, it's always nice to feel wanted. We have a jokey conversation that relieves some of the tension in my chest, and which also leads to the following comment:

Lol. You're literally funnier than every guy on the basketball team combined.

This is best compliment I could hope to receive at this point. I was about to cave in to temptation and check the online response to my nudes for the millionth time today, but this is enough to distract me for another minute or two.

Well, that isn't hard. Unlike every guy on the basketball
team, who are hard at all times. You know, due to
raging hormones and constant exposure to each
other's penises.

He doesn't reply to this for around half an hour, and I
actually start to freak out that I've offended him. I refresh
my emails several times—still nothing from the competition judges. I just want to know if I'm on the shortlist, damn
it! And if I do not receive word within the next forty-eight
seconds I am at very real risk of causing a Chernobyl-like
nuclear disaster through sheer nervous energy alone.

But then, Carson:

Hey, is your friend Ajita single? One of my firm-penised
teammates wants to ask her out, but I've seen her
around with that tennis chick. What's the deal there?

Always nice to hear my homegirl getting the attention
she deserves! However, this conversation is a minefield, so
I try to keep the tone casual and avoid any definite answers.

Yeah, I'm not sure firm penises are her jam. I mean,
neither are flaccid ones. Like, I'm just not sure penises
are her preferred genitalia. But your pal should ask
away, for I am not her spokesperson!

I then promptly fall asleep with the most absurd of smiles
on my face, dreaming of pizza with Carson Manning in the
not too distant future.

MONDAY, OCTOBER 3

<u>10:13 a.m.</u>
Things that have happened since arriving at school this morning:

1. Danny ignored me in homeroom. Sigh.
2. Ajita is out sick. She has food poisoning from consuming week-old pepperoni pizza, even though she's supposed to be vegetarian. I texted her to tell her that she is an extremely selfish and inconsiderate individual, but she just told me that she hopes I contract norovirus in the next few hours so I can join her on the sofa for a Comedy Central binge. That does not sound awful, in all honesty.
3. All the usual jeers and whispers and general assholery. It is quite baffling to me that people are still interested in my nudes, because as a solid 6/10 I'm painfully middle of the road. This is why I have developed a sense of humor to compensate, so I'm totally okay with my ranking as "above average but only just." However, I am totally *not* okay with

a random freshman boy who follows me around everywhere asking me to sign the iPhone case he's had made out of my leaked photo.

4. I flunked math. Shock of all shocks, quadratic equations and/or the ancient bastard who is Pythagoras are not at the top of my list of things I currently give a crap about.

5. Vaughan made a speech in the cafeteria in response to aforementioned jeers and whispers and general twattery. It went something like this: "Ahoy, gossiping fishwives! It is I, grandson of Benito Mussolini, evil dictator and abhorrent human being. I doth shall [again I'm not 100 percent clued up on doth usage but hopefully you'll let it slide] make it abundantly clear that I did not have sexual intercourse with this here Izzy O'Neill." I am paraphrasing slightly. The original was far less eloquent. Basically, he wanted everyone to know that despite all the evidence, he has zip zilch zero to do with this situation. And nothing screams "uninvolved bystander" like a public declaration of innocence.

6. I caved and checked the WCW website again. Nice new additions from a whole host of new contributors: a poll in which voters guess my weight, bra size, and body mass index based on the nude photo [these are weirdly accurate]; a strongly worded post about how decidedly unfunny I am [lol okay sure]; more amateur Photoshop jobs [in one, my face has been

superimposed onto a porn screenshot in which the actress is receiving a penis in every orifice].

7. Bumped into Carlie in the restroom, and almost as soon as she made accidental eye contact with me, she turned and speed-walked straight out of there. Thank you for the support, dude! I mean, I totally understand that as a new kid she probably doesn't want to taint her reputation by associating with the likes of me, but still. If she and Ajita do end up going out, I don't want things to be awkward between us.

8. Carson texted asking me to pick up our geography assignment, since he's covering a shift at the pizza place. This is sad news for two key reasons, the first being that I'll have to actually pay attention in geography, and the second being that there's no chance of Carson's signature cheer-up techniques turning my day around.

Sigh. I might go and hang out with Mrs. Crannon. She seems to be the last person at Edgewood who doesn't despise every fiber of my being.

2:45 p.m.

Crannon is also out sick. Am slightly concerned about the fact this coincides with Ajita's absence, and ordinarily I would cook up a delicious conspiracy theory about their passionate, clandestine love affair. But I'm just not in the mood.

Ho hum, woe is me, why must I go on? How can things possibly get any worse?

4:56 p.m.

Ha. Ha ha. HA.

Surely, Izzy, you have seen enough movies and read enough books to know that when the protagonist utters that doomed sentence, "How can things possibly get any worse?" things *invariably* get worse.

In my case, much fucking worse.

Someone sent a video of Vaughan's cafeteria speech to a local newspaper reporter, who uploaded it to the publication's website along with links to the gross Izzy-shaming blog, and a full background as to the involvement of a Republican senator's son in a small-town sex-scandal. Ted Vaughan has been approached for comment.

There's also an image gallery containing—you guessed it—the nude pictures.

It's had over 4,000 shares.

11:07 p.m.

Even though she's still a little sick, Ajita calls an impromptu but highly necessary girls' night to address the catastrophic developments today brought forth. I vow to ask her about Carlie, if the right moment arises, but I'm not going to force it. I respect my best friend too much to confront her about something she's not ready to share.

She answers the door in an R2-D2 costume, which is an unexpected perk of the evening, and I decide it'll be funniest to just pretend not to have noticed. So I greet her as normal and waltz into her house like I own the place. She plays along nicely, adding the occasional "beep-bop" for believability.

Her parents and sibling are all out at some tragic track meet [Prajesh is the next Usain Bolt, by all accounts] so we have the house to ourselves. We cozy up in her kitchen instead of the basement. It's really beautiful—sleek refrigerator with an ice machine, massive central island and breakfast bar, fresh lilies in a vase at all times. On the counter is a stack of freshly made anarsa, which are these freaking delicious buttery pastries Mrs. Dutta makes. She's left a note saying: *These are for your auntie's birthday tomorrow. I know exactly how many there are. If I find even one missing, so help me Ajita Dutta I will shave your head in the night. PS Remember to feed the goldfish. Mom x*

Ajita putters around making nachos—spraying grated cheese and rogue tortilla chip crumbs everywhere as she tries to stay in droid character—while I rant.

"I just don't get it," I say from my perch on a bar stool. "Why does anyone care about my sexploits? It's just so absurd."

"Agreed," she replies, sucking some spilled salsa out of the R2-D2 onesie. "I don't care either. I wasn't even listening to what you just said, for instance. You really are a hugely uninteresting individual."

"Right? And yet four thousand people give a crap about the fact that I slept with a senator's son. On a porch swing. And sent him nudes. WHY?"

She rams the haphazard nacho tray under the broiler and hops up onto the counter, which is where she always prefers to sit given the chance. She insists it's more comfortable than any sofa money can buy. She's an oddball, my best friend. "In all reality, though, how are you feeling about it? Because this cannot be easy."

I shudder. "The worst part is knowing how many actual adults will now see those pictures. When it was just the website, I assumed the damage would be contained to fellow high school students. Which was far from ideal, but it was easier to stomach than knowing parents and teachers and all sorts are now going to see my foofer." I groan. "Oh god. I just thought of something else. Nobody in this godforsaken town is going to hire me now."

This is terrible. Betty is going to have to work even longer just because her disaster zone of a granddaughter has rendered herself completely unemployable.

Ajita tries her best to put a positive spin on the situation. "I mean, you don't know that. I feel like you might have clout among owners of struggling dive bars. From their point of view, your incredible boobs might attract a whole slew of sleazy clientele as they arrive in hordes to attempt to woo you. Sales of Johnnie Walker will skyrocket."

I groan again, dropping my head into my hands. This all feels like a bad dream. Why can't I wake up?

"So Danny said you're mad at him," Ajita says, changing the subject in a bid to distract me from the fact that my future is evaporating before my eyes. "Something about a screenwriting course?"

"What? What did he say to you?"

She drops her gaze. "Uh, that he offered to help, and you were 'a bitch about it.' His words, not mine."

Red-hot anger flashes across my vision. It takes all my restraint not to charge through the French doors like a bull at a matador. "Arrrghhhhh. That is such bullshit. Oh my god. I can't even."

"Care to fill me in on the nonbiased, nonDannyfied version?"

Instead of spelling it all out, I just hand her my phone and let her read the messages herself.

"Jeez," she says, eyes widening. "Hey, Danny, might wanna cover up a bit. Your privilege is showing."

Exasperated, but also hungry, I pad over to the fridge and open it up, scanning for any potential snackage situations. "Do you understand what I was trying to say, though? Did I come off too harsh with all that stuff about not wanting or needing a rich person to buy me in?" I settle on the remainder of the grated cheese and start shoveling it into my face like popcorn.

"Not harsh at all," she says, giving the nacho tray a shimmy and dumping more guac on top. "It's like when I talk about racism, I'm not asking for one single white person to wave their magic privilege wand and fix one single symptom. What I'm saying is that I want the systemic racism to not exist in the first place. I want a cure, not a Band-Aid." She shrugs. "But a lot of rich white guys will never get that. They'll always make it about them. And why wouldn't they? Historically, it always *has* been about them."

Frustration is building in my blood to such a high concentration that not even rapid ingestion of cheddar can take the edge off. "Do you know, Ajita, I'm starting to lose all faith in the world."

"So how do we take your mind off it? I really thought the Star Wars costume would do it."

"What Star Wars costume?" I ask innocently.

"Yes, very good. Ha ha. Should we do some karaoke? I've also got a Chewbacca outfit you can wear for the occasion."

It really is incredible how much better singing along to Eminem's [admittedly highly problematic] greatest hits can make you feel. A personal highlight is our rendition of "Love the Way You Lie." I perform the rap segments while Ajita takes Rihanna's chorus. Magical.

Unfortunately her parents return at the precise moment Ajita is holding her brother's teddy bear over the gas stove, crooning "just gonna staaaaand there and watch me burn" as the burned nachos set off the fire alarm. But you take the wins where you can get them.

[I would show you the video of us dancing on the breakfast bar dressed as a Wookiee and a droid, but then I'd have to kill you.]

TUESDAY, OCTOBER 4

6:31 a.m.

Someone put a condom stuffed with a dog turd in our mail-box this morning. Dumbledore got confused, bless him, and thought it was an exciting new chew toy. And that's the story of how we're going to have to get a new couch.

10:44 a.m.

Ajita has her first tennis match today, and sends me a selfie from the team bus. Sitting next to her is, of course, the red-headed Lucifer. Their cheeks are pressed together and Carlie is slightly flushed.

Ajita hates unnecessary physical contact. I once wrapped my arm around her, and she threatened to saw it off at the elbow. And yet here she is with Carlie, faces mashed so tightly together it's almost as though they're attempting a skin graft.

12:58 p.m.

Betty let me stay home from school today. She's being all

cute and protective and bringing me things. She even knitted me a scarf now that the weather's getting cooler, and it is the single most ugly garment I have ever seen in my life—like roadkill, really—but I love it dearly.

I'm trying so hard to stay positive, to convince myself that this will all blow over, that the reporters will eventually get bored and move on to the next small-town scandal. But there's a dark part of my brain that likes to torture me by imagining what will happen if it *doesn't* blow over.

How can I stay in this place after graduation knowing everyone in it has seen me naked? Knowing they look at me and judge me and gossip about me over coffee or dinner? Knowing I'll never be taken seriously again? Knowing that because of one naked picture, I'll never be respected no matter what I do?

The fear is suffocating, but I can't shake it off.

1:35 p.m.

Meg, the precious cinnamon roll, requests to follow me on Instagram. Coming from anyone else I'd definitely think this was scandal-related stalking, but she seems sweet, so I decide to give her the benefit of the doubt and accept the request.

I click on her profile in return. There are a bunch of NFL-based photos—pics of players from the latest draft, and crowd shots from every game she's been to in the last year, i.e., a LOT. Interspersed with the football mania are reposts of amazing special FX makeup looks from top artists—the zombie Disney princess ones are especially amazing.

I follow Meg back. She seems cool, with way more awesome hobbies than I have. Then I start typing a "hey, wanna hang out?" message, but I lose my nerve at the last minute. Because if she doesn't reply, or the scandal has changed her mind on wanting to hang out with me, it'll make me feel so much worse than I already do.

Ugh. When did I become this cautious?

2:04 p.m.
Still haven't plucked up the courage to check the news.

2:12 p.m.
Whyyyyyyy???????

Whyyyyyyy did you let me check the news???????

The clickbait piece featuring Vaughan's speech has now amassed over 100,000 shares all across the state, and has been updated to include quotes from Ted Vaughan, whose political beliefs are as wrong as raisins in a salad [or really just salad as a concept]. He has this to say:

"The accusations of my son's involvement in this disgusting display of teenage promiscuity are outrageous and deeply insulting. His mother and I have dedicated our lives to raising this young man the correct way, and to insinuate his behavior has been anything other than exemplary for the past seventeen years is nothing but a vicious lie. As for Izzy

O'Neill, it's very sad that this is the kind of behavior our nation's youth engage in, which is why I continue to fight so hard to protect abstinence-only sex education."

Ted Vaughan is the kind of guy who's probably absolutely thrilled with this handy little PR boost his campaign so desperately needed. He then goes on about his abortion policies and what steps he'd take to fix us broken teens, which I can only assume involve systematic castration of the homosexual population and mandatory chastity belts for all unmarried women.

There's also expert analysis on the ineptitude of sex-education professionals across the country, a round-up of all the female celebrities who've had their nudes leaked, someone preaching passionately about abstinence being the only real form of contraception, and a lot of religious bigots condemning me to an eternity in hell.

And the photo of me having sex with Vaughan on a porch swing. Everywhere.

I'm trying very hard to process these developments, largely due to the fact that my name and face and private parts are now plastered all over the internet, but I feel strangely detached and unable to convince myself this is actually happening.

I have a text from Ajita asking if I'm all right, which makes me feel guilty since she should be focusing on her tennis debut. But no, she must care for her ridiculous human being of a best friend while said best friend cries into a bag of shredded cheddar.

Look, I know this is a little off-brand but I am seriously worried about you. There were reporters at school this morning asking people for quotes about you, and though I am surprisingly tough, there are only so many times I can bodily tackle our peers to the ground before my shoulder gives out, and FOR GOD'S SAKE WILL YOU JUST ANSWER ME, WOMAN?? Otherwise I shall be forced to call you and we both know how much you hate unsolicited phone calls when a simple text message would do. xo

If I had in any way processed what's going on around me, I might attempt letting my guard down for once. Now seems as good a time as any to let my best friend know I'm struggling. But to be honest, none of this feels real. Not in the slightest. I'm completely numb. So I fire off an eloquent and insightful message about my mental state:

Re: the reporters, I don't give a fuck. In fact, if you listen very carefully, you'll hear the sound of all the fucks I used to give exploding one by one, into tiny little fucklet particles that are imperceptible to the naked eye. Stop by after school? Love you.

Then she says:

Love you??? Are you sure you aren't dying?? It sounds suspiciously like you're dying. And I know you're a tireless curator of all the fucks nobody gives, but promise me you're okay? This press field day sucks on a whole new unprecedented level. You would have to combine an extraordinary blow job with a high-end

Dyson to even come close to how much this sucks. xo

Despite the enticing myriad of innuendo options available to me right now, I don't even have the energy to reply.

Danny texts me too:

Want a Mario Kart session with Praj and me? I'll even let you be Toad.

Part of me is glad he doesn't address the main issue. I'm beginning to think that nude picture will define me forever, that it's all anyone will ever see when they look at me. From mere strangers that's painful enough, but from the people I love? It's too hard to bear.

The semi-normal text message is a life raft, and I cling to it with everything I have.

7:28 p.m.

Having spent the whole day inside alone, having the numbness slowly wear off, trying and failing to fight the deep, gnawing shame eating my insides, I have to get out. Of the house, of my body, of my mind. I just have to get out.

In an attempt to cheer me up, Ajita makes it back from her tennis match—they lost spectacularly—and immediately insists on taking me shopping for sketch props with her mom's credit card. I have brief concerns over being recognized in the mall—which is where basically everyone from within a hundred-mile radius hangs out on evenings and weekends—but aside from the people I actually know from school, no one seems to notice me.

In fairness, most of the WCW website, and indeed the recent press coverage, has been focused on my body. Nobody is particularly interested in my face, and with my body covered up like it is right now, what else do I have to offer the world? Precisely nothing.

Still, every shop assistant who serves us, every cashier who swipes Ajita's parents' card, I wonder if they know. I wonder if they've seen me naked. I wonder if they laughed at me with their friends, or showed their colleagues in the break room. I wonder if they think I got what I deserved. I wonder if they know the intimate parts of my body that are now public property.

I feel powerless. Completely and utterly powerless.

We're now sitting in the food court drinking milk shakes [I go peanut butter Oreo, because I am very committed to my varied diet and believe in consuming equal quantities of fat and sugar] and planning a series of satirical Instagram posts using an avocado onesie. Although hipster foodies are absolutely harmless and probably very nice people, we can't resist an easy target. In fact it is often quite physically painful for us to try to refrain from making obvious gags, like the time I tried to give up "your mom" jokes and almost gave myself a stroke, thus it would effectively count as self-flagellation to attempt to control ourselves. This is, both medically and philosophically speaking, a thing. Trust me. I have an IQ of 84.

Once the hilarity wears off over the mental image of

me smeared on whole-wheat toast and topped with cracked black pepper, Ajita asks me ever so casually, "So have you thought any more about who started that website in the first place? 'Cause, you know. This is all their fault. Not yours. I don't want you getting bigheaded or anything, because your ego is already intolerable, but . . . you are wonderful. None of this is your fault."

Genuinely I almost cry at this, but manage to resist lest Ajita think I actually have emotions. "So, uh, what's going on with you?" I mumble. "How was the match this afternoon? Are you still a veritable prodigy in the making?"

The hope is that by segueing into a conversation about tennis, a) the attention will be shifted away from the undercurrent of emotions swirling around inside me, and b) Ajita will at last discuss what's happening with her and Carlie.

However, candid conversation is not the route my dear pal chooses. "Ah. Well, I hit a small snag when I got cocky with my powerful serve and ended up accidentally letting go of my racket mid-swing. It flew so far over the net that it knocked my opponent clean out. While this is not so great for her, on account of the concussion and all, I'm now convinced I'm not only the next Serena Williams but also an Olympic-standard javelin thrower. Prajesh is going to be so pissed when he realizes he's not the only track and field phenomenon in the Dutta family."

"This is excellent news. And Carlie? Is she still . . . your teammate?" I tread carefully, which is new territory for me. My conversational style is usually bull-in-a-china-shop-while-under-the-influence-of-narcotics. "After you nearly decapitated someone and all."

Ajita presses her lips flat together and stares at her straw. "Yup."

Okay then. Judging by my best friend's rapid and startling transfiguration into a brick wall, I'm guessing that subject is off-limits, despite the up-close-and-personal selfie she sent earlier.

"Hey, Danny messaged me yesterday," I say, moving swiftly on. "Asked if I wanted to play Mario Kart. In a super chill way, not, like, a date way. It was kinda nice for him to just be normal again."

"Thank nachos for that," Ajita replies. "I had many words with him. Told him to get his act together."

"You did?"

"I did. First I was all, 'Dude, why are you suddenly buying her all this shit. It's weird. You're weird. Why are you weird?' and he was all stuttery and Dannyish. But then I got it out of him that it's all part of his plan to win you over. Convince you to date him and such."

I grit my teeth. "That. Is. Bullshit. Why isn't the word 'no' enough for him?"

"Right? That's exactly what I told him. I said he should stop trying to win you over and just be there for you instead. That's what you need right now."

"Thank you," I say, with a sudden rush of gratitude toward her impeccable conflict management skills. "Okay, but wait. If all his weird behavior is just an attempt to woo me, why is he so up and down with me? Like why is he buying me stuff one minute and lashing out the next? The latter is only pushing me away, not getting me to drop my pants."

Ajita mulls this over, taking a swig of her s'mores shake. Next to her is a sign that says "Your Sandwish Is My Command." [Don't you dare laugh at this. It's the least funny name for a fast food restaurant in the whole word. Think of all the wasted opportunities! Lord of the Fries. Forrest Rump. The Codfather. I could go on.]

"That I did not ask him. But I think it might be frustration, and impatience. Like, in his mind he's trying so hard with you, and he's getting nowhere. If anything it's pushing him further and further from where he needs to be. And when he sees you give other guys the romantic attention he wants so badly, or when you don't immediately fall to your knees when he hands over his latest gift, he gets pissed. I'm not saying it's right. It's not. But if I had to put my money on an explanation for his behavior, that would be it."

"Makes sense, I guess." I pause, fumbling with the straw wrapper. "Did you invite him today?"

"No. I'd rather fuck a fruit bowl than look at his mopey face all night."

I laugh so hard at this I almost vomit.

9:04 p.m.

Sound the drama klaxon! Within the space of the last thirty minutes, the following hath ensued:

1. Vaughan called me [like, an actual telephone call, in this day and age! Who does he think he is??] to apologize for the media shitstorm he accidentally caused by making a cafeteria speech more ill-judged than the 2003 invasion of Iraq. I essentially told him to have sexual intercourse with the nearest cactus, and he called me a bitch and hung up.

2. Danny texted me about my secret girl date with Ajita. It went like this: "Thanks for the invite today. It was really great to hear my two supposed best friends were hanging out behind my back." He is such a man-child. Currently researching ancient witchcraft rituals in an attempt to cajole the universe into smiting him. [I do feel like smite is an underused verb, no?]

I don't have the emotional energy to deal with either.

11:02 p.m.

The day has left me feeling grubby and miserable, so I have a long, hot shower in an attempt to wash it all away. The website, the nudes, the press coverage. Danny. Everything.

Usually I'm in and out within five minutes, barely even looking at my body as I slather it in cheap shower gel and drag a razor wherever necessary, but tonight I examine it more closely than I have in years. It's been put under a microscope for the whole world to inspect, and I want to see what they see. It's sadistic, but it's an itch I have to scratch.

Cellulite and stretch marks around my hips and thighs. A giant mole on my left butt cheek. Swollen boobs because of the time of the month.

Imperfections that, up until a few weeks ago, were mine and mine alone. Until I shared them with two boys I trusted. Now the whole world sees them too.

I scrub for an hour but still can't wash away the dirty feeling.

WEDNESDAY, OCTOBER 5

8:28 a.m.

Just when you think life could not possibly get any more dramatic and palpitation-inducing, a gaggle of reporters flock to your neighborhood and bombard you on your way to school. Seriously, big fluffy mics, cameras, the works. Now I know how that Jenner girl felt back when people asked about her lips all the time.

"Miss O'Neill! Miss O'Neill!"

No. Go away.

"Izzy? Izzy, can you talk to us about Zachary Vaughan? Has his father made any effort to contact you directly?"

No.

"How does it feel to have your nude picture leaked? What warnings would you give other young women considering sending explicit photos?"

They just want to hear my side of the story, they say. Yes, but so do the other 631 bloggers/journalists/scumbags who emailed me personally to ask for THE TRUTH and THE

LIES and THE SCANDAL and for a verbatim quote on how much of a royal dick Ted Vaughan is.

And the thing is, I would consider selling my story, but I just fundamentally do not trust journalists not to twist every single thing I say to make me into even more of a laughing-stock than I already am. Plus, there aren't a lot of things in my life that I can control right now. At least I can control this.

Vultures, all of them. I just cannot begin to under-stand why they even care about my naked teenage body and unpalatable promiscuity. Aren't there wars happening or something? Are sex scandals really that interesting nowa-days?

Honestly, it's like running a gauntlet. Danny is nowhere to be seen this morning, but thankfully Ajita, aka my guardian-angel-slash-pit-bull, shields me from the flashing cameras as best as she could. It's a little like an ant trying to shield Hagrid, but I'm touched nonetheless.

In related news, in homeroom I'm going to rip off Vaughan's balls and stitch them to a sock puppet, and then I will explain to the reporters, using my innovative new mouthpiece, just how I feel about that unbelievable scumbag.

Then—because everything I thought I knew about myself and those around me appears to have been blown out of the water—I start to wonder whether he's really the one I should be hating here. Yeah, he made that ill-judged speech in the cafeteria that ended up hitting the news, and he has been a bit of a dick to me on several occasions [e.g., stomping on my flowers] but I sort of understand his reasoning. It all boils down to the fact that he's scared of his dad. And yeah, he does stupid stuff without thinking—in the same way I do, apparently—but I don't think there's any genuine malice there. Just fear, and a desperate need for approval.

Anyway, although I figure Vaughan is also being interrogated relentlessly about the nude pictures we exchanged, the key difference is that his family has an entire public relations office at their disposal. They have people to draft press releases, and spin doctors to expertly twist and distort the situation so they come out on top. Perks of being a politician's son. And while some of his teammates have teased him somewhat, generally he's being treated the same way he always has been.

I, meanwhile, am receiving 90 percent of the flak for a scandal I only had a 50 percent stake in. Perks of being a woman in modern America.

10:54 a.m.
Outside of Ajita, and possibly Meg, the only other student who isn't treating me like I have leprosy is, surprise surprise, Carson Manning.

We bump into each other by the water fountain before second period. He sneaks up behind me and squeezes my shoulders. "Hey, you. How you holding up?" He smells freshly showered—he must've just finished practice.

I wipe a rogue trail of water away from my mouth [seriously, is there any way to drink gracefully from a water fountain?] and turn to him, mustering up the most convincing smile I can.

"I'm all right, I guess. Trying not to look at the news."

He's wearing a gray hoodie and black jeans, and I want to rip them right off him. Good to know the whole sex scandal thing hasn't deterred the insatiable nymphomaniac inside me.

Carson rubs his forehead, looking anxious on my behalf. "Don't blame you. Please don't . . ."

As he trails off, he shakes his head.

"Please don't what?" I prompt him, rearranging my backpack. I have a terrible habit of hauling my books around on just my right shoulder instead of wearing it properly across both, so am therefore a few short months away from resembling the Hunchback of Notre Dame.

He looks around the busy corridor, where kids of all ages and social standings are staring at us, whispering conspiratorially. "Please don't think any of this is your fault. 'Cause it isn't."

A lump forms in my throat. "I'll try not to."

And then, despite all the stares and whispers, he gives me the biggest bear hug I've ever received.

He's so warm and comforting as he whispers in my ear, "You're tougher than they are. Hell, you're tougher than most people."

Before I can even reply, he pulls away, picks up the textbook he dropped, and after one last reassuring smile, sets off toward his next class.

These past few days have felt like my insides were being shredded with frozen icicles of shame, but Carson thaws them. Because he doesn't treat me any differently. He looks at me the same way he always has: like I'm funny and cool and someone he wants to be around. Like I'm a person, not a piece of meat.

Something in my chest aches, but not in a sad way.

11:35 a.m.

Just when I don't think things could get any worse, BuzzFeed gets ahold of the story. Yeah, so they blur out the porch swing picture. And they don't feature the nude at all. But still, it's not that hard to find the originals.

In any case . . . I'm global.

Well, the Vaughan family is global, but I'm caught up in the crossfire. Because revenge porn is still legal in my state, and such a high profile case involving a politician's son has attracted a storm of media attention and debate. And because I'm eighteen and thus not a child, they're allowed to show my pictures without being accused of child pornography.

Part of me is glad the issue of revenge porn legality is being discussed. I just wish I wasn't the catalyst.

Checked my Gmail for shortlist news [and to satisfy the paranoid part of me who's still worried the producers will see the nudes and put two and two together]. Nada, but I've had an influx of emails from yet more journalists and bloggers asking to interview me exclusively, and a smattering of hate mail, and also an offer from one of those vile tea detox brands asking me to promote their product to my whopping 213 Instagram followers now that I am apparently an icon for all that is wrong with the world.

Prior to today all I really received were emails like "Have you noticed how you have become so fat and hopeless?" and generous offers for $1 liposuction in outer Mongolia, but now the days of random spam are apparently over.

1:20 p.m.

Though I'm getting used to lunchtime being an unbelievably traumatic affair, today it reaches all new levels, now that I am known internationally as a slut of the highest order.

Kids listen in on my hushed conversations with Ajita and record our mumblings on their phones. We're only discussing which movie we wanna see this weekend, but still. They snap pictures and take videos and look at my nudes for the thousandth time while masturbating into their sloppy lasagna. [Again, I made this last one up, which you will not be at all surprised to learn. If you are currently consuming lasagna or any other baked pasta dish, I apologize for the mental image.]

I know citizen journalism is meant to be a positive movement, and for authentic coverage of protests and police brutality and natural disasters, yes, I can see the benefits, but this? Really?

Teens must send thousands, if not millions, of explicit photographs to each other every single day. Why is mine so damn interesting? Debating the legality of revenge porn is one thing. Showcasing my body for sport is quite another.

And, fellow students, do you really think Fox News is going to pay you for your under-the-bench photo of my crossed-over knees just because I'm having an unwanted moment in the limelight? Are you really that desperate for a few extra quarters?

Ajita tries her best to distract me and continue with our conversation about whether or not to see the big-budget thriller or the subtitled art-house movie, but eventually we give up and head for the woods to live out the rest of our lunch hour alone and in peace.

Well, you know, except for our gym teacher, aka CrossFit Monkey. But I'm starting to find him strangely comforting. It's like he doesn't exist in the same universe as the rest of us. Instead he lives in one where all he thinks about is how many jumping jacks he can do before he passes out, so chances are he hasn't seen me naked. Always a win.

2:14 p.m.
Miss Castillo goes all "O Captain! My Captain!" on us in English this afternoon. She's picked up on the air of general animosity and flatulence in the classroom, and tries to give us all a motivational speech about the importance of kindness, etc. Anyway it was kind of ruined by the chorus of "she doesn't even go here," but it was sort of sweet for her to try to make things a bit less crappy for me.

But then she corners me after class, waiting until everyone else leaves before sitting me down and smiling in the most patronizing of ways. "Oh, sweet child." In a very adulty way, I resist the urge to start singing Guns N' Roses at the top of my lungs, instead plastering a receptive expression on my face. "You've had a tough time, haven't you?"

Because of my dead parents, I've had this exact conversation with almost every single teacher in school. Soon as I mess up, by their standards, they take me to one side and instigate a long and painful exchange about my orphan upbringing. They take one long look at my over-worn clothing and unkempt scarecrow hair and think I'm a tragic Annie-like figure, and usually I don't have the heart to ruin the impression they have of me.

Another syrupy-sweet smile. "It can't have been easy, losing your parents at such a young age."

I shrug. What does she want me to say? "I've had thirteen years to get used to it."

Then she goes into full concerned-grown-up mode and I get a Shakespearean monologue about how the effects of deep trauma like losing parents can often take a while to manifest. Then: "All I'm saying is that nobody blames you for acting up, and you have a large support system around you no matter how this situation turns out, okay?"

There it is. That buzz phrase adults love: "Acting up." It's hilarious because they often use it in the context of behavior they themselves also participate in, such as sex and alcohol. One of the reasons I love my grandma so much is that she's never once uttered those three syllables in my direction.

Normally I'd let it go, but for some reason this bugs me so much more than normal. Probably because I'm guessing she hasn't pulled Vaughan to one side like this.

"Sorry, Miss Castillo, but can you define 'acting up' for me? I'm struggling to understand what you mean."

A sympathetic head tilt. "Our Lord does not support premarital sex, Izzy. You know that."

My ruthless snark rears its ugly head just at the right/ wrong time. "Oh! Well, fortunately I'm an atheist, and I have it on good authority that the scientific universe doesn't concern itself with the romantic activity of teenage girls."

Her hand flutters to the dainty cross necklace around her neck, as if it's an inanimate incarnation of "our" Lord himself, whose ears are too delicate to hear such blasphemy. Though I'm willing to bet that if said Lord really is all-seeing and all-knowing, he's witnessed a hell of a lot worse.

"He still loves you, Izzy. There's always forgiveness for those who ask. I hope you know that."

Smirk. "Awesome. In that case, I've got some more acting up to do before I have him wipe my record clean."

I'm taking it too far. I know I am. A little more meekly, I add, "Am I excused?" People in my hometown take religion very seriously, and poking the bear with offensive banter is not advisable unless you want to be chased down main street with a pitchfork. Which, at this point, is still a distinct possibility.

2:36 p.m.

Vaughan comes over to me as I'm grabbing a textbook from my locker, nudging my arm. Before I can even react to this astonishing development—since last time we spoke I told him to have intercourse with a cactus—he mumbles: "So I hear Castillo gave you The Talk. The Lord our savior, Jesus hates blow jobs, all that."

I snort despite my general revulsion toward the Vaughan name and everything it stands for. "She did. You got it too?"

"Yup." He shifts his backpack on his shoulder, white polo shirt crumpling as he does so. I'm not sure why he looks like he's participating in a surreptitious drug transaction every time we exchange words, but he's maintaining the trend nicely. "It was super fun. A wild ride from start to finish." A glimpse of the sarcastic, funny Vaughan I met on that porch swing shines through, and I can't help but picture him as a duck-billed platypus. [You know. A duck-billed platypus attempting to purchase crack cocaine.]

"Gotta say, I'm surprised Castillo bothered talking to you," I mutter, slamming the locker shut. A particularly tiny freshman tries to take a picture of us as she walks past, and I work very hard to resist the urge to flip her off. "Everyone else seems to be obsessed with dishing out all the blame to yours truly."

"Yeah, that's, uh . . . kinda what I wanted to say." He stares awkwardly at the ground. "I'm sorry it's blown up like this. Really. I mean, BuzzFeed? It's just insanity. And it's not fair how they're treating you."

This stuns me somewhat. "I . . . thanks, Zachary. For, you know. Not being too Vaughanish about it."

He gives me a pained smile. "Yeah, well. I know I acted

like a jerk before. When I first heard and all. But I don't want you to think I'm anything like my dad. Because I'm not, okay?"

I nod. "Okay."

2:59 p.m.

In the hallways and the cafeteria I am an A-list celebrity. Kids I don't even know seem to be torn between a) sucking up to me and trying to get all of the goss so they can sell it to *Us Weekly* and b) standing in front of me and doing impressions of a Labrador humping an Ugg boot. Some even attempt both, which I suppose is commendable in its own special way.

While waiting for math to begin, I give in and read one of the more enticing articles about me: "Why You Should Care About Izzy O'Neill's Nudes." It should be fairly obvious why I chose this particular feature, since I myself am struggling to understand what all the hoopla is about.

In a plot twist so obscene it's bordering on implausible, the feature is essentially a defense of me and my actions. First it opens with an image gallery of all the gross things politicians and journalists and sleazeballs the world over have been saying about me via Twitter. For example:

> Despite what Kim K wants you to think, feminism is NOT flashing your tits and vaj to the world. Have some class, ladies.

> Nothing less attractive than a slut. Put some damn clothes on, girl.

239

Those teen nudes are beyond disgusting. How have we raised our young generation so poorly? How did we FAIL so BADLY?

I know we're supposed to be outraged about these Izzy O'Neill nudes but ... HOLY HELL. Thanks for sharing #nicetits

Izzy O'Neill and Zachary Vaughan symbolize everything that's wrong with teen culture.

But then this kick-ass female columnist goes on to retaliate against every single one on my behalf, circling everything back to victim-blaming and violation of privacy. Sending nudes as an eighteen-year-old isn't a crime. Revenge porn *should* be.

Hear fucking hear.

6:59 p.m.
Finally, after a never-ending *Gatsby* rehearsal, I leave school feeling utterly exhausted. Like, if I do not sleep within the next 5.2 seconds I will disembowel a bitch very slowly and painfully using a ballpoint pen.

Was followed by reporters on my way home again, but I arrive relatively unscathed.

Remembering how refreshed and centered I felt after filming the granny stripper skit, I sit down to try to flesh out a three-act-structure plan for my latest comedy screenplay idea, but it's like pulling teeth. Except more painful. Everything I come up with is either dull and boring or incredibly clichéd. Normally I can visualize key scenes in my head, but tonight I have nothing.

Maybe I'm just too tired to focus on a big project. Maybe I should write a skit or two to get my writerly juices flowing.

Again, usually my mind is filled with hundreds of sketch ideas, and I just have to reach out, pluck one, and get it down on paper. But nothing funny or clever or imaginative comes to mind.

I scroll through today's news, hoping something will jump out and inspire a satirical idea. I read interviews with athletes and profiles of politicians and coverage from the Middle East, but nothing is remotely funny. Especially since I have to force my eyes away from the Most Read sidebar, which shows "Senator's Son in Sex Scandal" as the fourth most viewed piece of the day.

No. No no no. Shake it off, O'Neill. Do not engage.

What about a parody? What movies have I seen or books have I read recently that I could make fun of without much trouble?

Nothing.

My creative resource pool feels as dry as the Sahara.

8:03 p.m.

I text Ajita. For once, I want to actually open up about how I'm feeling. About the panicky, powerless sensation gripping my very bones.

Feeling kinda bummed. Wanna come over?

It takes her at least fifteen minutes longer to reply than it usually does.

Sorry, kid, Carlie and I are at the specialist tennis store in the city. I need a better racket, apparently. Can I call you later? xo

I shove my phone underneath my pillow and curl up under the covers, probably looking as pathetic as I feel.

THURSDAY, OCTOBER 6

<u>7:12 a.m.</u>

I have to go to school today, because I'm falling severely behind in basically every class. At this point I would rather sit naked on a traffic cone than walk those hallways, but the stubborn streak in me is screaming like a banshee: "Fuck you guys! Fuck you all! I'll never let you fuck with me!" Except they are quite clearly fucking with me, and I'm not handling it particularly well.

<u>9:08 a.m.</u>

Danny swings by my locker and apologizes en route to geography. "Hey. Sorry for freaking out that you and Ajita were hanging out without me at the mall. It was pretty childish." He rubs the back of his head bashfully.

I grit my teeth, resisting the urge to slam my locker shut. "Don't worry about it."

He sighs, fiddling with a loose strap on his backpack. We set off for class. His steps are longer and slower than usual, his mopiness seeping into his body language. "I have no idea why I'm so up and down at the moment. Probably 'cause everything at home sucks ass."

Not one to engage in games of Whose Life Sucks More, even though I would definitely win, I say, "You know where I am if you wanna talk about your parents or whatever. Just don't lash out at me again, okay? I really can't handle it right now, on top of everything else."

"That's fair." We walk in silence for a moment. I study my thrifted Doc Martens intently, staring at the scuffed burgundy leather. Then he adds, "I really am sorry, you know. About what you're going through. The media . . . fuck, they're so harsh."

"Yeah, Danny," I mumble, voice thick with impending tears. He gazes at me, eyes full of concern. "Yeah, they are."

3:51 p.m.

I can't believe what's just happened. Except I can, and that's what makes it even worse.

Math class is, as usual, a form of torture on par with those Russian sleep deprivation experiments. But I keep to myself, pretending to have the faintest idea what people are going on about when they say sohcahtoa, and generally watching the clock on the back wall as every second slips painfully by. Then, against all the odds, the school bell rings. Everyone has already started packing up, surreptitiously zipping up their pencil cases under the desk while coughing loudly, and I am no exception.

Before I can escape, though, Mr. Davies says, "Miss

O'Neill, can I see you for a moment?"

At the mention of my name, everyone's heads whip around, eager for a slice of my next humiliation. They're hungry for it now. The nude pictures whetted their appetites, and now they want more.

Standing just in front of his desk, I chew the inside of my lip, feeling as trapped and powerless as I have for days. "Yes, sir."

To the dismay of my classmates, he shepherds them all out and closes the door behind him. Meg shoots me a sympathetic look as she leaves, and I return a feeble smile. I'm fully anticipating another Castillo-esque lecture on my abhorrent behavior.

When he crosses back to the desk, he sits on the front of it, leaning uncomfortably close to me and with his legs spread. He is clearly still working very hard on his nonexistent reputation as a cool teacher.

When he doesn't immediately say anything, I ask, "What can I do for you, Mr. Davies?"

He nods weirdly, like he's appreciating something funny I've said or done. Smirking in an uncomfortable way I can't quite put my finger on. "You're handling this very well, Miss O'Neill."

"Sir?"

"All the media attention." He stares at me intently. "You're holding your head up high, and I like that." I can smell tuna salad on his breath.

I take a few steps back, putting some much-needed

distance between us, and lean against a front row table. "Umm, thank you, sir."

"You're not ashamed of who you are, are you, Izzy?" A creepy smile that makes the hair on my arms stand on end. "Not that you should be."

Then his eyes drop south, and that's when I know: he's seen the photos. He's picturing them right now. He's staring through my clothes, at the naked body he knows is underneath.

The old Izzy, the girl who existed before this all went down, might've answered back. Might've called him out, or told him to back the hell off. But she's gone now, and all I can do is run from the room, my eyes stinging and goose bumps covering every inch of me. Run down the hallway, run past a concerned-looking Carson, run out of the front doors until I'm gasping in fresh air like my life depends on it.

Standing on the front steps and trying to catch my breath, I want to claw my skin off. Despite all of the things that make me *me*—my personality, my heart, my sense of humor—I've been reduced to nothing more than a grainy filter and a pair of tits. To a mere sex object.

I wonder whether I'll ever stop feeling so dirty.

4:17 p.m.

I feel bad for pushing past Carson in the hallway earlier, so once I've calmed down in the bathroom—slathering lip balm all over my dry lips—I venture back out to my locker in the hope of bumping into him again. I get my wish, but not in the way I wanted. Not even close.

A handful of basketball players are gathered by the lockers opposite mine, and Carson is among them. They're all carrying their gym bags and heading to practice, by the looks of things. None of them see me as I cross to my locker and fiddle with the combination, hands still shaking from my mini-meltdown. I figure I'll try to catch Carson later, when he's alone. I'm not in the mood to deal with the shoulder jostling and inappropriate comments from his teammates.

Turns out I'm subjected to them anyway.

". . . pictures. Like, damn. Girl's got a body on her, right?" a short dude I don't really know is saying. He snickers and spins a basketball on his index finger while Carson fishes around in his locker.

My ears prick up. Are they talking about me?

Don't be paranoid, O'Neill. Probably just discussing some girl he's dating.

Baxter pipes up. "Seconded. That nipple piercing is . . ." He kisses the tips of his fingers to his lips as he smacks them, like a French waiter complimenting a bowl of onion soup. They all laugh.

"Not that I'd touch her with a ten-foot pole," the short dude chips in. "Not after the whole world's seen her naked. Supply and demand, right? If you're giving it away for free, ain't nobody gonna pay for it. Plus, she's probably riddled, right? Girl that loose gotta be carrying somethin'."

Now I know I'm not just being paranoid. They're definitely talking about me.

My cheeks burn as I bury my head into my locker. But despite being surrounded by empty peanut butter cup packages and untouched textbooks, I can still hear everything they're saying.

Or, in Carson's case, not saying.

He doesn't defend me. Not once. Just listens in silence as his friends destroy me piece by piece.

5:06 p.m.

The more I think about what happened with Carson in the hallway, the more hurt I feel. Up until today, he's made such a point of having my back, of not treating me like dirt because of the photos. But he sat and listened to his friends pick me apart without saying a word.

Does he really care about me the way he says he does? Or is it all just an act? Does he just want me for sex? Or is it more that he's worried his friends will judge him for being with me? I don't know which is worse. That's what this entire ordeal feels like: going from bad to worse and back again.

It's exhausting, and I want it all to stop.

7:56 p.m.

The vast hopelessness is overwhelming. My future sprawls before me like an apocalyptic wasteland.

I can't stay here, in this town with these people, and yet I can't leave either. Not just because I can't afford to, or because I don't want to leave Betty, but because now the entire country has seen me naked. The stares and the whispers will follow me no matter where I go, no matter what I do. I have nowhere to go. Nowhere left where nobody knows my name—or my body.

I'm completely and utterly trapped, a monkey in a zoo, the whole world watching in, laughing at my nudity, pitying the sadness in my eyes.

I'm not a girl anymore. I'm an animal in a cage.

10:14 p.m.
I'm just taking my makeup off when there's a buzz at the door. After a few seconds, guess whose voice I hear?

Danny's.

FRIDAY, OCTOBER 7

1:02 p.m.

Was so mad last night I couldn't even bring myself to type out the exchange with Mr. Wells. In fact I'm still so angry I'm in a vague state of furious nausea, like how I imagine Melania feels when she watches Donald remove his shirt.

So he arrives all sheepish-looking [Danny, not Donald Trump] and asks to come in, and Betty kindly offers him a whiskey hot cocoa even though he drove here. He declines and asks for some privacy with her granddaughter, which is pretty hilarious considering our apartment is about six square feet so there's no such thing as privacy [something I discovered around the same time I located the bald man in the canoe]. Anyway, Betty goes to the living room and promptly presses her ear to the flimsy cardboard wall, which I know because I can hear her trying to suck a poppy seed out of her false teeth from about a yard away.

"What's up, Danny?" I say in a very traditional and un-Izzy-like manner. At this point I am unsure what the tone of the conversation will be, so I play it safe. [In retrospect

I wish I had begun with "hello, you horrid little cretin" but you live and learn.]

Dumbledore watches with interest. Danny runs his hands through his wild hair, which is bordering on dreads at this point. I consider lecturing him about cultural appropriation but decide against it.

He eventually says, "I just . . . wanted to see you. Make sure you're okay, with everything that's going on. This news coverage is rough, man. I can't believe BuzzFeed picked it up. How are you doing?"

"Oh, you know, I'm all right. It sucks a bit. But you know. Fine." This is an understatement on par with "the political landscape in the Middle East is a little tense" but I'm not in the mood to go into specifics.

Honestly, he looks terrible. His skin is all flaky like a dry piece of pastry, and his eyes are red-rimmed. I thought I had trademarked this aesthetic last year when Ajita went away to teach textiles at a summer camp and I missed her so much I couldn't sleep, so it's strange to see it on Danny for a change.

After shuffling awkwardly for a few more seconds and absentmindedly brushing toast crumbs off our counter [Dumbledore nearly has a seizure with excitement and immediately begins vacuuming them up], he says, "Good. I'm glad. I just . . . um, I just wanted you to know that . . . well, I forgive you, Iz."

I was not even a little bit expecting him to say this. As far as I can remember, I have not wronged him in any way, other than maybe kissing him when I didn't intend for the kissing to be a recurring event. Last time I checked, this was a thing I am entitled to do, and something menfolk do all the time. Maybe not great to do it to your best pal, but still.

"I . . . what?" For once I am actually quite speechless.

"I forgive you. Really. I do."

"But . . . why?"

"Because I don't want there to be any bad blood between us."

Exasperated, I clarify, "No, I mean what exactly are you forgiving?"

He peers at me questioningly through his glasses, which desperately need cleaning. "Everything."

Maybe I am just exhausted, or hormonal, or my bullshit tolerance levels are out of whack, but I am ready to cut him at this stage.

"Define 'everything,' Danny. I dare you."

Wringing his hands together, he says, "Well, you know. Leading me on. Sending nudes. Rubbing you and Carson in my face. Crushing my flowers. Treating me like shit for offering you money. Do you really want me to make a list?"

"Sounds like you already have," I snap.

"What's up with you? I'm trying to be nice here."

"Right. You 'forgive' me for acting how every guy in high school acts. Because you're just such a Nice Guy."

"What's that supposed to mean?"

"Did you ever think maybe I don't want your forgiveness for those things?" I say. "We're not together, Danny. I can date whoever I like. I can make decisions about my own body without your approval. So shove your forgiveness up your ass."

Part of me expects him to just crumple—head in hands, dissolve into tears, the whole shebang—but he's obviously in the fighting mood too, because he just snarls like Remus Lupin at a full moon and says, "You know, after everything I've done for you, you should be grateful to have people like me in your life. Not every guy would put up with this shit, let alone *still* want to be with you. And the others? Well, where are they now? On CNN talking about what a waste of space you are?"

ARE YOU KIDDING ME—

"I should be grateful?" I yell. "To be treated with basic fucking respect? Get out of my house, Danny. Right now."

I swear I hear Betty whisper "oh snap" through the wall at this point, but I could be hallucinating due to sheer tiredness and frustration.

To his credit, he leaves.

So now I'm sitting in the cafeteria giving Ajita the full debrief, and she's just as mad at him as I am. She's explaining how Danny is in real genuine danger of her giving him a rectal exam using a bottle of ketchup when her phone bleeps. She looks down, instantly horrified.

"What? What's wrong?" I ask.

"Don't freak out . . . ," she says slowly.

"Always a great start."

She chews her bottom lip, eyes scanning something on her screen. Then, without even looking at me, she shakes her head in disbelief and says:

"Carson Manning sold his story."

The bottom falls out of my gut like a trapdoor opening. "Sold his story? What story?"

Then the worst moment of my life takes place.

Her face crumples. "You told him I was gay?"

4:44 p.m.

Carson spoke to one of the regional newspapers. They asked him for his insights on my situation, since he's been mentioned on the World Class Whore site, and I guess he needed the money, or has no soul, because he did it. He told them everything.

And I mean everything. Not just his opinion on all the shit that's already been covered, like that fateful night at the party [funnily enough, he doesn't mention the fact that he lasted less than forty-five seconds] and my nude pictures, but stuff that's happened between the two of us since. Me texting him to apologize for everything, and thus admitting sole responsibility, according to the article. Meeting him at the basketball courts. Telling tasteless jokes.

There's a direct quote, too. Calling me a whore.

Up until now, I've still been reeling over him not defending me to the basketball team, but as hard as that has been to swallow, I never could've imagined him doing something like this. Not in a million years.

There are screenshots of our text conversations in an image gallery attached to the article.

Hey, is your friend Ajita single? One of my firm-penised teammates wants to ask her out, but I've seen her around with that tennis chick. What's the deal there?

Yeah, I'm not sure firm penises are her jam. I mean, neither are flaccid ones. Like I'm just not sure penises are her preferred genitalia. But your pal should ask away, for I am not her spokesperson!

I doubt the reporter particularly cared about Ajita or the guy who wanted to ask her out. The piece is entirely focused on my disgusting manner in general, and the way teenage girls as a whole have lost all class, all self-respect and dignity—basically supporting everything the Vaughan family has been spouting ever since this atomic bomb of horseshit exploded all over my life. In fact I wouldn't be surprised if the Vaughans paid this reporter to write such a tacky feature, to be honest.

But Ajita was collateral damage. And for that I will never forgive myself.

Carson texted me as soon as the news hit. Insisting it wasn't him, insisting we'd both been screwed over, insisting he's not that kind of guy. Insisting he'd had his phone hacked, and that everything in the paper could've been gleaned from his text messages. It's true, I guess. Maybe he *was* hacked. Then again, maybe he wasn't.

I don't know what to believe anymore. I don't even think I care about Carson right now. All I know is how terrible I feel about what I've done to my best friend.

Why did I think it was okay to joke about it when Ajita herself has never addressed it? Why did I have a lapse in judgment so sudden and severe that I threw my best friend under the bus for the sake of a punch line?

All this time, the media has been talking about my string of hideous mistakes, about how I don't think through my actions, about how I'm so shortsighted and irresponsible that I can't see how disastrous the consequences of the things I do can be.

Until now I've resisted that line of thinking. Until now I've tried to own my actions, dismissing the idea that they were mistakes at all. So I had sex. So I drank beer. So I sent a nude. Those are things millions of other people, teenagers and adults alike, are doing every single minute of every single day. Knowing deep down I'm not a bad person is all I had left to cling on to, like a life raft when I'm drowning.

But this? Ajita? This *was* a mistake. This *was* a lapse in judgment.

This *does* make me a bad person.

I try to call her—my lovely best friend I'd do anything to protect, my lovely best friend who I've hurt so badly, my lovely best friend who might never forgive me—for the thousandth time since she fled the cafeteria in tears.

She doesn't pick up.

<u>8:59 p.m.</u>
I just got an email from LA. My screenplay made the short-list.

And I don't care. Not one bit.

SATURDAY, OCTOBER 8

8:15 a.m.

I barely sleep at all, thanks to the aggressive palpitations rippling through my chest. I think I finally doze off at around five a.m., and only a few hours later I'm awoken by a knock on the front door.

Bleary-eyed, still half asleep, I strain my ears as Betty pads over and opens it.

A low voice, male, sort of familiar. Not Danny's southern twang or Vaughan's clipped upper-class lilt. It's warm, gravelly, confident.

Carson.

I can't make out what they're saying, but Betty's tone is pretty harsh. I hear the door bang shut again, and a few seconds later she's perching softly on the edge of my bed. I roll over so I'm facing her, aware my eyes are probably all gloopy and gross from last night's tears. She strokes my hair, tucking the most unruly locks behind my Dumbo ears.

"Carson's here. He wants to talk to you."

I groan incoherently. Betty's all hunched over and sad-looking. This debacle has aged her massively, and I know she has to work today. Just another thing to add to my endless list of things to feel guilty about.

"He insists it wasn't him. That he didn't talk to the press. Do you believe him?" she asks quietly.

"I don't know," I mumble. "I'm losing faith in pretty much everyone. Even myself. Especially myself."

"Don't say that. Don't you ever say that. You're the best person I know, and I love you very much. I'll do anything to protect you." She kisses me on the forehead as a fresh wave of sobs cause my chest to almost cave in on itself. "I'll tell him to go."

"Thank you, Grandma," I croak. "I love you too."

9:10 a.m.
The entire world has gone insane. And not like good, quirky insane, like *The Rocky Horror Picture Show*, or Ajita after two beers.

Ugh, Ajita. My heart hurts whenever I think of her. I've sent her over a thousand texts and she won't reply.

I don't blame her.

I wonder if her parents have seen it. I wonder if she's currently fielding endless questions about it from her extended family. I wonder if I've ruined everything for her. I wonder if I was so far off the mark that it doesn't matter anyway. I wonder just how much damage I've caused.

Although it's not like I'm getting off scot-free. The porch swing picture was on the evening news last night, with all nether regions blurred out the same way BuzzFeed did.

The evening news! Seriously, I am just some random teenage girl with a penchant for nachos and peanut butter cups and sexual intercourse. Why would the host of a prime-time TV show invite some political analyst into the studio to discuss Ted Vaughan's campaign, and his flawed parenting, and the implications of his son's involvement in this stupid small-town scandal?

Why would Ted Vaughan use me as a launching pad to discuss his wacko opinions on abstinence? Is it because he realized none of this is just going to conveniently disappear, so his spin doctor twisted all the vitriol toward me instead?

Why would professional journalists use the word "slut" to describe an innocent eighteen-year-old girl?

Last night I cried so hard onto Dumbledore that his fur became all matted with snot and saliva, and Betty had to run him a bath in the kitchen sink, and I just watched them both and continued to weep hysterically about a) the unfavorable press coverage, obviously, b) my adorable grandmother and pet and how I would run through the fiery pits of hell and/ or a particularly hilly cross-country trail for them and yet am causing them untold stress, c) Vaughan turning out to be such a dick despite how chill he seemed at the party, but then coming full circle all the way back to semi-decent again, d) my eyebrow still not recovering from the overzealous plucking incident and how much it accentuates my lazy eye, e) people who attempt to use "jamp" as the past participle of "to jump," f) how my best friend in the whole entire world will probably never speak to me again and it's entirely deserved, g) how I had my very own guardian angel in the form of Mrs. Crannon and I've let her down, h) how I was starting to fall for Carson and yet he turned out to be just another fuckboy . . . et cetera, ad infinitum.

This is going to sound really morbid, but lately all I want to do is go to sleep and not wake up for a significant period of time. Not because I want to be dead or anything. I don't. I'd never give those toilet girls the satisfaction, for one thing. But being alive feels a lot more difficult than it used to. I'd really appreciate a prolonged stretch of time off, where I could wake up when all of this is ancient history.

You know what? I'd stay internationally reviled forever if it meant Ajita would forgive me.

Why did I do this? Seriously, what was my thinking when I was sending that text to Carson? That's the problem. I wasn't thinking. Not at all. And I've done so, so, so much damage through sheer negligence. It's deeply concerning— that I can screw up so epically and irrevocably, and not even be aware I'm doing it until it's too late.

Why am I like this? I know my generally apathetic and humorous nature can be endearing. But this is not okay. It's not okay that I'm like this.

I send Ajita one more message:

I'm so sorry. I'm so, so sorry. I love you. And I'm sorry. Please, talk to me. Or don't. Because I definitely don't deserve it. But just know how sorry I am. I'm so lost without you. xxx

MONDAY, OCTOBER 10

8:05 a.m.
As per our usual morning routine, Betty sits me down for a bowl of cereal and a much-needed heart-to-heart before I haul myself to Edgewood for another day of character assassination.

I'm crunching miserably through a bowl of Lucky Charms, and she's slurping the milk from the bottom of her already-demolished shredded wheat.

She finishes and smacks her lips. "Listen, kiddo, I know things are rough right now, but I promise you they will blow over. Do you realize how short an attention span most people have? By this time next month they'll have forgotten all about you. I know weathering the storm until then isn't going to be fun, but you have so much going for you. The screenplay, for example! That's such incredible news about being shortlisted. Mrs. Crannon must be so thrilled."

"I haven't told her yet," I mumble.

"Well, what are you waiting for? Get your ass into school, put a smile on that lovely face of yours, and tell your mentor that she has every damn reason to be proud of you. All right?"

"All right," I lie, knowing I'm still far too embarrassed to show my face in Mrs. Crannon's office. I'm not sure I'll ever be able to look her in the eye again. Whether I'll be able to look *anyone* in the eye. I'm struggling to meet Betty's worried gaze, even though I know she loves me unconditionally.

The shame is seeping into my bones. They feel heavy as I leave the sanctuary of my tiny home and go out into a world full of people who despise me.

Anyway. Long story short, I have to go to school and pretend to care about Tudor England. If I see Danny *or* Carson I plan to pull a full Henry VIII on their asses. I know we are not married so the metaphor doesn't quite work, but rest assured I will feel approximately zero remorse following the public beheading of those treasonous goats. I have brief concerns over probably not having the upper body strength to lift an ax above my head, but Ned Stark makes it look very easy. I'll keep you updated.

8:27 a.m.
More journalists hound me on the way to school, and it's infinitely worse without Ajita there to protect me. They follow me all the way to school with their fluffy microphones and TV cameras and notepads and flashing voice recorders, even though I don't say a word at any point. I am even very careful to maintain an alarmingly neutral facial expression, just in case they manage to flash a pic in which I look a) angry,

b) devastated, or c) like anything other than a stone cold ice queen with no soul, which is how I prefer to appear at all times.

Getting through the hallways isn't any better. Just a few weeks ago, barely anyone paid any attention to me. Not in a bad way, just that I've never been one of the popular girls, and apart from my semi-regular one-night stands and a YouTube channel nobody ever visits, there was no real reason to notice me. And although I would have appreciated a few more sketch show subscribers, that's the way I liked it.

All that has changed. Though nobody approaches me, everybody stares. It sounds like a cliché, but seriously. Everybody. Stares. Not one person manages to avert their gaze as I pass. I catch snatches of conversation—the usual buzzwords like "whore" and "slut" and "self-respect"—but don't allow myself the luxury of sticking around long enough to hear the whole shebang.

It's the most disconcerting sensation, being looked at but not engaged with. Hot and prickly, like you're an ant being roasted under a magnifying glass.

9:58 a.m.

Meg passes me in the hallway as I'm traipsing to class. She's wearing a New Orleans Saints jersey, and as she gets closer I notice she's matched her gold eye shadow perfectly to the fleur-de-lis in the logo. Come to think of it, her entire makeup look is on point—strong contour, immaculate nude lipstick, perfectly flicked winged eyeliner. Girl's got serious beauty game.

For a split second I worry she'll sneer at me like everyone else in the world, or even worse, she won't acknowledge me at all. But my fears go unanswered, because the moment our eyes meet, she grins widely, genuinely, and waves. I return her wave unselfconsciously, for the first time in . . . too long.

And then as I walk away, I'm overcome with grief over a potential friendship lost. I'd invited Meg along to one of my nacho sessions with Ajita, but now there are no nacho sessions in our future. Sure, I could ask Meg to hang out just the two of us, but she'd only ask what happened between Ajita and me, and I'd have to tell her the truth, and she would never smile and wave at me in the same carefree way again.

Who am I kidding? She probably already knows what I did. Everyone else does.

10:23 a.m.

Once again Ted Vaughan is using the whole nude picture fiasco as a vehicle for his deeply rooted misogynistic views, and has issued a statement about how he longs for the good old days when women were classy and respectful and served their male masters like quiet little mice servants with no personality of their own. Something along those lines. Knowing Vaughan Junior doesn't share his father's archaic views takes the sting out somewhat. Maybe there's hope for the future still.

It's really so irritating how I have become a poster child for all that is wrong with teen America. Some people try so hard to become icons, like those folks who go on reality TV shows and pretend to be completely devoid of brain cells, and yet here I am, minding my own business, and somehow the whole country suddenly knows who I am.

There are actual, genuine teenage heroes out there. People who fight for equality, fight against injustice, fight for human rights. Give *them* this much attention.

My newfound celebrity status makes school intolerable. Someone has graffitied "Izzy O'Neill for President!" in a toilet cubicle, which is completely insane and baffling on a number of levels, and then someone else has added "of the Whore Society" in pink highlighter. I will concede this is slightly amusing and far more innovative than most of the abuse being hurled my way, but still.

While I'm peeing and admiring the semi-originality of the libel before me, I hear a couple of girls enter. Their voices sound young—freshmen maybe. Their conversation goes something like this:

"So we were just texting, like, back and forth, you know? Like the banter was flowing so easily, he's really funny, like super hilarious, and I was just bouncing off him, you know? He's just so easy to talk to, so different from other guys our age, you know?"

"I know, yeah," Girl Two says emphatically. At this point I am extremely relieved that we have established the knowledge of Girl Two.

"And then out of nowhere he starts trying to sext me! Like asking what I was wearing, what I'd do if we were

267

together. It was so awkward, but I just played along because I didn't want him to think I'm frigid, you know?"

Good grief.

"Oh my god, Louise! I can't believe you!"

"I know! Then, you'll never believe this, he asked me to send a picture. I was like, eww, no! I wouldn't want to end up like that Izzy O'Neill girl, you know?"

"Ugh, I know. I'm surprised she hasn't killed herself yet."

The looks on their faces as I exit the stall at this point are comedy gold, but for some reason, I don't feel like laughing.

10:59 a.m.

Neither Ajita nor Carson seem to be in school. I'm relieved about Carson, because although I don't want to admit it to myself, I was actually starting to care a lot about him, and I'm pretty devastated that he turned out to be even worse than the rest of them. And I hate, more than anything, that Danny was right.

So yeah, I'm glad Carson isn't here. As much as I want to tear him limb from limb for what he did, I'm just not really up for a big confrontation.

In fact, I'm not really up for anything anymore. Although usually I am more hyperactive than your average cocker spaniel [this is an absurd and blatant lie. I am and always have been lazy to my very core], these last few weeks have drained the life out of me. Energy is a thing of the past.

When I'm walking out of biology class after a highly traumatic dissection of a pig's heart, I see the last person I expect to bump into at school: Betty.

She's leaving the principal's office, and looks absolutely furious about something. Principal Schumer, a stern fellow with a big gray mustache, goes to shake her hand, but she totally shuns him and storms away. She nearly knocks over a gaggle of girls gathered at the water fountain like giddy geese. [Check out that alliteration. In the unlikely event you are studying this book for a high school English class, please do feel free to point out my astonishing grasp of literary devices. Between you and me it was just a happy accident, but your teacher doth not need to know this.]

Betty finally spots me gaping at her and approaches with a look of righteous anger in her eyes. "Izzy! Darling granddaughter! Why did you not inform me that your principal is a cretinous goblin with the worst breath I have ever encountered in my life?"

She's speaking so loudly that everyone within a thirty-mile radius can hear, but I'm truly beyond caring at this point. To say my reputation is in the gutter would be an understatement of epic proportions, so really how much worse can a mad raving loony of a grandmother make things?

"Betty-O. Dare I ask what you're doing here?" I say, in an attempt to appear calm despite my forever-churning insides.

A strained smile. "Well, Iz-on-your-face, I—"

"Hilarious new nickname, by the way."

"Why thank you, I do try. Anyway, I thought I'd have a chat with your principal about his complete lack of action in determining the founder of the World Class Whore website, and his apparent disinterest in the way you're being treated in this godforsaken sanctuary for cretinous goblins."

A small crowd has gathered to listen to our conversation, including Mr. Davies. To the average onlooker, it appears he's abandoned an AP class just to observe this unlikely scenario: a lunatic grandma set loose on the halls of a so-called cretinous goblin sanctuary. But I know the truth. He's probably watching his back; making sure I haven't ratted him out.

"And? What did he say?"

She turns beet-colored at this point. "Funny you should ask! He said that while the website is being investigated, the school has limited resources and cannot prioritize instances of a self-inflicted nature."

"Self-inflicted?! That's victim-blaming. And revenge porn is a big deal. It's illegal in a lot of states."

"Exactly what *I* said, Iz-on-your-face, but the twat goblin just made some sanctimonious remarks about self-respect. He also said that while revenge porn isn't illegal in our state, having sex in public *is*, and we should be thankful nobody is pressing charges."

"It was on private property!"

"I know, I know. But he seems to think that we should, I quote, 'lie low and not make this any worse than it already is.'"

I puff air through my cheeks. "Shitting hell."

"Yes. Shitting hell indeed."

The murmuring crowd remains gathered around the principal's office long after Betty departs in a ragey flounce. I hope my comment about victim-blaming strikes a chord, even to just a handful of them.

When Betty leaves, I head straight for the woods. It's the only place on this godforsaken campus that you can find any space to breathe. And I'm desperate to get away from the eyes, the constant eyes on me, the never-ending stares that follow me wherever I go. It's suffocating.

But when I get to the clearing, Danny's there. He's sitting on the ground, back against the tree I leaned against when we had that first confrontation all those weeks ago, right after I accidentally kissed him.

His head is in his hands, skinny shoulders shaking. Is he . . . crying? I haven't seen him cry since we were twelve years old.

A twig crunches under my foot, but his ears don't prick up. He hasn't seen or heard me yet, and all I want to do is to turn and walk away. The last words he said to me burn through my mind.

"You know, after everything I've done for you, you should be grateful to have people like me in your life. Not every guy would put up with this shit, let alone still want to be with you."

Just walk away, Izzy. Walk away.

It's not that easy, though. When you've been so close

to someone for so long, seeing them hurt or sad breaks you a little bit. It's an animal instinct to protect them. They're your family, and even if you're mad, even if you've been in a fight, it all gets put on the back burner if one of you is upset.

"Danny," I say carefully, not wanting to give him a shock. But he doesn't hear me. Louder: "Danny?"

He freezes, caught in the act. Then sniffs, wipes his nose, and says, "Go away, Izzy."

"No," I reply, defiant. I edge closer. "You're upset. We can put the fight on pause. What happened?"

"Why do you even care?" His voice is sad, but slightly venomous. "I mean nothing to you."

"You know that's not true," I say, persevering through his stubbornness. "You're my best friend. I care when you're hurt."

I step forward until I'm right beside him, but he still doesn't look up at me. He just stares straight ahead, teeth gritted.

"What happened, Danny?" I try again. "Talk to me. Is it your parents?"

For a second he looks like he's considering telling me, but eventually he shakes his head, dissolving into fresh tears. "Please. Just go."

So I go.

12:36 p.m.

Lunchtime. Cafeteria. I'm sitting alone on a bench, trying to eat my grilled cheese and tomato soup in peace. I've accidentally put too much salt in the soup so every time I have a spoonful my face resembles a bulldog sucking a lemon, but in the grand scheme of things I'm sure this is not the greatest tragedy I'm facing. Still, it's taken me a good fifteen minutes to even make a dent in the bowl, and at this point it's all cold and lumpy.

Carlie and her gang of tennis-playing cronies are sitting at the bench behind me, and for the most part I'm barely listening to what they're saying because for all their chitchat about balls, it's not the entertaining kind. But then I hear something that pricks up my ears.

". . . That Ajita chick. Is it true? Are you two having a thing?"

"Ugh, god no," Carlie says, as though she's never heard anything more disgusting in her life. "She's so annoying. She follows me around like a lost puppy. I only invited her to tryouts to be polite, and now that she's on the team I can't get rid of her."

The underlying anger I've been trying to bury for weeks begins to bubble a little hotter.

"Really?" another girl asks. "You seemed to be having a nice time in the woods together last week, and if the leaked texts from that Izzy slut were anything to go by . . ."

The whole table giggles. God, I hate high school.

"Shut up, all right?" Carlie snaps like the stick of celery she's gnawing. "Why would someone like me be interested in someone like her? She thinks she's hilarious, she's got these weird Indian parents—"

Something inside me splinters. As calmly as I can muster, I stand up, pick up my bowl of cold, oversalted soup, and pour the entire thing over Carlie's head.

Gasps and squeals ripple around the table as Carlie screams. Lumps of unblended tomato trail into her open mouth and down her cleavage. It smells like a sauce factory explosion. People all around the cafeteria stop and stare, pointing disbelievingly.

Standing over her like a disapproving parent, I sneer at Carlie, whose smugness is now completely obscured by red chunks. Loud and clear and full of strength, I say, "You will never, *ever* be good enough for Ajita Dutta."

And then I storm out. Or at least, I try to. Before I even reach the door, someone grabs my arm. Mr. Richardson.

"Miss O'Neill. Principal's office. Now."

2:25 p.m.
"You could've given her third-degree burns." Mr. Schumer's angry voice is even quieter than his normal voice. He's intimidating in that cold, calm way, like President Snow in *The Hunger Games*.

His office is impossibly neat and orderly, and he never has the radiator turned on, so I can practically see my breath. It's like a morgue.

I sit in front of his desk, refusing to be sheepish or remorseful, because I'm not. "But I didn't burn her. The soup was cold."

"You didn't know that."

I match his calm, measured tone. "I did. I'd been eating it thirty seconds earlier."

There's a silent stand-off, in which all we can hear is the buzzing of the strip lighting and the vague sound of the road outside.

"Why did you do it?" he asks, but I can tell by his voice there's no right answer. He clearly thinks I'm some uncontrollable monster.

"Because they were disrespecting my best friend." On the chair next to me is Betty's scarf. She must've left it here earlier. Nothing but a coincidence, of course, but it gives me strength. It feels like she's here with me. I pick it up and wrap it around my neck, inhaling her scent—whiskey and cocoa.

He leans back in his chair, robotically, not breaking eye contact. "Just because someone acts in a way you don't agree with doesn't mean you have the right to punish them for it."

I scoff. "See, that's what I'm having a little trouble wrapping my head around, Mr. Schumer. Because a few weeks ago, I, too, acted in a way some people didn't agree with. And ever since that moment, the world has done nothing *but* punish me, and if your conversation with my grandmother is anything to go by, that doesn't bother you at all."

Again, our principal says nothing. I jut my chin out defiantly. Before I can talk myself out of it, I add, "And since it's such an important subject to you, maybe you want to have a word with your faculty about respect. A certain math teacher can't keep his eyes off me. Especially when he keeps me behind after class just to make inappropriate comments."

His eyes narrow. The light catches on his expensive watch and flashes in my face, but I don't flinch. I power through. "Don't you want to know which teacher I'm accusing of sexual harassment, Mr. Schumer? Or should I just go straight to the school board with my complaints? I don't mind either way."

Looking grimly down his nose, he replies, "You can try. But after your antics, I'm not sure there's a single board member who would take your allegations seriously. Miss O'Neill, it doesn't escape my attention that all this is a little convenient. You're just remembering these inappropriate incidents now, when you're facing disciplinary action? Accusing my staff of harassment will not get you off the hook."

My blood spikes red-hot, and I fight the urge to clamber over the desk and tear his face off.

"I should suspend you immediately. But I won't."

I snort. "Let me guess. Because I'm a tragic orphan?"

"Something like that."

We stare each other down for a minute. That doesn't sound like much, but there are certain times in your life when you realize just how long a minute is, such as when waiting for another driver to let you slip into their lane during a traffic jam, or when waiting for a microwave meal to cook. This is one of those times.

I feel like he's waiting for me to apologize, but I won't do it.

Eventually, he says, "You may go. But if this happens again, I won't be so lenient. Your behavior has already attracted a wealth of unwanted attention to our school, Miss O'Neill, and by continuing to act up, you're only making it worse for yourself. I know you've had a troubled upbringing, but there's only so much understanding we can give before we have to take action."

Now I feel like he wants me to thank him for letting me off the hook, but again, I won't do it.

I walk out without a word.

4:47 p.m.

Desperate to have my faith in the world restored, I stop by Mrs. Crannon's office after the final bell. Instead of candy wrappers, she's surrounded by balled-up tissues and a tube of menthol oil, and her nose is redder than a baboon's behind. Bless her.

And yet at the sight of my weary expression, she's the one offering me sympathy. "Oh, Izzy. You poor thing. How are you doing?"

My skin crawls. The idea that this warm and kind woman has seen my vagina is so sickening, so gut-wrenching, that I can barely breathe. But I'm getting used to having the wind knocked out of my lungs, and I try to push past it.

Swallowing hard, I perch on a desk instead of condemning myself to several minutes of torture-chair hell. "I'm okay, I guess. I just don't know how I'm supposed to respond to it all, you know?"

She blows her nose like a trumpet, mumbling against the tissue. "Well, I think only you can answer that. There's no right answer. Just do what feels most comfortable, and know that you've done absolutely nothing wrong. Those of us who truly care about you know that too, and don't look at you any differently."

Even though she's being sweet, my cheeks burn with embarrassment as I let it really, truly sink in that my middle-aged drama teacher has seen me naked. You know those dreams you have when you're a kid that you accidentally go to school without any clothes on, and everyone stares and there's nowhere to hide and you just want to die?

That's my reality.

I can't do this.

I'd planned to chat with her about my screenplay, but I'm too mortified. I leave without even saying goodbye. Maybe she calls after me, but I can't hear anything over the blood roaring in my ears and the self-loathing rippling through my veins.

4:59 p.m.

I almost don't see him.

I'm hurrying down the hallway in the arts and social sciences building, chin tucked to my chest and heart beating wildly, dreaming of the moment I hit the fresh air but knowing deep down it won't make me feel any less dirty.

Mercifully, there are no other students around. Because it's so quiet, the soft remixed reggae floats out into the corridor even though the door to the art studio is closed. It's so out of place, so incongruous. It takes me back to Baxter's party, sipping beer on the soft couch with Carson pressed up against my shoulder. Before . . . everything.

I stop in my tracks. The art studio is just down the hall, and while the door is shut, the blind over the window hasn't been pulled down. Curiosity gets the better of me and I edge closer, the music growing louder as I do. It's not as intense as it was at the party; it has that tinny quality you get when you play songs through your phone speakers. But it's definitely the same song.

Carson has his back to the door as he paints, working on a giant canvas propped up on an easel. As I creep toward the unblinded window, I try to get a better look at what he's painting, but his body obscures the middle of the canvas. Around the edges, in the background of whatever he's shielding, is the star-spangled banner, painted in the same red and white I saw speckled on his shirt back when he kissed me in the hallway; the same blue that stained his hands.

A brush in his hand, he dabs away at something I cannot see, leaning close to the canvas and examining his work in painstaking detail. I'm transfixed, but I also feel like I'm violating his privacy. He once offered to show me his work someday, but like I say. That was before.

I'm about to walk away, to leave him to the painting session he's obviously skipped basketball practice for, when he swivels his body to the side, reaching for some more paint. His shirt lifts up as he does, exposing a strip of toned torso, but for once that's not where I'm looking.

Painted in deep turquoise on the center of the canvas is

the Statue of Liberty, piggybacking on an African American slave. The slave is sweating with the exertion of carrying the statue, and bleeding from whip wounds on his chest. Behind him are hundreds of other slaves, getting smaller and smaller as they fade into the background; into the fabric of the American flag. The colors are vivid and textured, and the light and shade are so expertly manipulated that the statue's torch seems to shine only on her, not the slaves below.

Damn, Carson is *talented*. He's good at basketball—hell, he's great at it—but this? This is another level. It's so good I can barely breathe.

The soft reggae remix ends. Before the next song begins, Carson twists back to the canvas, and he catches sight of me in the corner of his eye. Our gazes lock through the window. Something unreadable crosses his face. My gut instinct is to go to him, to tell him how incredible his work is. How incredible *he* is.

And then I remember. He betrayed me. He sold me out.

As I shake off my awe at his talent, another song starts, and I walk away toward the fresh air I thought I craved. But at the sight of Carson, I know the truth.

All I crave is him.

6:13 p.m.

Betty has gone out to one of her ludicrous evening classes. They run them for free at the community center—I think Monday nights are yoga finger painting, where they have to paint nude pictures of each other while holding impossible poses. Laugh all you want, but Betty now has the flexibility of a double-jointed circus freak, and the paintings get less creepy the more you look at them.

So yeah, she's out all night, meaning I have some time to do some digging around on the internet to see if I can figure out who exactly made my life a living hell—and why—since the school board apparently gives precisely zero shits. Betty's absence is doubly beneficial because a) I can cry all I want in the process without worrying her, and b) I don't have to share the Wi-Fi, which is a bonus because she's always downloading movies illegally despite the fact that she's never once been able to successfully open any of the files. She is the world's worst pirate.

I make myself a pumpkin spice latte using bargain basement coffee creamer, and settle down onto the couch with Dumbledore and a box of tissues at the ready [which means a very different thing to teenage boys, I've come to understand]. And then I open the World Class Whore website.

The first few pages of the blog are just links to all the media coverage surrounding the scandal, posted anonymously by "fans" of the page, plus comments about my whoredom—again, not from the site's owner, but from the page's followers. Even though it still stings, I'm not interested in this. I need to go back to the beginning.

I hit "previous page" until I hit pay dirt. The very first post. The picture of me having sex with Zachary Vaughan on a porch swing, the one originally uploaded by the site owner. Below it are 1,704 comments.

Crap. When I first found this site, the picture only had two comments, both from anonymous users and both fairly standard iterations of what a slut I am. But 1,704? How am I supposed to sort through all these?

I start with the top-rated comments. Trawl through dozens of posts about how nobody will ever take me seriously after this, about how I've ruined any hope of a career, about how I deserve to burn in hell for all of eternity because I'm having sex outside of marriage. Huh. Maybe I should make Castillo a possible candidate.

What I'm really looking for are replies from the owner of the WCW blog themselves, anything I can use to glean hints from, but there are none. In fact, the only thing they uploaded was the original image. Everything else is from other contributors.

A quick flip through Facebook shows me Vaughan has applied to Stanford. There are 403 likes and 189 comments on his status, not one of them mentioning his dick pic. I don't know why I'm even surprised.

I open a new tab: Twitter. I haven't checked it once since this all kicked off, and I'm not sure I'm emotionally prepared for the inevitable deluge of hurtful libel being thrown my way. But then I think: How much worse can it possibly be? Everything horrible that could potentially be said about me has already been thrown out there in the public domain.

After scanning my tags, searching my name, and scrolling through the feed for ten minutes or so, I'm not surprised by the insults. There really is nothing new. Not from the hundreds of politicians and right-wing journalists and religious organizations condemning me, nor from the regular people reacting to the story, nor from the schoolkids I genuinely believed were my friends. The tweet from deadpan queen Sharon—"Am I the only one who doesn't see the appeal? Girl should rly lose some weight before her next nude leaks"—hurts a bit, especially after I took her under my wing and invited her to appear in our sketches, but I move on as fast as I can.

Ted Vaughan is louder than them all, vehemently posting every hour about me and his angelic son. I'm scum, I'm a whore, I have no self-respect, I'm everything that's wrong with modern teens. I'm out to destroy his son's life, to sabotage his future career, to make him look like the bad guy when really I'm the one who is at fault. Blah blah blah.

But what I am surprised by is the sheer number of people defending me. There's support from other teen girls fighting in my corner, saying I'm beautiful and unapologetic and deserve respect no matter what. From feminist organizations discussing consent and misogyny. From columnists exploring gender inequality and slut-shaming, demanding that Zachary Vaughan be held to the same level of public scrutiny for his dick pic.

For every negative comment, there's a positive one to match.

It should feel good, but it doesn't. It's too much. This is all too much.

Betty is out. Ajita and Danny both hate me. Even

Dumbledore is more interested in licking his own asshole than cuddling with me.

The whole world is watching me suffer. Enjoying it, even. Everyone knows who I am, everyone has something to say about me. And I have never felt more alone in my life.

8:24 p.m.
After my eleven millionth text to Ajita goes unanswered, desperation sets in. And even though he's been the High Duke of Jerkdom lately, and even though, back in the woods, he told me to leave him alone . . . I cave and message Danny.

Can we talk?

Part of me is terrified of his reaction. He's been so erratic lately, so volatile, that I have no idea whether he's going to kiss my ass or bite my head off. But few minutes later:

Sure.

So he's on his way to my apartment right this second. I'm scared, and hollow, and I just want more than anything not to feel like this anymore. I have no idea whether meeting with the guy who's been a douchebag for the last few weeks is going to make it better or worse, but at this point, I'm willing to try anything to ease this awful emptiness.

This sounds like wishful thinking, but I miss Ajita so much that the shame of the leaked nudes fades into the background. It's like a bullet wound in my chest, and I know that sounds dramatic, but it genuinely physically hurts.

11:13 p.m.

Danny and I hang out on my sofa for over an hour, watching Dumbledore chew his way through Betty's old slipper. Since said slipper probably has some kind of venereal disease, I make a mental note to get the dopey pooch checked for STDs next time we have a spare six thousand dollars to throw at a veterinarian. [I am obviously kidding. At last check, the slipper does not have syphilis, and neither does Dumbledore.]

At first it's kind of awkward. I don't address the fact that I found Danny crying in the woods for mystery reasons, and he doesn't address the fact that I outed our best friend by accident. I don't address the fact that he's been a hot-tempered asshole, and he doesn't address the fact that I kissed him then rejected him within about five seconds. We just make small talk about the logistics of how an inanimate slipper might contract gonorrhea. [You don't want to know.]

Then, once Dumbledore has lost interest in the festering foot holder and drifted off to sleep and a strange silence fills the room, I finally break the embargo on Serious Topics. The olive branch is extended. The white flag is waved. And as I make my peace offering, a tiny amount of the weight on my shoulders feels lifted.

"I'm sorry that things are crappy for you right now," I mumble, fiddling with the stitching on my ancient pajama shorts. "You don't have to talk about it if you don't want to. But I'm here if you do."

He nods furiously, as though trying to force back a fresh deluge of tears. "Thanks. And right back at you. I'm sorry you're in such a bad place."

Rubbing my face, I sniff pathetically. My hands smell of cheap dish soap. "After what I did to Ajita? I deserve it."

"Don't say that, Iz." His voice is soft and gentle for the first time in weeks.

"No, it's true." I swallow the ice cube bobbing in my throat. "I deserve to feel this low. I deserve to feel like my insides have been hollowed out. I deserve it all, Danny. Nobody can convince me otherwise."

TUESDAY, OCTOBER 11

<u>**10:43 a.m.**</u>

Thanks to the tomato soup fiasco, which Carlie's parents immediately told the press about, journalists have started making comments about my grandma's parenting abilities, or supposed lack thereof, and Betty herself had to talk me down from heading over to the local radio station and Hulk-smashing the hosts.

As many of the most vile insults usually are, these comments are disguised as concern. Sort of like when fat-shamers preach to plus-size models about their health when really they're just judgmental reptiles who don't like to look at stretch marks lest they choke on their meal replacement shakes. These reporters are framing their comments as condemnations of social services and its supposed failings, in the context of how an impoverished elderly woman was granted custody of her orphaned grandchild, and whether or not she was emotionally equipped to raise me after going through such a trauma herself, and whether it is in fact Betty O'Neill's fault that her granddaughter is such an indiscriminate whore.

You should add that to your résumé. "Izzy O'Neill: talented writer, below-average mathematician, indiscriminate whore. xo"

At this point I have to imagine what Ajita's commentary would be. I think I nailed it.

Betty's acting like the public disapproval of her parenting skills isn't bothering her, but I know it's getting her down. Normally she sings upbeat Motown in the shower, and though this morning's rendition of "Everybody Hurts" with improvised rap segments was beautiful yet haunting, I'm worried.

I read the shortlist email one more time. About how I have three weeks to act on the next round of feedback before they select the finalists. About how I show a lot of promise, and about how the judges are sure that a bright future in screenwriting awaits.

I still don't care.

5:46 p.m.
Holy fuck. I know who's behind World Class Whore. And . . . holy fuck.

My phone buzzes on our kitchen table. I'm in such a daze, sipping a long-cold cup of cocoa and staring sadly out the window, that I almost don't read the email that's just landed in my inbox. Almost.

> Izzy . . . I have something to tell you. Something that's been eating me up inside. Something you have a right to know.

It was me. I started the website. I took the picture of you and Vaughan at the party, and I uploaded it.

I'm sorry. I'm so, so sorry. You rejecting me hurt more than I ever could've imagined. And then I saw you and Carson kissing in the hallway. It destroyed me, Izzy. And then the sadness made way for anger. And then . . . yeah. I fucked up. I fucked up so damn badly.

I never meant for it to escalate the way it did. And you have to know the rest of it, the nude picture, outing Ajita, and all the awful comments . . . they weren't me. I promise. I would never do that to you and Ajita. I could never. Anyway, I've deleted the site now. I should've done it a long time ago.

Last night you said, "I deserve to feel this low. I deserve to feel like my insides have been hollowed out. I deserve it all, Danny. Nobody can convince me otherwise." Hopefully this will make you see that you don't deserve to feel that way. I do. You? You deserve all the happiness in the world.

I love you, and I'm sorry.

Danny

The pain takes my breath away. The betrayal carves out my insides until I'm empty.

It was Danny all along.

My former best friend has ruined my life, sparked a

national sex scandal, made me feel like a worthless piece of shit—all because I rejected him. All because I put him in the Friend Zone.

He thought he'd earned the right to my love. And when I didn't give it to him, he retaliated by tearing me apart.

I think a dark part of me always knew it was him. I believed his denial because I wanted to; because it was easier than confronting the fact that my best friend had betrayed me.

No. Looking back, he never did deny it. Not once did he say, "No, I didn't do it." Instead he said:

"What are you accusing me of?"

"I can't believe this. I genuinely thought that when you asked to talk to me, you'd had a change of heart. About . . . us. But no. You're actually accusing me of setting up that blog."

"Fuck you, Izzy O'Neill."

He never denied it. And still, I turned a blind eye. Let myself believe that I really knew the guy standing in front of me. That he cared too much about me to let rejection and jealousy stand in the way of our friendship. That he had seen me cry over my dead parents for so many years, and he would never do anything to hurt me.

I should be convulsing with anger right about now. I should be ranting to Ajita, or screaming in Danny's face, or seeking elaborate and brutal revenge on that pathetic prick. But I'm not. I don't have the energy, or the conviction. I don't even reply to his email.

I am destroyed by his betrayal.

And, beneath it all, bereft. I've lost both of my best friends.

I think of the Danny of this summer. Funny and smart and protective and loyal. Happy. Lately there have been glimmers of Old Danny—playing dumb games, taking Prajesh under his wing, goofing around when Carlie shut us out of her conversations with Ajita, wrapping his arm around me when I was being attacked in school—but there's no denying it. He hasn't been happy for a while. He hasn't been Danny.

Maybe it's because of me. Maybe it's his parents. Maybe something else; something so far below the surface he'll never let anyone close enough to see it. And yeah, that sucks. It sucks that he's going through a hard time. But sadness is not a get out of jail free card. It doesn't allow you to treat the people around you like human punching bags. Like they exist solely to make you happy again.

All of this is Danny's fault. He's become spiteful and jealous and cruel. I know that, deep down. And yet a part of me, the part forged in this firestorm of hatred, still wants to blame myself.

I loaded the gun. He just pulled the trigger.

7:09 p.m.

I decide to go over to Ajita's and beg her to talk to me. Can you feel homesick for a person? I have a constant pit of guilt and sadness in my gut. I need her. It's selfish, but I need her. I need her to not hate me anymore. There's no way I can survive this otherwise.

I arrive at her house on my rickety old bike, and it takes me a good ten minutes to pluck up the courage to walk up the drive and ring the bell.

Her mom answers the door, dressed for celebration in a red sari. She doesn't say anything, just looks at me sternly. She is absolutely terrifying. She's short, as short as Ajita, and incredibly round. Knowing how intelligent she is just adds to the stress. I'm intimidated both physically and mentally.

"Hi, Mrs. Dutta," I choke out, through the driest of throats.

"Izzy. What do you want?" The house is weirdly silent behind her. Usually there's so much going on, with Ajita's brother playing super loud video games and their five cats running around and knocking things over and generally wreaking havoc on the Dutta household. But today it's like a cemetery.

"Is Ajita home?"

"No. She's not."

I don't buy this for a second. "Okay. Do you know where I might find her?"

Mrs. Dutta sighs and takes off her glasses, rubbing her eyes wearily. She looks tired as hell. "I'm not sure my daughter wants to see you, Izzy. Not after the lies you've been spreading about her."

Lies. So Ajita denied it to her parents, whether or not it's true—which I still don't know for sure. It makes sense. They're hugely traditional, hugely conservative. I doubt her coming out at the age of seventeen would go down all that well.

"Please. I just want to explain. To apologize. Please, Mrs. Dutta."

"What is there to explain? Was it just an attempt to shift the attention off yourself for a minute? Is that it?" A heavy sigh. Her words are harsh but her tone is soft as she holds up her palms. "But it's not my place to judge. You can do what you like. It's your life to ruin. Just don't involve my daughter, okay?"

My heart is shattering into a thousand pieces. "Please," I whisper, more desperate by the second. "Let me talk to her. Five minutes is all I ask."

A strange expression flits across her face. I think it's pity, and I hate it.

"My heart goes out to you, Izzy. It does. You're just a kid, and you've been through a lot. Losing your parents at such a young age . . . I wouldn't wish that on anyone. But it only excuses so much. And this? This is inexcusable."

I'm about to get down on my hands and knees and beg when I hear a group of babbling voices behind me. Fear flashes on Mrs. Dutta's face before a giant fake smile emerges, I'm guessing for the benefit of whoever's behind me on the driveway.

Turning to see who she's smiling at, I see a group of Hindu women, around Ajita's mom's age, dressed in beautiful saris of turquoise and violet and peach. I rack my brain for the date. Is it Navaratri? Diwali? They're both in the autumn, but I'm not sure which days the festivals fall on this year.

God, I'm such a shitty friend. I should know this, but I've been so self-involved lately I've barely been able to look past my own reflection. No wonder Ajita hates me.

Hissing through her teeth, Mrs. Dutta mutters, "Go. Now."

I bite my lip to prevent a heaving sob from escaping, and I back away toward the women. They all stare right at me, silence falling on the small group. One of them, wearing a gorgeous sari of cerulean and seafoam, shakes her head and tsks.

Pushing past them with my head tucked to my chest, I can't look them in the eye.

As I'm mounting my bike, limbs trembling as I clamber over the seat, I hear snatches of their conversation from the doorway.

". . . sorry we didn't come by sooner, but what with all the rumors . . ."

". . . it's been such a scandal in the community . . ."

". . . we didn't know if you'd want to see us, that's all," says the woman who tsked at me.

Mrs. Dutta's airy voice dismisses them. "All slander, I can assure you. Nothing but spiteful lies."

The magnitude of what I've done hits me all over again. One careless text has shaken Ajita's entire world—her family, her community, her life.

Whether it was true or not, this was not something she

was ready for. This should've been on her terms. I stole that from her. And I will never forgive myself.

7:48 p.m.

I don't go straight home. Instead I pedal slowly around town in a strange sort of haze, completely immune to what's going on around me. I move on autopilot, only aware of my surroundings in some kind of subconscious way.

I must cycle carefully because I don't get hit by a truck or anything [which I suppose would've been nice in a poetic way, being killed in the same manner as my parents just as I'm 100 percent sure I've disappointed them as much as I possibly can in the short time I've spent on this planet], but there's no active thought process behind the cars I swerve to miss, or the pedestrians in the cycle lane I ding my bell toward.

The noise of the street—engines and brake pads, laughter and gusts of wind and the beep of the crosswalk—is just a vaguely muffled din. All I hear is Mrs. Dutta's voice echoing vividly through my head.

"It's your life to ruin. Just don't involve my daughter."

My eyes sting from exhaust fumes and tears.

"This? This is inexcusable."

Is it really? Am I really beyond redemption? Surely people do worse things than I do every damn day, and yet they don't feel like this—like a complete and utter scumbag who doesn't deserve the air she breathes. Do they? Or do they just do a really good job of hiding it?

A horn blares behind me, but I barely register it.

Once when I was having a low self-esteem moment—just a standard teenage drama about my lopsided boobs, even before they were on display to the world—Ajita said to me, "Izzy, it is not okay that people who wave the Confederate flag feel good about themselves and you do not." Is that still true?

If this was happening to someone else, I'd tell them to maintain their pride and self-respect. So you sent a nude, and had sex with a couple guys, and kissed your best friend even though you did not wish to let him enter you. So what? You behaved like a standard teenager. It's not your fault that the whole of America is inexplicably interested in your exploits just because one of your conquests was a senator's son. It's not your fault you were not in love with your best friend, and he couldn't handle it. It's not your fault this is happening to you.

Even the things that *are* your fault. The Ajita thing. You messed up. Badly. You didn't think before you spoke. You're not the first person to do that, nor will you be the last. In fact someone else is doing it right now, right this very second. Forgive yourself.

But somehow, those rules don't seem to apply to my situation. Me? I'm a scumbag. A complete and utter scumbag. All self-worth I once possessed has evaporated, and right this second, right here in the middle of a busy road in the middle of town, all I want—all I deserve—is for a sinkhole to open up beneath me and swallow me whole.

Of course, the universe doesn't work like that. Nobody who wants to disappear actually does. It's always the people like my parents, the people who have everything to live for, who get hit by drunk drivers and are eradicated forever.

The thought of my parents jolts me painfully back into the present. I'm sitting stationary at a green traffic light, cars behind me tooting angrily, some jerkwad leaning out of the window and yelling about how much of a dick I am. Yeah, dude. I know. Believe me, I know.

I start pedaling again, unsure where I'm even going. The mall's nearby. Maybe I could go for a Cinnabon. The idea seems so absurd, so ridiculously normal, that I almost laugh. Almost.

Instead, I turn a corner, and the first thing I see as I round into the street is a stab in the gut.

Ajita and Danny. Together. Without me.

She throws her head back and laughs at something he said. They carry coffee cups, and I know what's inside them without having to guess: peppermint hot chocolate for Ajita, Earl Grey tea for Danny. His hair is clean, for once, and there's color in his cheeks. Maybe his confession freed him while destroying me.

I expect to feel a rush of hatred toward him, a tide of bitterness over what he did to me. But all I feel is emptiness, and a self-loathing so powerful it knocks the wind from my lungs.

Because I feel like they're both better off without me. Their worlds are better without me in them.

8:36 p.m.

Betty's out again. Ping-Pong tournament. You know when Forrest Gump gets back from Vietnam and is suddenly phenomenal at Ping-Pong? That was Betty after she lost her daughter and son-in-law. Unspeakable trauma, but on the plus side, she became very talented at the most pointless sport in the history of pointless sports. [No offense to Ping-Pong players. But really. What is the point?]

Feeling as hollow as, well, a Ping-Pong ball, I open up my laptop and boot up Final Draft to start editing my screenplay. I've read the opening pages so many times that I've lost all concept of whether or not they even make sense, but the judges emailed me a ton of feedback with the shortlist announcement, so at least I have some semblance of direction for the revisions. I'm grateful for the distraction, to be honest. It's keeping my tiny pea brain occupied when the rest of my world is falling apart.

I launch my email browser to retrieve the feedback, and the "Inbox (308)" aggressively reminds me of just how many people know about my scumbag tendencies. Sorting through them is too daunting, so I just search for the producer's name. Frown. It still says "Inbox (1)." I wasn't expecting to hear from them again until after the deadline for submitting revised screenplays, which isn't for another month.

Hi Izzy,

Hope you're well. I'm just dropping you a brief email with a quick competition update.

After much consideration and discussion, the

judges have made the difficult decision to withdraw your entry from the Script Factor shortlist. The recent press coverage following some indiscretions in your personal life will likely attract unfavorable attention to the competition, which is of great concern to us. We've worked very hard over the years to build a certain kind of reputation in the industry, which is why we're so highly thought of today (and thus why reaching the later stages of the competition is still something to be very proud of!). As a result, any threat to that reputation is taken very seriously indeed.

Particularly due to the sexual nature of your screenplay, we've been forced to reevaluate your position, and regretfully we've made the decision to remove you from the running.

I understand this is disappointing, but we hope you continue to persevere in the screenwriting world. You have a lot of potential and the judges saw something in your work that we don't often come across.

We'd like to invite you to reenter the competition in a couple of years—once the controversy surrounding your personal life has settled down (which we're sure it will), and we'll be more than happy to welcome you back to Script Factor.

All the very best,

Tom

9:02 p.m.

Every time I feel like I can finally catch my breath, like I might actually survive this, something even worse steals the air from my lungs.

Oh my god. Losing everything and knowing it's all my fault is excruciating.

9:06 p.m.

When this all first kicked off, I had the fleeting thought that the competition producers might find out about the scandal. But I dismissed it as standard issue Izzy melodrama. They wouldn't possibly see the nudes, and if they did, it'd be them who should be embarrassed. I distinctly remember thinking that. That *they* should be mortified to be caught looking at a teen girl's nudes.

And yet now the embarrassment and downright shame is enough to drown me.

How the hell do I tell Mrs. Crannon? She'll be devastated. I can't stop thinking about that fifty-dollar bill. I know the money is such an insignificant thing, compared to everything else, but I've been raised to appreciate its value. I've been ruled by it. Fifty dollars to me is the whole world. I agonize over that unbelievable show of love and support and confidence in me—in honor of Mrs. Crannon's wonderful father. Her dead father.

I've let them both down. But not nearly as much as I've let Betty down. After everything she's done for me, everything she's given up, every last sacrifice she's made. Every extra shift she's picked up, every painkiller she's swallowed, every chance at retirement she's turned down. Every time she's put my needs before her own. She's worked and worked and worked so I can afford to stay in school, so I can afford to write screenplays in my spare time, so I can have shoes and toothpaste and running water. So I didn't have to live with the Wells when my parents died. So I could keep being me against all the odds.

I owe her the world and this is how I repay her.

9:14 p.m.
My phone bleeps. At first my heart leaps, hoping it's Ajita finally returning my messages, but instead a text from a number I don't recognize flashes on the screen.

Kill yourself, slut.

I hit delete as soon as I see it, but it's too late. The words are already burned into my brain.

9:16 p.m.
I've got something special, Tom said. They'd be happy to welcome me back. I should persevere, despite the fact that I'm the lowest form of scumbag imaginable.

My conversation with Ajita about how maybe People Like Me don't belong in Hollywood feels like an eternity ago. I was right. People Like Me *don't* belong. Unless you're perfect and classy and perfect and eloquent and perfect and poised and perfect and *rich*, you don't belong. This email confirms that.

Look at Vaughan. He's done everything I've done. He drank beer, had sex, sent a nude picture. And he just applied to Stanford without fear of rejection. Why is his life worth more than mine, just because he's rich and male?

My heart hurts. Imagine being deemed so lowly and awful that not even your talent and hard work is enough to keep you afloat in the career you want more than anything. Imagine one lapse in judgment stealing everything from you.

One moment can change everything. In the time it takes to send a nude, or in the time it takes to crack a joke about your best friend's sexuality, or in the time it takes for your car to be crushed by a drunk driver, your whole life can come crashing down around you.

One moment can change everything, and that's the most terrifying thought in the world.

How do we even function knowing that? Knowing how tenuous our existence is, how fragile our happiness? It's debilitating, when you really think about it. And now that I've thought this thought, I can't ever unthink it.

9:21 p.m.

I used to believe I could handle everything by myself; that I didn't need help from anyone. The last few weeks have shown me how completely and utterly wrong that is. I do need people. I need my friends and my Betty. I need them so much. The irony is that I've learned this too late, and I'm already losing everyone.

I can finally admit that I need help, but nobody has the energy left to give it.

I feel so fucking alone.

9:27 p.m.

As I toss and turn in my bed, agonizing over every second of the last few weeks, my mistakes gnaw at me from the inside. All I want is a time machine.

I've figured it out, why people just sometimes spontaneously combust: regret. It's enough to set you alight.

Too much. This is all too much. And I'd do anything to make it stop.

9:30 p.m.

It's now, in probably the darkest moment of my life, that my phone bleeps again.

I almost throw my phone at the wall because I'm so sure it's more hate, so sure it's another message telling me to end it all. But just in the vague hope it's Ajita, I look.

Another unknown number, but a different one.

Hey, Izzy! It's Meg. From math class? I hope everything's okay with you. I know you must be having a rough time, but I just want to say that I think you're so strong and brave for the way you're handling it all. Sorry it's taken me so long to work up the courage to text you... I didn't want to come on too strong! Anyway, I'm around next weekend if you wanna hang out at some point? x

Some of the tensed-up muscles in my chest relax. I'm not alone. I'm not.

With every scrap of resilience I have left, I force myself to bury the dark thoughts—thoughts about permanent ways in which I could make all of this stop—and keep breathing.

I dry my damn eyes, pull back the covers, knowing tomorrow can't possibly be as bad as today.

WEDNESDAY, OCTOBER 12

7:20 a.m.

I wake up with my standard raccoon eyes and scarecrow hair, but I wake up. And things feel a little brighter.

Pulling on a crumpled sweater and some jeans, I deliberately avoid my reflection in the mirror, knowing I probably look a bit like the Wicked Witch of the West. The apartment is silent. Betty must be out, or still in bed. I grab my phone and purse and head for the door.

I'm not going to school today. There's somewhere much more important I need to go. Somewhere I haven't been since I was thirteen; since Betty let me stay home from school because of a paper cut.

Outside, it smells of wet grass. The sun is weak and watery, but there's no wind. The streets are that kind of Sunday morning quiet—barely any cars, barely any people, just the odd jogger and dog-walker. And pigeons. Lots and lots of pigeons.

My bike's ancient gears clank and groan as I pedal almost robotically, staring two feet in front of the handlebars at all times. I feel tapped out, emotionally and physically, and it's sort of nice just focusing on the slight ache in my legs as I crest the hill I haven't been to in so, so long.

The cemetery sits on the only hill in our town, which is generally as flat as Kansas. There's a tiny church, which seems empty—I think it's too early for morning mass—and one giant oak tree shading the oldest tombstones in the graveyard, most of which are covered in thick moss. They've all been tended to immaculately, though, and the grass is neatly trimmed. One fresh grave near the entrance is covered with bouquets of flowers and notes. It makes me sad to look at, so I turn away. I've got enough grief of my own without absorbing a stranger's.

There's a bench I used to come to a lot when I was eleven or twelve and I first got my bike. It was the first time I was really allowed to go out alone, without my grandma with me, and I used the opportunity to visit my parents a lot. I know I could've done it when I was younger, with Betty by my side, but I always got the sense she dealt with things by not thinking about them and just pushing through. Seeing the spot where her dead daughter was buried in the dirt would make it pretty hard to do that.

Overlooking my parents' gravestones—modest and plain, side by side, the exact same death date—is a memorial bench, made of a dark stained wood. It sits with its back to a short stone wall, basking in the low autumn sun. Far enough from my parents that I don't have to read their names and birth dates, but close enough that I can still feel their presence.

Everything looks exactly the same as I remember it; exactly as I pictured it would be. Except for one thing.

Betty is sitting in the spot I used to, right in the middle of the bench where the plaque is. Her white-gray hair is wrapped in a purple paisley scarf, and she's leaning her arm on a walking stick I haven't seen her with in years. I've always suspected she used it when nobody was watching; when nobody could witness her needing help. She's as stubborn as me.

She doesn't look up as I prop my bike against the wall, nor when I perch next to her on the bench. If she's surprised to see me here, she doesn't show it.

"How you doing, kiddo?" she asks, cradling a thermos of coffee in her hands. She's wearing at least three silver rings on each finger, kooky old bat that she is.

"Concerned that my grandmother is wearing more rings than, I don't know, Saturn. But other than that, fine." [I know, it's incredibly frustrating that I just had an epiphany about needing the people I love, and yet I'm cracking jokes and masking the hurt like I always do. Hey. Old habits die hard.]

The lie is not the least bit convincing. She snorts. "Right. Sure. And I'm Harrison Ford."

"I wish," I say.

"Me too. Then I could have sex with myself."

307

Once upon a time, in a land far, far away, this would've given me a laughter-induced stomach ulcer. But not today.

I sneak a sideway glance at her face, on the hunt for signs of crying, but her cheeks are dry and her eyes aren't red-rimmed. She just looks tired.

I sigh. Here goes. "I'm just . . . overwhelmed. So overwhelmed it's hard to process everything."

Preparing for her usual up-by-the-bootstraps, bravado-boosting pep talk, I square my shoulders. But it never comes.

After a long pause, she says in a small voice, "Me too."

And then the unthinkable happens. She lays down her stick and her thermos, and wraps her arms around me, kissing the side of my head. Then she tucks a lock of my hair behind my ears, and strokes my cheek with her thumb. She smells how she always smells; of whiskey and cocoa.

"It hasn't been easy, has it?" she says, voice thick.

I don't know whether she means the last few weeks or the last thirteen years, but either way the answer is the same.

"No," I admit. "I guess it hasn't."

Letting go of the embrace but leaving one arm draped over my shoulders, she picks up the thermos again, offering me a sip. I gratefully accept.

"I feel like I've failed you, Izzy," she says, voice full of a regret I hate to hear.

"Absolutely not," I insist. "You've given up everything for me. I'll never be able to repay you. I'm so grateful to have you."

A tight smile. "But I've never given you an environment in which you could talk about your emotions. You've felt like you always had to put on a brave face, always had to be cracking jokes, because that's the way I dealt with my pain. And you had no choice but to do the same."

I let these words sink in. I guess it's true. I've never thought Betty made me the way I am, but I suppose I learned a lot from watching her. Every single part of my personality contains elements of her, including her flaws.

Finally, I say, "Well, every kid is screwed up somehow by whoever raises them. And if I had to be screwed up by anyone, I'm glad it was you."

We both laugh at this, but it's different from our usual defiant laughter. Softer. More real.

"We're going to do better, okay?" she says, gazing not at me but at my mom's grave. "We're going to talk to each other about how we're feeling. And we're going to cry when we need to. And we're going to admit that sometimes, life just isn't fucking funny."

I take a deep breath, then let it out slowly. "Okay. Agreed."

We both watch as a janitor leaves the back door of the church with a mop and bucket, emptying the dirty water over a wall and into the field behind.

"I miss them," Betty says quietly. "Your parents. They were wonderful people." Her voice is even thicker now. A tear slides down her cheek. And then another. And then her shoulders are shaking and it's me with my arms around her. "I could use their advice sometimes, you know? Their reassurance that I'm doing right by them. With you. With everything."

A massive lump forms in my throat, and before I can help it, I'm sobbing too. And then the thing buried deep inside me—the part of me containing painful questions about how different my life would be if my parents had lived—cracks all the way open.

If my parents had lived, maybe I wouldn't have felt so vulnerable on that porch swing with Vaughan. Maybe I wouldn't have needed a distraction, and so maybe I wouldn't have slept with him. And then there would have been no nude photo to leak.

Hell, maybe if my parents had lived and I weren't the way I am now—sarcastic, defensive, closed off—I might have been the kind of person who would've fallen in love with Danny the same way he did with me. Our families were always close. I can only imagine how excited both sets of parents would be if the two of us ended up together. And in a universe where the two of us ended up together, there would have been no World Class Whore website.

And most of all, if my parents had lived, maybe I wouldn't feel so completely and utterly broken. There would be none of this pain. Different pain, yes. I'm under no illusions that if my parents were still alive, my life would be perfect. But I can almost guarantee I wouldn't hurt anywhere near as badly as I do now.

The tears keep coming and coming, but it actually feels good. Cathartic. Betty and I hug each other tight. She sniffs. "You're a wonderful person, Izzy. And I'm just . . . proud. To call you my granddaughter. And I know your parents would be proud of you too."

More tears spill down my cheeks against my will. "But I messed up, Grandma."

She shakes her head fiercely. "No. You didn't. The fact that everyone is so damn interested in the sex life of an innocent teenage girl is more a reflection on them than you."

I snivel pathetically into her purple tunic. A pigeon watches with interest. "I know, but . . . I haven't told you the worst part. About Ajita."

"I already know, sweetheart," she says softly.

I'm genuinely shocked. "You do?"

"Yes. Mrs. Dutta called me."

A coil of anxiety tightens in my belly. "Oh god. What did she say?"

"She was mad. Of course, she had to explain everything from beginning to end, because as you know I do not understand the interweb, and had not seen the article in question." A pause. "Is it true? About Ajita?"

"I don't know," I whisper. "That's the problem."

Betty strokes my hair and takes a sip of coffee from the flask. "Mmmm. Mrs. Dutta seemed to think it was impossible. Literally beyond the realms of possibility. I tried reasoning with her—saying she should be open to the idea that it might be true, and try to have an honest conversation with her daughter—but . . . well. I didn't get the impression that would happen, somehow."

I rub my eyes, which have finally stopped leaking involuntarily. "I wish I could be there for her. Ajita. In case it is true."

Betty frowns. "You can be."

"How? Mrs. Dutta won't let me see her."

A disappointed tsk noise. "You and Ajita have been best pals for so long. Are you really going to let her homophobic mother dictate your friendship?"

I pause. "I feel like you want me to say no here, but have you met the woman? She's terrifying."

She glares at me sternly, which she has literally never done before in my whole life. "Izzy."

"I know."

And I do.

THURSDAY, OCTOBER 13

7:32 a.m.

As part of the plan I made with Betty to intercept my Lieblingsfreund ["best friend" auf Deutsch, because even in my worst times I am an educator of the masses] on the way to school, I get to Ajita's house stupidly early. Seriously, early is stupid. Never trust morning people. They have deeply rooted psychological issues, and as a person with deeply rooted psychological issues, I consider myself something of an expert on the matter.

Parking my bike across the street [and slightly around a corner so Mrs. Dutta cannot gun me down with an assault rifle], I pull out my flask of coffee, and I wait.

7:33 a.m.

After waiting for roughly forty-five seconds, I find it completely unreasonable that Ajita has not yet surfaced, and consider aborting the mission in lieu of a good old "hide in the bush and cry until you spew" session, but I tough it out.

[I know. My bravery is astounding.]

While I wait, I think about the screenplay competition. Yeah, it sucks that I got kicked out. It does. Mainly I feel bad for Mrs. Crannon, and a little for myself over the lost opportunity. But something Carson once said soothes me like cooling gel on a migraine.

"You can love a thing without necessarily dedicating your life to it, y'know?"

I love writing. I love performing. I love making people laugh.

The school system, and society in general, would have me believe I therefore have to make a career out of it—have to use my interests and talents to plow money back into the economy. That I have to be *productive*, above all else. A gerbil on a wheel, powering the machine with my success.

And yeah, it'd be cool to sell a screenplay to Hollywood; to hear actors speak my words on the big screen someday. But if that never happens, I think I'll be okay. My passions bring me enough joy to sustain me, even if they stay at hobby status forever.

Because what matters to me above all else? The people I love. And there's not a damn thing wrong with that. If people cared more about being kind than being successful, the world would be a much better place. That's why I need to mend things with Ajita. That's why I need to protect Betty no matter what I have to give up to do so.

I don't think I would ever have had this epiphany if it weren't for Carson. A sharp pang echoes in my chest when I think of him; of the night we spent playing at the basketball courts, meeting his mom and walking home together. Of the way he made me feel warm and fluttery and safe. Of his beautiful, painful art.

Danny confessed to starting the website. But there's still the question of who uploaded the nude from my phone. Was it the same person who sold me—and Ajita—out to the press?

Carson. Sweet, funny Carson. Could that boy really have betrayed me? Yeah, my best friend did it to me in the biggest way imaginable, so it's not beyond the realms of possibility that Carson did too. But before I cut another person out of my life, I'd like to know for sure.

8:19 a.m.

By the time I finally see Ajita rounding the corner toward school, I'm so jittery that I've splashed coffee all over my jeans. I'm just mopping the worst of it off with my roadkill scarf when I see her, all wrapped up in a jacket and carrying a stack of textbooks, which is incredibly alarming on account of the fact she's never voluntarily opened a textbook in her life. She looks like someone out of *Gilmore Girls*.

It takes her a split second to see me, but when she does, she stops in her tracks and stares at me vacantly. As if she has no idea who I am.

"Ajita . . ."

Her massive brown eyes shine dangerously. She looks like she's about to burst into tears, and I hate myself so much for causing that pain. She bites her lip and stares at the ground, clutching those books so tightly her knuckles go white.

315

"I'm sorry. I'm so sorry." My voice wobbles as I talk. "They say you're not supposed to ruin an apology with an excuse, which is a relief, because I don't *have* an excuse. Not a single one. That text message was just . . . wrong."

A cold silence stretches out between us. Then: "That's the thing, though," she whispers. "You weren't wrong."

There it is.

I hug her. I can't help myself. She looks so cold and sad standing in the middle of the sidewalk, surrounded by dead leaves and empty bags of chips and cigarette butts.

"I wasn't ready, Izzy," she mumbles into my shoulder. "I'm still not."

"I know," I say, unleashing her from my bear grip. She's crying a little. I am too.

"Everything's just so . . . uncertain. I don't know who I am; who I want to be. *What* I want to be. And this . . . it's just so confusing. It's like this gray cloud over my future. Everything my family wants for me—to be a wealthy doctor, to marry a successful man from our community, to provide 2.5 grandchildren—I just don't know if I can give it to them. Or if I even want to." She scrunches up her face and shakes her head. "I hated you, you know. When I first saw it. I hated you so much."

"That's fair. I hated me too."

"I still do, a little."

"Again. Fair."

Pressing her lips together, she finally looks up at me. Her eyes are still glistening and red-rimmed. "I need you, though. You're my best friend. And I'm kind of going through a thing that I need a best friend for." A frown. "And you are too, right? So I'm guessing you feel the same. About needing me, and all."

"Yes. It's kinda gross, isn't it. Admitting we need each other."

A smile, albeit smaller than her usual Cheshire Cat beamer. "So gross. Just like your face."

"I would retaliate with 'just like your mom,' but I think she has several snipers pointed at me right at this very second. One wrong word and she'll give the command."

She sniffs back a snot bubble. Neither of us are particularly attractive criers, but her nose takes on a life of its own when faced with a tear-inducing situation like this one. "I also have the authority to sanction your murder, so I'd tread carefully, Izzy O'Neill. Very carefully indeed."

"Noted. Do you have the authority over other killings? I have a hit list I'd like to start working through."

"Sure. Who's first? Carson?"

"Nah," I say, draining the dregs of my coffee. "Carlie, please."

Ajita smiles genuinely now. "I heard what you did. Thank you for sticking up for me. I can't believe Schumer didn't suspend you."

I nod. "Yeah, I was kind of hoping he would, to be honest. I could do with a week off. But I think he knew that's what I wanted, and the bastard didn't give it to me. So rude."

"I never did like him." She sniffs against the cold wind.

"So you and Carlie are . . . ?" I prompt.

"Over." She grimaces. "We talked. Apparently there was never anything there for her. Just harmless flirtation. Except it doesn't feel all that harmless, you know? It fucking sucks."

I nod, hating the pain she's going through but glad she's finally talking about it. "Okay, so Carlie is first on the hit list."

"Yup. Who next?"

"Danny," I mutter. "He started the World Class Whore website."

Ajita's eyes flash wildly. "Wait, he did *what*?"

"Yep. He confessed. Sucks, huh?"

All her sadness evaporates in lieu of world-ending rage. "That little son of a . . . how dare he! And to think . . . to think! He's been playing the victim all this time, manipulating the crap out of me, out of both of us, and . . . he's the one who's to blame for all this! He ruined his best friend's life out of *jealousy*?! OH MY GOD, WHERE'S MY MOM'S ASSAULT RIFLE WHEN YOU NEED IT?"

Voice small, I mumble, "I still feel like I kind of deserved it."

Ajita stops abruptly. "Don't you dare. Don't you *dare* ever think that. You're an amazing person, and Danny is a shitty person, and you don't owe anyone your love, okay? Except me. You definitely owe it to me."

I laugh. "I think I'm okay with that."

Her words soothe my conscience like aloe vera on a burn. Even after everything I've done—leading Danny on, accidentally outing my best friend—to hear that I still don't deserve to be shamed means everything in the world. If I'm going to spend the next few months rebuilding my self-worth from the ground up, it makes it so much easier to know my best friend will be by my side, laying the foundations right there with me.

10:02 a.m.

As Ajita and I leave math class, we notice Carson lingering on the opposite side of the hall—the first time I've seen his face since he spoke to the press, although he's been texting me at regular intervals to promise me it wasn't him. I want to believe him. God, I want to believe him.

Before he spots me, Ajita grabs my arm and hauls me back into the classroom, nearly knocking out Sharon the deadpan queen with her backpack. Which wouldn't have been terrible on account of her horrid Twitter rant about my displeasing body shape.

We hunch behind the door and tactfully avoid Mr. Davies's glares by pretending to rummage in our purses for tampons, which we all know is a surefire way to get male faculty members off your case.

"Shit, Ajita, what am I going to do? Should I confront him?" I mutter as I slip quietly into cardiac arrest. "Carson, not Mr. Davies."

She considers this for a moment while dangling a paper-wrapped supersize emphatically in front of her face, like she's trying to hypnotize me on behalf of the period goddesses. "Look, Izzy, boys are like buses."

"They all come at once?"

"No, they're cheap, unreliable, and smell like day-old dick cheese. Point is, you're awesome, and none of these pricks deserve you. Not Danny, not Vaughan, and not Carson. Just go and give him a piece of your mind. You've got nothing to lose."

I frown. "What about my last remaining strand of dignity?"

"Don't be ridiculous. You lost that last summer, when you touched your foofer after chopping chilies and had to squat in a bowl of Greek yogurt."

"I have no idea what you're talking about."

"Don't you remember the touching funeral service I held for said dignity? Betty said a few words, Dumbledore peed on the casket?"

By now I am just so desperate for this conversation to be over that when she shoves me back out the door, I'm beyond caring what happens in the next few minutes of my life.

Carson's eyes meet mine and sheer terror flits across his face. I stride up to him, trying to forget Ajita's profoundly disturbing observations about dick cheese.

"Izzy, I—"

"What the fucking shit, Carson? Selling your story? Are you actually kidding me?"

Literally everyone on the planet is looking at us. Drivers on the highway have abandoned their vehicles to get a better look. Every drone in the world is pointed in our direction. Extraterrestrial life-forms have finally breached the earth's atmosphere and nobody has noticed on account of the fact everyone is focusing on this pathetic sex scandal in small-town America.

"You don't under—"

Red-hot anger bubbles through me. "I don't understand? I don't understand needing some extra cash? Really? You're really saying those words to me right now? For fucking, shitting sake, why—"

He looks genuinely devastated that I'm cursing so fluidly at him. "I can explain. Please. Let me explain."

"Okay. Go."

Carson seems taken aback by my bluntness. "Right here?"

Small crowds have gathered around us now, and I don't know whether surviving several shaming rituals in the last month has toughened me up a bit, but I actually don't even care who witnesses this exchange.

"Why not? You'll probably sell your story again and all of these people will find out all the gritty little details anyway, so it might as well be public."

He shoots me a genuinely pained expression, wincing like I've punched him in the kidneys. "I didn't sell you out. I promise. You gotta believe me."

"No? So how'd the press get those screenshots?" I'm starting to yell now, and the corridor is quieter than it's ever been so my words echo around the lockers.

He almost whispers, "It wasn't me, okay? It was my brother. He knew we were texting, so he grabbed my phone while I was at work and read everything. The money he got for it paid our rent. I'm sorry. I'm so sorry. But it wasn't me."

Something in the way he's clenching his fists and staring at me so urgently tells me he's desperate for me to believe him. I remember the way he acted in the days after the website was made. He didn't treat me any differently, didn't talk to me with any less respect. He was sweet and reassuring and gracious.

And the way he is with his mom and siblings. The guy I saw looking out for his family is not a guy who would willingly ruin my life.

And I know money is tight for his family. I know desperation can make you do questionable things. If it was his brother . . . I guess I could understand it. It fits.

And I really, really want to believe him. Because my list of people who aren't weapons-grade douchebags is getting hella short.

When I don't say anything for a moment, he adds, "And you know I would never, ever call you a whore. Not even if they paid me a million dollars."

I smirk despite the situation. "Well, that's just dumb, Carson. A million dollars would solve both of our financial problems forever. I'd let you brand the word 'whore' on my ass cheek for a million dollars."

"That could be arranged!" someone jeers from a few feet away.

Another snarks, "Let's crowd-fund that shit!"

Everyone laughs.

This next part, I say more quietly. "You didn't stand up for me."

"What?" he says, matching my soft tone. He steps forward, closing the gap between us. He looks like he might take my hands, but decides against it, leaving his to curl at his sides. "When?"

"In the hallway. When Baxter and your other teammates were discussing the pictures. 'If you're giving it away for free, ain't nobody gonna pay for it.'"

His face falls. "You heard that?"

"It's all I've heard for weeks."

"Oh god." He closes his eyes. "I should've said something. I nearly did. I just hate confrontation, you know? Makes me sick. But it's not an excuse. I should've told them to shove it, and I'm so sorry I didn't." He opens his eyes again, running a hand over the buzz-cut hair on the back of his neck. "You gotta believe me, though. I had nothing to do with that article. I was as shocked and disgusted as you were, I promise. Please believe me."

Random people start shouting "Believe him!" and "How can you resist that face?" and "What the hell is going on here, why are none of you in second period?" [I think this last one was Mr. Davies, which is 100 percent justified.]

I pause for dramatic effect before replying, "I'm thinking about it."

Dimples form in his smooth brown cheeks, like they always seem to when he's smiling at me.

He mumbles, "Yeah? So, uh . . . what about that pizza

sometime? 'Cause I'm kinda tired of us pretending we're not into each other."

The dumb part of my heart that inconveniently fell for his puppylike nature all those weeks ago flutters.

"Who says I'm pretending?" I smile. "But I never say no to pizza."

4:56 p.m.

Ajita orchestrates a meeting between Danny and me in the woods after school.

She bids me farewell, saying, "Good luck, old buddy old pal. Meet you in the diner in a half hour? There'll be a s'mores milk shake waiting for you." A sly smile. "Oh, and Meg's coming too."

For the second time today, my stone heart melts. I love my friends. The old ones and the new ones. The real ones, who don't make websites condemning me to an eternity in hell just because I'm not attracted to them.

When Danny arrives, wringing his hands together in fear and, hopefully, guilt, I step out from behind a tree like a Bond villain revealing themselves. [It is probably quite clear that I have not watched many Bond movies, but I assume this is the sort of thing that happens.]

I summon the voice I finally found in the cafeteria, right before I poured cold tomato soup over Carlie's head. The voice forged over the course of this month of sheer hell, of a thousand tiny fuck-ups, and of a lifetime attempting to repair the hole my parents' death left in my world.

Before Danny has a chance to even blink, I spit out, "How could you do this to me?"

I don't have to force the venom into my voice. I just remember how low I felt after that screenplay email, before Meg messaged me, before I finally asked for help . . . and the anger comes rushing back.

"Izzy, I—"

"No. You don't get to talk. You've done enough damage, and there's nothing you can say to make this better. *Nothing*. You nearly ruined my life, Danny. Did you know that I've been kicked out of the screenplay competition? Did you know Betty is being attacked by journalists and politicians every day? Did you know that now, when I walk down the street, it's so excruciating knowing how many strangers have seen me naked that I just want to disappear? Did you know that on Tuesday night, after it felt like I'd lost everything, I genuinely wanted to not be here anymore?"

He drops his backpack to the ground and leans back against a tree, face splitting apart with regret.

I keep going, tears now streaming uncontrollably. "Why would you do this? Why would someone who claims to love me want to ruin my life? You only just deleted the site. You could've done it weeks ago, before this got so bad. Because it's been *so* bad, Danny. Have you enjoyed it, seeing me in this much pain?"

He still doesn't say anything, just rubs his face with his hands, looking like he might throw up.

I scoff, throwing my hands up in the air, letting my voice

rise above the trees. "Or was that your goal all along? To annihilate my sense of self-worth so that I'd collapse into your arms and beg you to fix me?" I raise my voice and scream so loudly a flock of birds fly away from a nearby tree. "You nearly killed me! Is that what you wanted?"

This gets a reaction. He pushes off the tree trunk and flies toward me so fast I actually recoil.

"No, Izzy! All I wanted was *you*!" His eyes are shining too, but he yells like he's made of pure anger. "How do you think I feel? I love you so damn much, Izzy, and just because I'm not Channing Tatum I've been relegated to the Friend Zone for the rest of eternity. I have to watch you chase the same good-looking *assholes* that every other girl wants to fuck, then pick up the pieces after they inevitably screw you over."

My eyes narrow and I fight the urge to spit at him. The tears are starting to dry up. "Oh my god, I'm so sick of your entitled bullshit. You didn't get what you wanted, so you lashed out with the sole intention of hurting me. Hurting me for not wanting you. How do you think *I* feel, Danny? My supposed best friend thinks I'm obliged to go out with him just because he *wants* me to?" I clench and unclench my fist. "Yeah, I messed up when I kissed you, and I'm sorry if that led you on. But stop with this poor little Nice Guy crap. You really think being 'Friend-Zoned' is worse than finding out someone you thought valued you as a whole person just wanted to fuck you? If my friendship is not enough, then fuck you. Just . . . fuck you."

Danny snarls in an ugly way. Then he says: "You know

326

what? This isn't about me. This is about you, and your complete inability to be emotionally available. Are you even capable of love, Izzy? Or are you just too damn scared to let yourself feel anything? You're . . . you're dead inside."

This is like a stab to the chest. I genuinely double over a little bit. "So the only reason I could possibly not be attracted to you is psychological damage? I can't believe you'd . . ." I trail off, speechless for probably the first time in my life. And then I find my voice again.

"What do you want me to say, Danny? That I'm so completely broken and fucked up that I've come all the way back around to detached?" I gasp as I choke on a sob, but I keep going. "That there's a gaping parent-shaped hole in my life? That I use humor as a coping mechanism? That yeah, I *am* terrified to fall in love because of what happened to my parents?"

"Iz—"

"No, Danny. Stop. You're hurt, and you're lashing out at me again, and you think it's justified because you believe you have a *right* to have sex with me, a *right* to my love, but just . . . stop. We're done. Our friendship is done. Which is totally fine, because it turns out it was never enough for you anyway."

And then I walk away. Because for the first time in too long, I genuinely believe this is not my fault.

I do not deserve this. Not one bit.

FRIDAY, OCTOBER 14

<u>9:05 a.m.</u>

As soon as I get to school, I go straight to Mrs. Crannon's office. I checked her schedule, and first period on Friday morning is one of her only frees of the week.

She seems surprised to see me, as she's tucking into a delicious-looking Danish pastry. I briefly wonder if Mr. Rosenqvist is trying to win her friendship with Scandinavian delights. I would *so* be here for a Crannon-Rosenqvist buddy comedy.

"Hi, Mrs. Crannon," I say, standing awkwardly in the doorway. "Do you a have a sec?"

From behind her towers of books, she says, "I'll always have a sec for you, Izzy. Take a seat!"

I'm feeling brave, so I plonk myself down into the iron maiden chair without a second thought. I'll apologize to my buttocks at a later date.

I take a deep breath, forcing myself to look at her rather than twiddling with my zipper as I usually do during serious conversations. "Can I be honest with you, Mrs. Crannon?"

One of her warm smiles lights up the room. "Always."

"Okay. Well, ever since everything blew up with, you know, the pictures and everything, I've been too ashamed to come and talk to you."

"Izzy! That's—"

"Please, let me finish." I feel bad for interrupting her, but if I don't say this now I never will. "I know this might sound crazy, because you're my teacher and not my mom or anything, but I've been fighting the feeling that I let you down." I pause. "I made the shortlist." Her face lights up, and she goes to celebrate, but I stop her. "No. They kicked me out a few days later. They found out about the . . . scandal." I swallow the wave of shame that rises like nausea.

Her face collapses in sympathy. "I'm so sorry, Izzy. I can't believe they'd do that."

I shrug. "I've been surprised by a lot of things these past few weeks, but that wasn't one of them. I get it. They don't want the bad publicity."

"But still. You're a talented young woman, and you deserve a shot, no matter what's going on in your personal life. Which, by the way, you should never feel embarrassed about. We've all had sex. We've all sent risky pictures. It's nothing to be ashamed of."

She says this last part so sincerely, without even blushing or mumbling or showing any sign of discomfort, that it emboldens me to carry on.

"Thank you. Really. You've been so supportive since day one, and I'm so, so grateful. I'm sorry you wasted your dad's fifty bucks."

"Wasted? Izzy, did you get great feedback from the judges?" I nod. "Is your script better for it?" Nod again. "And has it given you faith in your ability?" My face says it all. She smiles. "Well then, I'd hardly call that a waste, would you?"

2:46 p.m.

Ajita, Meg, and I are in Martha's Diner, being poured fresh OJ by my wonderful grandmother. Yes, at quarter to three on a Friday afternoon.

Half an hour earlier, we're all in English class together, listening to Castillo trying in vain to make Emily Brontë even half as interesting as Charlotte by talking about the feminist undertones of *Wuthering Heights*.

That's when Sharon pipes up with a pass-agg comment definitely aimed in my direction. "I think it's interesting how everyone seems to think feminism in the twenty-first century is better than it's ever been. I think it's just the opposite. Women had so much more class back when the Brontës were writing. They'd probably be horrified to see how some girls behave these days. You know, sleeping around, sending tacky nude pictures, and all that."

Everyone shoots me the same judgmental/pitying/snooty looks as usual, and something inside me snaps.

I stand up haughtily, gathering my belongings. "I'm leaving."

330

"Dude . . . what?" Ajita looks up in shock, just like every other member of the class.

"I'm not going to sit here and listen to ignorant assholes say crap like that about me. Especially if the person who's supposed to be in charge of the class just lets it happen without saying a word." I shoot Castillo a look so withering it makes Medusa look mild-mannered. "So, in conclusion, I'm leaving."

I just threw cold tomato soup all over Castillo. You know, metaphorically.

I gather up my stuff and shove it into my backpack as fast as I can, stray highlighters scattering everywhere, but I don't care. Because Ajita is doing the exact same thing. She's coming with me.

Castillo finally finds her voice. "Now, listen here, girls. Don't you dare walk out of that door, or I'll have you suspended."

Ajita shrugs as if she has literally never cared about anything less in her entire life. "So now's when you speak up? Not when one of your students is being bullied relentlessly by her peers, but when she finally decides to stand up for herself? Shame on you, Miss Castillo. Shame on you."

And with that, we stride confidently toward the door. Everyone just stares in utter amazement.

Meg's in the back row. As Ajita passes, she adds, "Meg, are you coming?"

Delighted to be involved in the protest, Meg grins ecstatically and wheels herself out after us, abandoning everything on her desk. Literally abandoning her pencil case, textbooks, everything. Amazing.

Castillo calls meekly after us, "But wait . . ."

We barely hear. We're too busy whooping down the corridor like we're the most badass bitches on the planet.

So now we're slurping milk shakes [I went strawberry cheesecake, Ajita and Meg both chose mint Oreo] and chatting and feeling all fired up. The diner is almost empty, since it's mainly a hangout for high school kids and all the non-rebellious ones are still in class.

"You know what?" I say, raising my voice over the clatter of pans from the kitchen, and the crooning of Elvis Presley emanating from the nearby jukebox. "I'm tired of lying down and letting stuff happen to me without resisting."

"Damn straight," Ajita says. "It's time we stood up for ourselves, you know? It's time we threw cold tomato soup everywhere. Why should I let my own mother bully me into silence over a major part of my life? Why should we let people make us feel like crap?"

Meg jumps in. "What's that Eleanor Roosevelt quote? Nobody can make you feel inferior without your consent."

"YES!" Ajita and I both yell. She smacks the table so hard in agreement that the salt shaker nearly headbutts its peppery cousin.

"I'm sick of it," I continue. "I'm sick of feeling like I live in a lose/lose world, and that there's nothing I can do about it. As a woman, you're damned if you do and damned if you don't. A slut if you send the nudes and a prude if you don't.

A whore if you have sex and frigid if you don't. A bitch if you fight back and submissive if you don't."

"We should reclaim the word 'bitch,'" Ajita argues, her eyes alight with passion. I love it when she gets like this. Meg watches in awe of her fiery new pal. "It's been used to silence opinionated women for too long. Women who have beliefs and goals and things to say. Women who won't stand for injustice or mistreatment. They're labeled bitches by men—and other women—who feel intimidated."

I nod along like one of those bobbing dogs middle-class people inexplicably have in the back windows of their cars.

Meg speaks up. "Bitches bite back. And men hate that. Society hates that." A charming little milk shake mustache has settled on her upper lip, but we're both taking her as seriously as a president addressing the nation.

A spark of an idea forms in my head; dim at first, then brighter than an exploding sun. I gasp. "We should start a website. A community of teen girls who refuse to stay silent any longer. And it could be called . . ." I grin. "Bitches Bite Back."

Ajita laughs excitedly. "That. Is. Awesome."

"I really think it would resonate with so many young women," Meg agrees. "From all walks of life. What teenage girl can't relate to being called a bitch?"

We all look at each other, magic and milk shakes in the air.

"Let's make this happen."

It's hard to believe that less than a month ago, my life was entirely different from how it is now.

I hadn't had my screenwriting dream almost within reach—and then snatched away again. I was just beginning to crush on Carson, and I hadn't yet slept with him or Vaughan. Danny was still my best friend. Ajita was still in the closet. Meg wasn't in my life. I wasn't the center of a national sex scandal. My naked body wasn't on display to the entire world, and journalists weren't gathered around the school. Betty hadn't told me she was proud of me. I hadn't had my life torn apart on a public website made with the sole intention of ruining my life. And I hadn't stitched my life back together with the help of the people I love the most.

Shame. It's a peculiar beast, especially when it happens in public. It leaves you powerless. It strips you of everything you thought you knew about yourself, forces you to examine the very core of your being. Do I like who I am? Am I proud of my choices? How can I become better?

I don't regret sending the nude picture. I don't regret having two one-night stands. I do regret hurting Ajita with an ill-judged joke.

That's what truly matters to me: the people I love. And it took a fuck-up of epic proportions to realize that.

A month ago, if you'd asked me what three things I wanted to be, I'd have said: funny, cool, well-liked.

What do I want to be now? Bold. Fierce. Honest.

A fighter. A revolutionary. A bitch.

Because the way the world treats teenage girls—as sluts, as objects, as bitches—is not okay.

It's the exact opposite of okay.

OLD WHITE MEN LOVE IT
WHEN YOU SLUT-SHAME
POSTED BY IZZY O'NEILL IN
BITCHES BITE BACK

Slut-shaming: in which a woman is labeled a "slut" or "whore" for enjoying sex (or even just looking like they might) and is subsequently punished socially.

Interestingly, only girls and women are called to task for their sexuality; boys and men are congratulated for the exact same behavior. This is the essence of the sexual double standard: boys will be boys, and girls will be sluts.

Unless, of course, you're not a slut, in which case you are some variation of the following: a frigid bitch, a cock-tease, a boring prude, or matronly purveyor of the Friend Zone.

Basically, if you're a woman, you're damned if you do and damned if you don't. If you refrain from any expression of sexiness, you may be written off as irrelevant and unfeminine, but if you follow the male-written guidelines, you run the risk of being judged, shamed, and policed. It's super awesome.

You might think: But Izzy, given this set of circumstances, isn't it preferable for a girl or woman to abstain from sexual expression? To that I say: nay. Putting aside the inherent sexism of this assertion, it shouldn't make any difference whether a girl or woman is sexually active, or even utters any expression of sexuality. The problem is the way in which society interprets this perceived behavior. Because here's the thing: slut-shaming is not really about women's sexuality. It is grounded in the belief that men have the right to assert themselves, and women do not.

It's not a new phenomenon—just ask Monica Lewinsky—but in the social media age, it's becoming more toxic than ever. One scroll through my Instagram feed on any given day proves this. Hordes of (usually male) users comment on young girls' selfies and bikini shots, dubbing them whores and sluts just for showing a little flesh or wearing red lipstick (this normally follows failed attempts to hit on these girls, may I add—it's amazing how much slut-shaming is derived from rejection-induced bitterness). Don't these girls know nobody will ever respect them now?

As an aside, I actually really admire people who slut-shame on the internet. Usually when someone has a low IQ they try to hide it, but these guys just throw it right out there in the public domain.

Never mind that these same dudes then go and spend five dollars a week on top-shelf glamour magazines with oiled-up naked models splashed on the front cover. You can *buy* tits, but you can't *have* tits. That would be absurd!!

In fact, I think in the manual they hand out to girls at birth, the chapter on sexuality should start with the disclaimer: unless an old white man can profit from your sexuality, you better hide it, because if it can't be exploited, it will be punished.

Our sexuality is a commodity, and thus the principles of supply and demand can be applied. If we're sexy but untouchable, we're in short supply. Demand goes up. And because demand goes up, the aforementioned old white man can charge more money for it. But if we give it away freely? If we actually have sex—and have the audacity to enjoy it? Supply is booming. Profit margins die. Old white men can't make as much money, so they get out their sticks and beat us into slut-shamed remission. And the rest of the society buys into it.

When you're a young girl, your developing sexuality is a loaded weapon. You should polish it to a shine for the sake of the male gaze, but you shouldn't seek any enjoyment from it yourself. Play with power, as long as you never claim it. Enact desire, as long as you don't follow through.

I call bullshit.

THE FRIEND ZONE IS
AS REAL AS NARNIA
POSTED BY IZZY O'NEILL IN
BITCHES BITE BACK

The Friend Zone: an imaginary area filled with self-professed Nice Guys who've been sexually rejected by women they've been Nice to. See also: a convenient social construct designed to comfort men who cannot cope with rejection. See also: a manipulative tool used by Nice Guys to make a woman feel guilty for not wanting to have sex with them.

The Nice Guy Phenomenon: in which self-entitled men believe that if they spend enough time with a woman and aren't explicitly terrible to them, it's unfair when the woman doesn't then suck their penis and/or fall in love with them.

Poor Nice Guys. It must be so difficult, putting all that effort into pretending to be a decent human being without being rewarded with sex or love afterward. They listen to our problems, buy us gifts, shower us with compliments, talk to us about all the other horrible guys we're dating, and yet! And yet we still don't tear our clothes off and fall into their arms. We keep going for those other dudes, the ones with charisma and personality. The ones we're attracted to, the ones who make us laugh, the ones who make us feel good. It is just so unreasonable and infuriating. They must really regret falling for such a Bitch.

To that I say: cry me a river. You should be nice because it's the right thing to do. If you're nice because you want something in return, you're probably not that nice at all.

I mean, maybe we can blame Hollywood. The invariable message of most romantic comedies is that men can be as lazy or slutty or awkward or obnoxious as they like, but as long as they're relatively nice and keep trying, they'll get the girl in the end. The below-average and perilously flawed man always ends up with the beautiful girl if he puts in a little effort and isn't an outright dickhead to her. The bar is so low that Nice Guys who watch it must see it and think, huh. I can do that. And if I do, I'll get any woman I want. Who is *she* to say no? Who is *she* to have a choice?

But I've got a news flash for you, Nice Guys: the world doesn't work that way. Sure, it'd be great if you could get anything you wanted—a job, a promotion, a mortgage—by being a semi-decent person and trying hard, but that's not reality. Just ask the millions of disadvantaged people around the world who face discrimination based on their gender, race, sexuality, class, and disabilities every day.

That's probably why the Nice Guys are so angry. In a system that inherently favors them, it's the first time they aren't automatically getting what they want just because they want it. Their privilege is no longer doing the heavy lifting, and they're mad about it.

This entitlement has to stop. The world owes you nothing. Girls owe you nothing.

We *do* like good guys. You just aren't one of them.

EPILOGUE

Dear Izzy,

I'm a screenwriting agent based in West Holly-wood, and was a judge during the shortlisting phase of this year's Script Factor. I championed your screenplay from the get-go. It's clever, topical, and downright hilarious. You have big talent, and should be very proud of your work.

However, I've recently learned about the dis-qualification of your entry. I strongly believe this is a terrible (and, frankly, cowardly) decision on the part of the organizers, and I can't even begin to imagine how disappointed you must be.

Next time you're in LA, give me a call. I'd love to meet with you in person to discuss the future of your screenwriting—and the possibility of represen-tation at our agency.

You're going places, Izzy O'Neill, and I'd like to be on that journey with you.

All the very best,

Eliza Kennedy

ACKNOWLEDGMENTS

Acknowledgments are weird. It kind of feels like an Oscar acceptance speech, except I'm alone in my pajamas at three in the afternoon, eating popcorn and trying to resist the lure of video games and *The Office* reruns. Ah, author life.

First up, the hugest shout-out to my literary agent, Suzie Townsend. We've worked together for five years, sold eight books during that time, and it's not hyperbolic to say I wouldn't have a career without her. And the rest of the New Leaf family—in particular Joanna Volpe, Cassandra Baim, Pouya Shahbazian, Maíra Roman, and Veronica Grijalva. The best agency on the planet, truly.

Obviously this book would not be a book without my incredible editors on both sides of the pond: Catherine Wallace at HarperTeen, and Alison Dougal and Liz Bankes at Egmont UK. I may be biased, but you all have great taste. Thank you for believing in Izzy—and in me.

Over the last few years, I've met some incredible writing friends, both online and in real life. My agent sisters Victoria Aveyard, Emma Theriault, and Claribel Ortega. Rebecca

McLaughlin, Pitch Wars mentee turned lifelong friend. My ambitious badasses Sasha Alsberg and Francina Simone; our group chats and Skype hangouts give me life. The world is not ready for us. *yacht emoji*

There are so many others, and to have enough paper to thank them I'd have to murder an entire rain forest, so let's just say: the entire YA community on both sides of the Atlantic—authors, bloggers, readers, reviewers, agents, editors, event coordinators, and all-around champions. Thank you for welcoming me with open arms.

Then there's the unfortunate bunch who have to put up with me in real life, which I assure you is no mean feat. Firstly, to my dog, Obi, who cries whenever I work and thus validates any and all procrastination. Mum, Dad, Jack, Gran, Harry (who is also a dog), and the rest of my huge, mad family. The best pals a girl could ask for: Toria, Nic, Hannah, Lauren, Lucy, Steve, and Spike. And Hilary, even though you technically come under the Mad Family header, you're really in a category of your very own. To Millie—I hope the world is a better place for young women by the time you become one.

To Amy Poehler, Tina Fey, Mindy Kaling, Serena Williams, and J.K. Rowling. I am not friends with you but like to pretend I am.

And to Louis, who will be my husband by the time this is printed. Wtf. Thank you for the nacho-fueled life talks, terrible puns, hilarious cases of the zoomies, karaoke-filled road trips, endless back tickers, always doing the dishes, and for making me smile no matter what. There's nobody else I'd rather have by my side.